Insatiable

Insatiable

ERICA RIDLEY

DELACORTE PRESS

Delacorte Press
An imprint of Random House Children's Books
A division of Penguin Random House LLC
1745 Broadway, New York, NY 10019
penguinrandomhouse.com
getunderlined.com

Editor: Bria Ragin
Cover Designer: Angela G. Carlino
Interior Designer: Cathy Bobak
Production Editor: Jamie Johnson
Managing Editor: Tamar Schwartz
Production Manager: Shameiza Ally

Library of Congress Cataloging-in-Publication Data is available upon request.
ISBN 979-8-217-11741-3 (trade pbk.) — ISBN 979-8-217-11743-7 (ebook)

The text of this book is set in 11.2-point Warnock Pro.

Manufactured in the United States of America
1st Printing

The authorized representative in the EU for product safety and compliance is Penguin Random House Ireland, Morrison Chambers, 32 Nassau Street, Dublin D02 YH68, Ireland, https://eu-contact.penguin.ie.

For Lacey—
I can never thank you enough
for just being you.
XOXOXO

1

August 1886
Scottish Highlands

Scarlet-soaked storm clouds loom overhead like the wool of blood-spattered sheep. I sprint over the hill, protecting the contents of my basket as best I can with my free hand.

Those who say *Red sky at night, shepherd's delight!* are not seventeen-year-old girls racing home through empty fields. I must return before nightfall has a chance to wring the last shimmer from the sun and leave me stranded alone in the darkness.

Anything can happen in the shadows.

Rivulets of sweat stream down my spine as I hurry to the barn to deposit the last batch of dried grass. When my brother Hamish is home from school, it's his job to bind blocks of hay to feed the livestock over the long winter . . . But it was also his duty to cut and dry the fields of grass to begin with, yet I'm the one with calloused hands and a spasming back.

With a grunt, I toss the basket into the barn and yank the heavy wooden door closed. The setting sun will glower with dangerous beauty for at least half an hour more, affording me enough time to make it home safely.

It's reckless to linger alone and unprotected after dark. The capricious fairies who lurk out of sight won't protect me from trouble. Their whims and their magic are more frightening than any human mischief.

Soon, I barge through the open doorway of my home with aching feet and a drumming heart. The hearth smokes faintly, the scent of soil and grass clinging to my mother's skirts. She turns, broom in hand, and smiles at me. Relief floods the last remnants of fear from my tense muscles. I am home. I am safe. I am loved.

It should be enough.

Before Mother or I can utter a single word of greeting, raucous laughter erupts from the sitting room. Hamish and Father relax in comfortable armchairs, sipping mugs of ale as they play yet another round of draughts on the square table between them.

"Catriona, *wait*," hisses my mother, but I'm already crossing the threshold.

I used to sit on my grandmother's knee in this room to hear her clever tales. The whispered ones that were passed down from grandmother to granddaughter for generations.

My father and brother are neither so old nor so wise, but their stories are irresistible all the same.

Hamish is fifteen and has spent the past two years at his boarding school in Inverness, studying to become a solicitor.

Words cannot convey the depth of envy that causes.

I've never even been to Inverness, or to any big city, really. I've only left our small village in my parents' company during holiday celebrations in the next town. I cannot imagine the sights Hamish has seen, the food he has tasted, the friends he has made.

The cramped schoolhouse next to our church—both run by the same ancient minister—cannot possibly hold a candle to the sprawling grounds of the Royal Academy of Inverness. I've memorized every word my younger brother says about the buildings, the professors, the sporting clubs, the cèilidh dances. His experiences match the stories our father tells of his own years there, before he returned home to become a tanner and take over this farmland from my maternal grandfather.

Hamish won't have to come back at all, unless he's of a mind to do so. My brother will go to university and become important and rich and happy. He'll enjoy a career he likes and marry a lass he loves. He'll *know* things, and *have* things, and *do* things. All because he happened to be born a boy.

My eyes water at the unfairness.

Hamish glances up from the black-and-white checked board as though the waves of bitterness and jealousy rolling off me had reached all the way across the sitting room to tousle his hair.

We have the same big, thick black curls, though mine are stuffed in a lopsided bun, whilst he keeps his cropped closer to his head. Our skin is a similar shade of golden brown, neither the deep brown of our mother's nor the bone white of our father's. Both of us have wide smiles and apple cheeks blessed with dimples. Bright brown eyes and curling black lashes. Strangers can tell we're siblings at first glance—though that's where the similarities end.

I need only to look over my shoulder at Mother by the fireside to know where my future lies.

Father twists in his seat to see what has captured his son's attention. "Catriona, there you are!"

As if I spent all day from six in the morning to eight o'clock at night breaking my back in the fields because doing Hamish's chores in addition to my own seemed more fun than drinking ale and playing draughts.

"Here I am" is all I murmur.

Father clucks his tongue. "You are rather unkempt and windswept. Won't catch a husband that way, will you?"

He always says things like this. As if it were possible to harvest fruit and shear sheep and cut hay whilst corseted and bustled into a floor-length silk gown.

But I know better than to argue with a man.

"Won't catch one today," I agree lightly.

"We'll see." An unsettling twinkle in my father's eyes sends gooseflesh skittering down my exposed skin. The words themselves aren't unusual, but the way he said them . . .

"I was telling Father about me winning the caber-tossing competition," Hamish says, oblivious as always to any tense undercurrents. "Plenty of lassies were there to cheer my team on, though I daresay *you* would've spent the day indoors making dour crocks or weaving a creel."

He doesn't mean this with malice, I remind myself for the thousandth time. Hamish conflates what I do with what I *wish* to do because the only women he knows are me and our mother, and all he's ever seen us do is work.

Then again, he's spent nine months of each year in Inverness since he turned thirteen. The boarding school may be all male, but the city isn't. Surely some young woman somewhere in Scotland has the freedom to do as she pleases?

"Pottery isn't boring," I reply. "Some artisans have remarkable craftsmanship."

Hamish's eyes glaze over.

"You began after the hammer throw . . ." Father prompts, all interest in me forgotten.

Hamish lights up and is off and running again, prattling on about his endless heroic wins at feats of strength.

I place my hands at the small of my back and attempt to rub some feeling other than pain into the sore muscles.

This is but a wee a taste of what's to come. Once Hamish goes back to school next week, Mother and I will no longer have to cook and clean for him . . . but his chores will fall to us. Or just to me.

But he's here right now. Couldn't this tale of physical prowess have waited until suppertime?

It's not that I wish my brother to be stuck out in a field all day. It's that I wish to heaven I had the same opportunities he does. Though I'd never say so aloud. Even thinking the word *wish* makes me flinch.

In the Highlands, there is little more perilous. Never say

the word without retracting your foolish statement and invoking God's protection. Ever. If one of the many fairies overhears your wish, they might choose to grant it . . . in the worst way possible.

According to legend, a mother once wished for enough money to feed her family—only for all three of her babes to turn into tiny figurines of gold. I heard a hundred more such stories at my gran's knee. Wishing invites disaster.

So I *dream* of a better life. One in which I'm as educated as my brother. I long to become an educator myself someday. A governess or a boarding school professor . . .

Mother appears in the doorway. "The stew will be ready in fifteen minutes."

Father wrinkles his nose. "I don't feel like stew."

My muscles tighten. He doesn't feel like the specific dish he said he wanted this morning at breakfast, causing my mother to change her plans for the day and spend the hot August afternoon bent over a fire instead?

"What do you feel like, my love?" Mother asks with infinite patience.

She's had forty years of practice. I've only had seventeen. With luck, there are many more decades to come, for us both.

"Chicken tonight," Father replies. "Catriona, go and butcher a few for your mother."

My mouth falls open. I *hate* killing animals.

"But th-that's Hamish's chore," I stammer. "He loves breaking their necks. And he's sitting right here. Until he goes back to school—"

"Father and I are playing a game," Hamish chirps, swinging his mug of ale out of the way so he can hop one of his wooden pieces over one of Father's. Hamish chortles. "Look, I'm king!"

I step forward, my eyes flashing at the stupid game of draughts.

Father glares at me. "Catriona, would you disobey a direct command?"

"Of course not," I mumble, regretting daring to speak up at all. I thought I'd buried that pointless urge long ago.

"Good lass." He raises his glass toward me. "I'll have a surprise for you when you return."

My mother stops me at the door. The last glow of sunset is almost gone, so I expect her to tell me to be safe. Instead, she glances over my shoulder at Father and Hamish. "Be kind to them."

"Why must we?" I demand, matching her hushed tone. "Because Father and Hamish are wounded or stunted or otherwise incapable of awareness and empathy and mercy?"

"No." Her expression is pained. "They should be capable."

"Then why should I be the one to—"

"Because sometimes family is the best thing you've got," she says softly. "And other times . . . family is *all* you've got."

My fingers clench. "It's not enough."

She touches my cheek, then turns back to the hearth. "You and I can eat the vegetable stew. Just fetch enough chickens for Hamish and your father."

"Yes, Mother." I stalk out to the pen. Without the benefit

of sunshine, the wind is cold and unforgiving. I should have grabbed a cloak, but I won't be long. This isn't a task I care to linger on.

I visit the chickens every day and have never once given them a reason to fear me. They are fellow living beings, with lives and hopes of their own. We're the same. Like me, they'll never leave their pen. We're all trapped.

The first family story I remember hearing was that of my grandmother's grandmother, a bonny lass named Davina.

One day, after many years of relentless childbirth and cooking and cleaning and tending the livestock and tilling the land, weary Davina glanced out the open kitchen window at a glorious sunset and absently wished aloud for wings to fly away and enjoy the evening.

In her dreamy state, she forgot to retract her words and invoke God's protection. A fairy, hidden in the brush beneath the windowsill, overheard Davina's wish . . . and gleefully turned her into a chicken.

Moments later, Davina's husband—my great-great-grandfather—came home from having a pint at the pub. Upon discovering a chicken in the kitchen, he assumed the bird was meant for his supper . . . and slaughtered her.

The warning has passed down from mother to daughter ever since.

A prophecy of tragedy to come.

I prefer to believe that my great-great-grandfather didn't murder my great-great-granny. That Davina flew out that window, even if she only made it as far as the farmyard on the other side.

Then again, had she done so, Davina would have been captured and deposited in the henhouse with the others. Her wings permanently clipped, if she made any further attempt to fly away.

Is a lifetime encaged, laying eggs for the man who owned her, so different from the human existence from which she'd sought escape?

Perhaps the sweet, gentle chickens surrounding me so trustingly right now aren't brainless farm animals but my own kith and kin, descended from the same maternal womb.

Only for my father to force me to wring their necks so that he can spear morsels of their flesh into his mouth along with his next pint of ale.

I kneel onto the dirt amongst the birds. "I'm so sorry."

They rub against me, comforting me. It doesn't work.

Killing the first chicken would be too easy. They recognize me on sight. I'm the one who feeds them, who sings to them, who loves them. They gather around me in perfect trust, fluttering their wings against my skirts like feathery hugs.

How can I destroy a creature like that?

I spring to my feet, startling them. They cluck and flap their wings in confusion as I back away to the gate and throw it open wide. I cannot save all the chickens of the world, but I can save the ones here. Sometimes family is all you've got.

"Go!" I shoo them out of the pen and into the night. "Fly away, cousins! Be free!"

They waddle off in noisy wonderment. Melting into the dark forest. Vanishing into thick shadows.

My father is going to be *furious.*

But in the future, if he wants any other living thing on this farm killed for his supper—he'll have to do it himself.

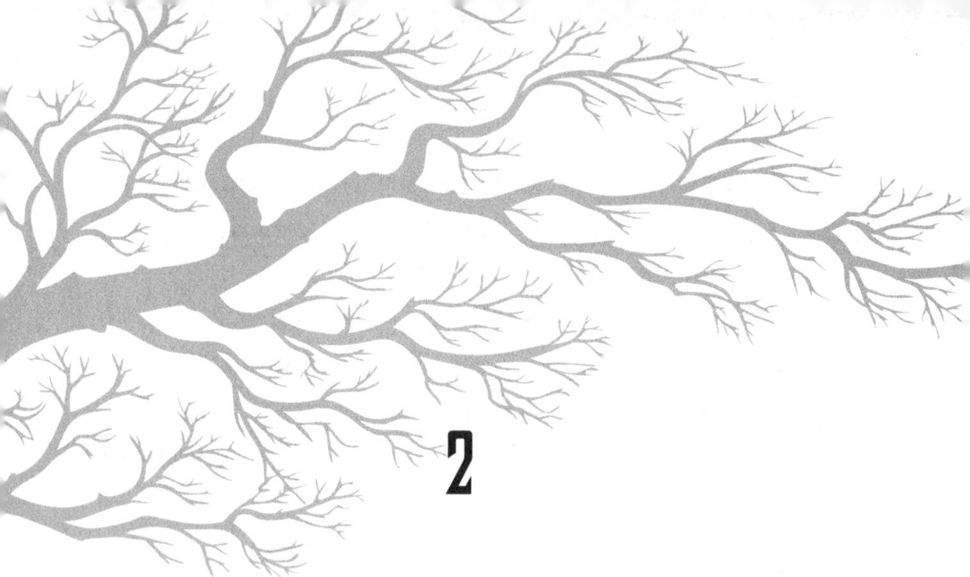

2

When I return to the house empty-handed, my mother doesn't ask me what happened. She closes her eyes and sighs.

I shift my weight. "What if they're our cousins?"

She looks at me. Not with shock or humor or disappointment, but with resignation. She doesn't say I'm wrong.

Maybe I'm not.

Perhaps Davina's daughter passed down a tale of her mother being murdered after having a wish partially granted because that fate seemed *kinder* than admitting Davina-the-accidental-hen had lived the rest of her short life in worse captivity, and we've been eating her other children ever since.

"Catriona," shouts Father from the parlor. "Get in here."

I glance at my mother. Did he see my grand rescue from the window?

She doesn't meet my eyes. Instead, she whispers, "I'm so sorry."

She sounds like me, about to slaughter a pet chicken.

"Catriona!" Father repeats, louder this time. He doesn't *sound* angry. He sounds . . . smug? Proud? Giddy?

I hurry into the parlor. "Did you win the game?"

His eyes are twinkling again. "The best game of all."

I slide my gaze over to Hamish.

He points at the draughts board, then at his chest, mouthing, "*I* won the game."

Then what—?

"Sit," Father commands, gesturing toward the hardback chairs Mother and I use when we knit socks or card wool for yarn.

I sit.

Mother sits beside me.

"I've wonderful news," says Father.

Thunder cracks outside, loud enough to rattle our windows. The storm foretold by the dark clouds is here. Rain pours down.

"You may not have the wherewithal to think about your future," Father begins.

Oh, I've the *wherewithal.* All I ever do is think about the life I yearn to have! Unfortunately, I can't do anything about it.

Father leans back in his comfortable chair. "Since you were born, I have worried about you"—Translation: He despaired the moment he realized his firstborn didn't have male anatomy—"and I'm delighted to inform you that I've managed to secure your future."

I blink at him in confusion.

"I see you don't understand," he says gently.

Father's voice is always gentle when he speaks down to his meek, helpless, female-brained daughter. Never mind that I was the brightest child in the schoolhouse, or that if my further education is lacking, it's because I wasn't allowed to *have* one.

"I've made you a match," he explains with obvious pride. "You weren't going to attract any husbands on your own, so I took it upon myself to procure one for you."

My flesh goes cold. "Wh-what? Who?"

"Seumas Grant," he replies with satisfaction.

"The *butcher*?"

Bile rises in my throat. Father isn't providing for my future. He's signing me up for a living hell. A lifetime as the marital property of someone who will empathize with me even less than my own father. A man who wouldn't hesitate to wring the neck of a helpless bird, even if he *knew* it had once been his wife.

"Seumas has had his eye on you for some time now," Father continues. "We've been negotiating long enough that he's willing to forgo a dowry altogether to wed you."

"Congratulations," I choke out.

Seumas the butcher is almost as old as my father, and so much worse in every way. If killing chickens makes me sob into my pillow, I can't marry someone who slaughters animals as a profession. He'll come home drenched in their blood. Wearing gore-spattered clothing I'll be expected to clean. Touching me with hands stained red, dark crescents of clotted blood beneath his fingernails.

It's my personal nightmare.

"You can't," I whisper, but this is a lie. Arranged marriages are common and rarely designed to benefit the bride.

"Does this mean we can have all the fresh meat we want for free?" asks Hamish.

Is that the reason?

Our family isn't poor. At least, we have enough money for Hamish to attend a prestigious boarding school. Maybe we're counting on Hamish becoming a success in the big city and sharing his wealth with the rest of us. Between that day and now, a lot can happen.

"Anyone but Seumas," I try again. "Please."

Father isn't listening. He's droning on about how it's the perfect match because Father is a tanner and Seumas is a butcher, and between the two of them, no part of any animal will go unused. Every organ, every drop of blood, every scrap of skin . . .

"Why don't *you* marry him, then?" I burst out.

The parlor turns as frigid as the Highland winds raging outside.

"What did you say to me?" asks Father, his voice sharp.

"That I don't want to marry him!" I slide from the chair to my sore knees on the hard wooden floor. "Please, Papa. I'm begging you—"

"This isn't your decision. The arrangement has been made. You'll do as I say."

Hot tears spill from my eyes. Not in sadness, but in rage. At him, for not caring what I might think—worse, for not believing me even *capable* of rational thought—and bitter anger at the world, at my own self, because he's right about one thing.

I'll have to do as he commands. A lifetime of misery awaits.

Unless I can change his mind?

"What about Duncan?" I blurt.

Hamish perks up. "Who's Duncan?"

"A nice lad her age who sits behind us at church," Mother murmurs.

In the few years we shared together at the schoolhouse, Duncan never spoke more than three words to me or to anyone else. Lately, he blushes every time I catch him watching me.

"His father sells cheap tallow candles that smell like burnt lard," Father says flatly. "There's no advantage to marrying Duncan."

"I *like* him." Surely that's an advantage. Shouldn't my happiness factor into the choice?

"I like meat," says Hamish. "I'm looking forward to that."

I glare at him.

He grins at me. "I'll even dress nice for your wedding."

I could throttle my brother. "I don't give a rotten egg about who wears what to the wedding! I'm concerned about all the other years I'll have to survive after the vows. I want a life I can look forward to. A future I choose for *myself*."

"Catriona," Father says in warning.

I crawl toward him on my knees. "Please, let me have a life first. Or at least an education, so that I can forge my own path."

He appears exasperated. "Women cannot—"

"Women *can*," I interrupt desperately. "Mary Somerville—"

Father flings up his hands. "Not this again!"

"A Scottish woman," I say even louder, "and the first female member of the Royal Astronomical Society."

"Honorary member," Hamish corrects me.

"Eliza Wigham," I continue stubbornly. "Scottish abolitionist and suffragist."

"Not successful at it," Hamish puts in. "Females won't ever have the right to vote."

"And a good thing, too," Father replies, "if this is a female's idea of a compelling argument. You're not those lasses, Catriona. You'll never be one of them."

"Sophia Jex-Blake," I crow in triumph. "A few years ago, she was part of the first group of seven women to study medicine at the University of Edinburgh."

"An Englishwoman," Father says dismissively.

"And the university repealed all their degrees," pipes up Hamish. "Too many people protested."

"Too many *men* protested, you mean," I mutter.

Protest sounds so civilized, when in fact those seven brave, pioneering women were bullied, assaulted, and terrorized on a daily basis. The newspapers printed lurid details of the Surgeons' Hall Riots week after week.

Father's voice is sharp. "It doesn't matter if Queen Victoria herself trains to be a barrister. *You* are marrying the butcher."

"I'm seventeen!" I cry.

My flimsiest argument yet. By law, girls can marry as young as twelve. The only other lass in the schoolhouse with me—my closest friend—married last year at fifteen. I haven't seen her since.

She and I wouldn't have been there at all, if Scotland hadn't passed a law several years ago mandating education for lassies and laddies until the age of thirteen. That only gave us a few short years of education, but it was long enough to learn how to read. And to dream of more.

"That's true," agrees Father. "You're seventeen. A second ago, that made you old enough to be a surgeon and a suffragist and an astronomer. Which means you can also be a wife and a mother."

"I'm old enough to go to school," I clarify. "To learn how to be something that will help others. I'd like to be a professor."

He sighs. "Catriona, I'm not immune to your youth or your perspective. Which is why I've negotiated an extended betrothal with Seumas. You won't wed until you're eighteen."

Hamish's spine shoots up, and his mouth falls open. "I have to wait an entire year for free beef?"

"You're the one in school," I snap. "Become a fancy lawyer and buy your own beef."

Father sends Hamish a quelling look before returning his firm gaze to me. "I surmise this arrangement isn't as you might have wanted—"

He surmised that, did he? What phenomenal male intellect. Full marks in deducing the obvious.

Of course this isn't what I want. So much for following a passion, exploring the world, starting a career. Now it seems I'll never leave this village.

"Don't sulk," Father scolds me. "It's unbecoming and unnecessary. All an education would do is fill your pretty head with silly ideas."

I open my mouth.

He barrels on before I can share a few choice words.

"Your mother can't read and never missed it for a moment," he says with confidence. "She's never once aspired to anything grander than serving me, because there *is* no higher post for a woman than wife to a man."

Even without looking at the hard wooden seat behind me, I can feel my mother deflate like an old balloon. After twenty long years, her husband still doesn't know her. Or, believes all he has to do for a thing to become true is to say it out loud with authority.

Hamish smirks. "I wish you could attend a boarding school, if one would even have you. You'd come crying home before the end of the first week and *beg* to marry the butcher. After the first day!"

A growl of thunder rattles the windowpanes.

I flinch. "Hamish! You know you shouldn't say—"

Mother erupts into a coughing fit, distracting me from my brother's thoughtless words. I thump her on her back with growing concern for a long moment before she's able to regain her composure.

Hamish doesn't even acknowledge the interruption.

"You wouldn't survive an hour in one of my classes," he says with a laugh. "Educate a *girl*? The headmaster would laugh you right out of—"

Lightning fills the room, and thunder shakes the windows again, matching the fury inside my heart.

I scramble to my feet. "Of all the ignorant, immature, mean-spirited things you've ever said—"

A knock shakes our front door.

We all fall silent, staring at one another. Who would be foolish enough to venture out-of-doors in a storm this violent?

Actually . . . I cock my head to listen. I can't hear the rain anymore. The nails shivered in the timber seconds ago, but suddenly, it's so quiet that I could almost believe the world outside these walls ceased to exist.

The knocking sounds again, louder this time. A draft slithers under the door, carrying the chill of damp earth.

"Don't stand there, Catriona." Father makes an impatient shooing gesture. "Go answer the door."

Hamish leaps up from his armchair and races to beat me to the entryway. He is the one to turn the handle and fling open the door.

On the other side stands a tall, thin stranger with dark skin and a dry cloak and black eyes shadowed beneath the equally dry brim of a black top hat.

I glance over his shoulder. The storm is gone. It looks like it never happened at all. The ground is dry. No breeze rustles the leaves of the trees. Stars fill the cloudless sky.

Something is wrong.

Hamish puffs up his chest. "May I help you, Mr. . . . ?"

The stranger looks bored, in as much as his half-visible expression can be read. "Ross. Reporting to take Miss Catriona Cameron to school, as requested."

I stare at him. "What did you say?"

"School?" my brother repeats, flabbergasted. "No one requested that."

"I've the papers right here." Mr. Ross lifts a black-gloved hand. A sheet of tri-folded parchment pokes from his fingers.

Hamish snatches the paper from the stranger.

"I'm so sorry," I tell Mr. Ross with embarrassment. "I'm Catriona Cameron. My brother—"

"It says you're to report to boarding school," Hamish exclaims. "On the Isle of Skye!"

"What? Let me see." I pluck the paper from his fingers and scan the contents in confusion. Floodbane Academy? Never heard of it. "It says . . . they approved my application."

Hamish goggles at me. "I didn't know you'd applied."

I didn't.

Though as far as mistakes go, this is the best one that has ever happened to me. I hate that I must confess to Mr. Ross that I won't be—

"Did it work?" murmurs my mother's voice behind my ear.

I spin to ask her what on earth she's talking about, but the urgency in her brown eyes gives me the answer. It's the same expression she wears when passing down tales from my gran.

I wish you could attend a boarding school, my brother had snarled at me.

Without retracting his words.

Without begging God for protection.

And tonight, the fairies decided to grant a young boy his wish.

"It's happening," I whisper back in shock.

The fairies are trickster sprites. They love to grant wishes in the opposite way from how they were meant. My brother's intention was to shame me. To assert that girls neither deserved nor could qualify for the same advantages as boys.

Instead of shaming me as well, the fairies are offering me

what I've always wanted. A path that didn't even exist until Hamish opened his mouth.

"Floodbane Academy?" My brother seems to be equal parts flummoxed and impressed. *"You?"*

"She can't go," Father says flatly. "Seumas won't marry her if she gets some fancy education."

"Unsurprising. Seumas doesn't give a pig's knuckle about my brain," I retort, clutching the letter to my chest for dear life. This academy on the Isle of Skye may not compare to the esteemed Morrison Institute for Young Ladies in Edinburgh, but I'll take it. Hell, I'd take a wooden raft across the Atlantic before I'd subject myself to a miserable marriage.

"You're not going anywhere," Father repeats, his face red. "I won't pay a penny for it."

Exactly the same words he spoke when he sent Hamish off to school, and Mother tried to convince him to send me as well. The Morrison Institute for Young Ladies isn't a finishing school for future aristocrats, full of embroidery and waltzes. Not only are the students taught to be future educators themselves, but the headmistress also prides herself on placing the brightest of each class in paid positions upon graduation. A school like that would have changed my life.

I guess so would marrying the butcher.

"Parents needn't pay," says Mr. Ross, pointing a black-gloved finger at the letter in my hand. "She's received a full scholarship. All Miss Cameron needs to do is climb into the carriage. If she'd like to, that is."

As if on cue, a horse neighs outside. I didn't even notice a vehicle before, but there it is: a sturdy four-wheeled carriage resting behind two large geldings.

"I'll pack our valises," Mother suggests. "Obviously, I'm coming with you to see you settled in."

Of course she is. My heart warms. Mother was my first and best educator. The lessons she taught me will be with me always. Although I'm about to embark on a new chapter, I'm not ready to let go of her hand yet.

"Nobody is packing any bags," Father roars. "I said Catriona shan't go anywhere. I've an agreement with the butcher."

"I never agreed," I say. Father neither hears me nor cares to.

"No need for luggage." Mr. Ross glances at a pocket watch tucked into his gray waistcoat. "Uniforms and other necessities are provided to all students. To make it back to Skye safely, I must leave within the next few minutes. With or without you."

I look over his shoulder at the waiting carriage.

Father growls, "Don't you dare."

Mother steps between the two of us, setting me free.

I leap past Mr. Ross before my father can stop me, racing to the carriage as though my life depends on it. My future very well might.

If the fairies are willing to offer me wings . . .

I shan't refuse an opportunity to fly.

3

Though I cannot hear the driver's boots on the ground behind me, when I arrive breathless at the carriage, Mr. Ross is right there to hoist me up.

My father swears from the front doorstep. He must think words alone can cage me.

"Get back here. I forbid your education!"

Can he stop me? The fairies have already made the impossible, possible.

"I'll disinherit you!"

From what? I've no dowry and was about to belong to some other man.

"We'll disown you for the rest of your life!"

He can try . . . but no matter what Father threatens, I'll never lose my mother.

She sprints toward me.

Mother arrives at the carriage as Mr. Ross takes his perch as driver. Before he can whip the horses into motion, she presses something small and pointy and warm into my outstretched palm and closes my fingers around it. My strong, brave mother blows me a kiss as we drive away, tears streaming down her smiling face.

I stare until the sloping hill swallows her up. The farm where I've lived since birth disappears from sight. Only when all I see are the stars and full moon do I face forward in my seat and uncurl my fingers, careful not to let the bracing wind steal my sole treasure.

This is my mother's parting gift: a small metal cross, half as tall as my pinkie, dangling from braided twine. My mother's grandfather was an ironworker. He forged this pendant for my great-grandmother, for protection. She corded the yarn for the necklace from the sheep on these rolling hills.

Like our legends and stories, this necklace has been passed down from mother to daughter for generations. Always for protection. Which, until now, meant always on a wedding night. For what could be more dangerous than becoming the property of a strange man?

Apparently, my mother thinks my impending education might be as perilous. I cannot imagine why. Boarding schools are gender-specific, which often includes the professors themselves. I'm unlikely to see any men at all, much less one with the legal right to own me.

Or perhaps nothing is more terrifying than watching your baby chick attempt its first flight from the nest.

I loop the necklace over my head and slip the cross beneath my bodice, to nestle it against the bare skin above my heart. An organ currently flailing against my ribs.

All right, it's not just mothers who panic without their daughters. The coach has been traveling for less than ten minutes, and already I miss her so much I could cry. If only we'd been spared a moment for a final embrace! No hug, no cloak, an empty belly—

"There are two baskets behind your seat," Mr. Ross says without turning around. "One has blankets and outerwear, and the other contains nourishment for the long journey."

I stare at the back of his top hat. It's as if he overheard my thoughts.

Ridiculous. Naturally, I must be thinking about supper and warm clothing. He arrived at dinnertime during a storm. I tilt my head and frown. Little is stronger than a Highland wind. Yet Mr. Ross's top hat perches immobile atop his head. With my wild black curls flapping at my ears and the loud clomping of the horses' hooves as they drag the wooden carriage wheels over dirt and rock, I shouldn't have been able to hear his soft speaking voice at all. Nonetheless, the gusts of air themselves somehow carry each syllable to my ears.

I kneel on my seat and turn around. The carriage is a rectangular box with a collapsible hood over the rear half. Wide enough to seat two people hip-to-hip on the bench, with the driver's high seat up front, and room for a small trunk or two behind.

Or in this case, two large, woven willow baskets. Sitting where my valise would be, if I'd been allowed to bring one. I place both baskets onto the bench beside me.

I open the first and discover a pelisse in shimmering yellow. An odd choice, for an ankle-length coat. Yellow shows dirt, and here in the Highlands, colors have meanings. During harvest, yellow signifies a healthy yield. But at other times, yellow symbolizes sickness or caution. It's a color to be avoided, unless you wish to summon illness and bad fortune.

The pelisse unfolds to reveal two more surprises.

First, it appears tailor-made for my precise form. There's even a fancy vent in the rear to accommodate a bustle, if I were the sort of lass who minced about in the latest fashions instead of hauling bales of hay across fields.

Second, there is a large, embroidered patch covering most of the left breast. It's a coat of arms containing four interlocking symbols. An annulet, signifying strength. A lynx, symbolizing vigilance. An arrow, signifying readiness. And a cauldron, symbolizing willingness to battle. Or witchcraft, depending on your interpretation.

"That's the academy's coat of arms," says the driver without turning around.

"A bit paranoid and bloodthirsty, isn't it?" I jest nervously. "Are the girls at this school meant to be military warriors? The boys' schools must quake in fear."

"Floodbane Academy is an all-boys school," Mr. Ross answers.

The pelisse falls from my fingers. "Wh-what?"

"Until now," he clarifies. "Unless you'd rather go back home."

My stomach bottoms. Mother was right to worry. The fairies couldn't allow me to have a peaceful, joyful education. Damn Hamish and his cursed wish! But I *cannot* return to the life that awaits me at home.

"Am I . . . the only lass?" I croak.

"There are six of you," he replies. "If you all show up."

"I'm going," I whisper.

My intestines churn. *Am* I making a wise decision?

Country folk like me tend to follow tradition without question. My father tried his best to provide me with the only future he understands.

My fingers curl into determined fists, and my spine straightens tall. Succumbing to infinite misery because someone else cannot envision an alternate future isn't the answer.

This coat of arms is for *me*, now, too. For all six of us girls. We will be strong. Vigilant. Ready for anything. As many women before us strove to do, we shall battle our way to an equal education.

"The rest of your uniform is in your room on the isle," Mr. Ross comments.

I shove my bare arms into the pelisse. "There's more clothing for me?"

"A fortnight's worth in an armoire. Your scholarship includes food and other supplies, for as long as you reside at the academy."

Fairies truly have no limits.

In this case, I choose to interpret their gifts as a good omen. If I learn enough at school, if I make all the right connections . . . I will not only escape marriage to the butcher, but also be able to provide a better life for my mother with my future salary as an educator.

My stomach growls, so I open the second basket. I gasp. The basket is filled to the brim with all my favorite treats. Fresh bread, somehow warm from the oven. Fruits I could have sworn were out of season. Pudding pots with clootie dumplings and cranachan.

"Don't expect to eat like that at the academy," the driver warns. "That's to tempt you into its walls."

"I was as hooked as a fish the second you said 'scholarship,'" I inform him, my mouth full of raspberries and honey. I'm glad he can't see me shoveling sweetened berries and whiskey-soaked oats into my mouth like a pig feeding at a trough.

When we crest another hill with the roof folded back and the open air all around, I cannot help but feel exposed. Out here, I'm an easy target in a bright, moonlit clearing.

For an unsettling moment, I'm no longer sure whether I'm running away or being kidnapped.

"How long is the journey?" I venture.

"About ten hours."

I nearly fall out of the open carriage. *"Ten hours?"*

"Try to sleep if you want it to go faster."

We're already further from home than I've ever been. If this were daytime, I'd stay awake so as not to miss the swaying of a single blade of grass. But I'm trundling alone in a carriage helmed by a strange man, as he ferries me from my home to a remote, sparsely populated island.

My skin prickles. "How far is Floodbane Academy from its closest mainland village?"

I'm expecting an answer like *two miles,* but instead Mr. Ross replies, "Three hours."

"What do people do in the event of an emergency?" I stammer.

"Pray," he answers grimly.

Goosepimples scurry across my flesh. My throat has gone dry.

The horses snort white clouds into the air. At every rut, the carriage wheels jump, and the axles groan. The night's muggy breath clings to my suddenly clammy brow.

"Don't do this," Mr. Ross says quietly.

I jerk my startled gaze to the back of his top hat. "Don't ask questions?"

He shakes his head. "Ask far more. Listen to the answers. You seem a sweet lass. Floodbane Academy isn't always a nice place. You should choose a different life."

Uncertainty tickles my skin.

"This *is* my different life," I manage. "I *am* choosing it."

He makes no further comment. For the next hour, we travel in silence, save for the occasional eerie cry of a bird of prey, triumphant at having captured and killed its unsuspecting supper.

I try not to think about the sound tiny bones must make as they're ripped apart by talons and crushed between strong beaks.

"Does the Isle of Skye have lovely beaches?" I ask in a small voice.

At first, Mr. Ross doesn't respond. Perhaps he didn't hear me.

But then he says, "Not anywhere near Floodbane."

A flash of disappointment shoots through my chest. There must be other wonders to behold.

"What *is* near the campus?" I try again.

"Cliffs," he answers without hesitation. "Fog. Deep, freezing rivers. Steep hillsides. Uneven, rocky terrain. Thick forests. A few swampy bogs. And watch out for adders. They're the only venomous snakes in Scotland. We have an infestation."

At this point, I'm unsurprised that poisonous serpents are crawling all over my new school. Probably as invisible in the fog as the sharp cliffs leading to freezing rivers.

I've never felt more unprepared in my life.

"It's not too late," he offers.

I swallow hard. "You'd take me home?"

His shoulders twitch in the moonlight. My question has made him chuckle. "I was never going to take you back home."

My clammy fingers grip the yellow pelisse. "But you said—"

"I've been summoned to perform a job. In this case, deliver you to the academy. Should you choose to leap out of the barouche and return home on foot, I'd make no attempt to chase you. My role isn't to abduct schoolgirls. It's to provide transportation."

Grimly, I fold my hands over my chest and fight a shiver. If I feel exposed in this tall sturdy carriage, it would be a thousand times worse picking my way alone through the dark Highlands on foot. It's too late for that.

But I have no second thoughts. At home, I haven't even the illusion of choice. This is my path now. A better one. Floodbane Academy is going to change my life in ways I cannot even imagine.

4

An anguished shriek pierces the air overhead, and I open my eyes to inky blackness. I cannot fathom how my driver, Mr. Ross, can tell where we're heading. Yet he urges the horses ever faster through this thick molasses of nothingness.

"What was that noise?" I whisper.

"Nothing," comes his disinterested reply.

I don't believe him.

Spiderwebs envelop me—in my hair, on my face, in my mouth—and I'm shrieking, flailing, spitting . . . only to realize that they're not spiderwebs after all, but the ghostly mist of early morning.

The darkness hides my embarrassment. Floodbane Academy is a boys' school. I cannot allow my male classmates' first impression of a female student to be a display of hysterics. I must stay strong, or at least look that way.

No matter how much I may tremble inside.

The horses make a sharp turn, and the carriage drifts

precariously to one side. I recall Mr. Ross's warning that the campus is surrounded by steep cliffs, and deep, freezing rivers, and dark, dangerous forests.

The first hint of light trickles through the thick foliage. Trees part to reveal a wide, packed-dirt road, and up ahead . . . My breath catches. Time ceases to tick forward.

Floodbane Academy. This is it. My final destination.

Even if the school's name hadn't been written in script on the massive wrought iron gates before us, there would be no doubt that I've arrived somewhere worth visiting.

No thatched roofs and rotting wooden walls here. The academy is a fortified castle of shimmering pearlescent stone, with four tall turrets stabbing up into the brink of dawn. Mist clings to the towers like smoke from a battlefield. The clouds bloom red, like blood spilling beneath the sea. The sun's white-hot rays pierce my pupils as if I'm unfit to cast my eyes upon a future this bright.

I squint to protect my vision, though nothing could tear my gaze away from my new home. It's built fine enough for a king, and big enough to house the grandest army. It must hold a ballroom, a gymnasium, a library the size of my old church . . .

"This is where I'm going to live?" I exclaim in delighted wonder.

Mr. Ross chuckles. "No."

Rather than go through the majestic gates, he takes a weed-matted trail leading away from the school.

I yelp in alarm. "Where are you going?"

"Female housing."

The horses duck beneath a copse of drooping branches, to lead us back into darkness. This time, I see how the wheels are scraping the trees. A crooked branch comes close to taking off the top of my head. This trail isn't meant for carriages. Not a single weed or thornbush has been cleared aside to make way for the new crop of students.

"You're certain they know we're coming?" I ask, hesitant.

"They all know."

His words should reassure me, but instead, they sound ominous.

"Duck," Mr. Ross advises as the horses get a burst of speed.

I dive to the floor to avoid being decapitated by passing tree branches.

Eventually, the carriage rattles to a stop. When I raise my head, I find a different structure. One I shall *not* confuse with the academy.

It is the house in every fairy tale that one dares not enter. The lair of witches in the woods. The gateway to hell from sweat-soaked nightmares.

A narrow two-story structure of thin, unrelenting gray, mottled with dead vines and great scabs of caked-on dirt. Bones so derelict, the sneeze of a hummingbird could send the place shuddering in a thousand directions, burying its residents beneath two tons of rotted rubble.

"Female housing," Mr. Ross announces. "The ride is over. Get out."

I gape at him. This man cannot be serious.

Mr. Ross stares back. He is deadly serious.

"Bloody fairies," I mutter, not caring if the wretched creatures hear me.

They can't let anything be easy. Not even a wish come true.

Mr. Ross flings open the carriage door, plucks me out like a wobbly baby tooth, and tosses the baskets to the ground next to me.

Not grass. Tangled weeds, thick enough to twist an ankle. It would take ages to turn this dirt into land that could be used to grow something good.

Without wishing me well or even sparing a glance over his shoulder, Mr. Ross and the carriage disappear into the thicket, leaving me alone with panicky nerves in front of a house that may or may not be haunted.

Swallowing hard, I lift a basket in each hand, determined to ignore the foreboding creepiness.

I'll be fine. Won't I?

5

Weeds tug at my hems as I inch toward the daunting abode. My long brown skirt and pristine new ankle-length yellow pelisse hide the trembling of my legs.

No one opens the door. Obviously, there's no butler stationed to peek through the curtains, ready to greet me. The windows are too coated with grime to permit the tiniest ray of sun.

I'll knock in a moment. First, I need to determine what I'm going to say. *Good morning, I'm here because my brother made a mean-spirited wish intended to shame me*? Presumably the other five lasses were chosen based on some combination of academic merit and valuable social connections. The type of girls who have never heard of my small village.

My skin itches. I was so busy worrying about whether the male students and faculty wanted to have young women here, it didn't occur to me until now that my own housemates might not be welcoming.

There's only one first impression. Do I curtsey? Have I ever curtsied? Is it better to try and risk falling over, or to stand stiff-legged and risk appearing rude? If I want to make fast friends with them all, is the wiser course to—

The door swings open to reveal a young white man so pale and dour, his narrow face looks prematurely embalmed.

"You're late," he snarls. "Yet another disappointment."

I'm so startled to find a boy in the female housing that my brain forgets everything it ever knew about the English language. All that stutters from my mouth are a few nonsensical syllables, mumbled so faintly even I can't hear what I'm saying. Perhaps for the best.

The scowling young man sighs with exaggerated impatience, grabs my elbow (but neither of the baskets) and hauls me over the rotting threshold into the shadowy gloom of my new domicile. The interior smells of old wood and mildew, heavy with disuse.

"I . . . wasn't sure . . ." is all I can stammer.

"I bet you weren't," he says sourly. "None of you little chits knows a bloody thing, nor will you by the time this ill-advised experiment is done, and Floodbane Academy returns to the respectable institution it was when it first opened its doors to the best and brightest lads in Scotland. Exclusively."

My jaw drops at such open hostility.

Quickly, I adjust my plans. Instead of finishing my schooling here at Floodbane, I vow to do whatever it takes to transfer into the far more appropriate Morrison School for Young Ladies . . . if they'll accept me. And if I can somehow earn enough money for tuition.

Who am I kidding? It's Floodbane Academy or nothing.

"Ignore Mr. Fraser," drawls a bored female voice from deep within the gloom. "This fourth-year prat is nothing more than a messenger boy for Headmaster MacKenzie."

He whirls to snap at her. "You don't belong here. None of you! And mark my words, you'll be gone soon enough."

A happy squeal fills the air, followed by a high-heeled stampede of two dainty booted feet across creaking wood. Mr. Fraser leaps aside as two arms crush my face to a plump bosom, enveloping me in a warm bear hug, the likes of which I haven't experienced since my late granny passed.

"Do I know you?" I mumble into soft muslin and warm flesh. She smells like roses and spiced cider.

"I'm Ishbel, your new roommate!" she crows, releasing me from her joyful embrace to pluck the heavy baskets from my hands and place them to one side. "Our room is the smallest one in the back, with the tiniest window!"

Said as though it were the greatest fortune ever bestowed. Perhaps it is. The smaller the room, the fewer rotten floorboards through which to fall through and break my neck.

Now that my eyes have become accustomed to the darkness, I see Ishbel more clearly. She's half a head taller than me, with beauty that Renaissance painters spent their lives trying to capture with oil on canvas. Big brown eyes, gorgeous brown skin, generous curves, a smile that could light up a room—and is actively doing so. My belly flutters. I find myself smiling back helplessly, charmed at her unexpected but welcome delight at my arrival.

Her name will be impossible to forget. Ishbel is the belle of the ball. A person seemingly as beautiful on the inside as she is out. *She* could be the good omen I've been hoping for. Instead of feeling shabby in her presence, cowering in some dark corner, I hug her back.

I shall savor my adventures here at Floodbane Academy. These will be the stories I pass on to my own daughters, and their daughters after them. Not cautionary tales of when our wings were clipped and we were slaughtered in our own kitchens, but exuberant memories of how we women became stronger together, and how it all started with a simple kindness.

"I'm Catriona," I offer.

Ishbel beams at me. "I know. Shall I introduce you to the others?"

"You needn't bother," snaps Fraser. "None of you will stay long enough for your names to matter."

"Names don't matter," agrees the earlier bored voice that advised me to ignore Fraser. It's a blond the size of a blade of wheat. She doesn't bother to look up from a knife she's sharpening with a whetstone. "I'm here for an education, not to make friends."

"That's Sorcha," Ishbel whispers. Sort of. Her whisper could wake the dead. "Sorcha has repeated 'Every woman for herself!' at least five times in the past hour."

"Eight," Fraser corrects her. "I'd be done giving this pointless orientation by now, if you chattering chits would shut the—"

"We're all in this together," Ishbel interrupts. "The six of us girls are a team, *and* part of the greater academic community."

Fraser and Sorcha snort in tandem, like a pair of horses.

"As I was saying, before the latecomer arrived . . ." Fraser glares at me. "As legend—and history books—have shown, tragedy strikes these grounds every quarter century. This campus is overdue for a plague. If you survive until half-term in October, I advise you to go home for the holiday and never return. Not if you value your life."

I stare back at him. *Marvelous. Uplifting.*

"His whole speech has been like this," Ishbel murmurs behind her hand. "The food in the refectory will cause some combination of vomiting, diarrhea, and swelling, not that we're invited to eat there with the lads."

"You must take your meals here in female housing," Fraser confirms severely. "And cook them yourselves."

"I don't mind directing the household. I've been practicing all my life in order to please my future husband." A plump redhead curtsies prettily. "I'm Fiona, by the way."

Fraser scoffs. "How long has your life been, fifteen years?"

"Doesn't matter." She bounces on her toes. "Thanks to the elite connections I'll form here at Floodbane, once I graduate, I'll no longer need to lift a single finger for anyone. My future husband shall spend the entirety of *his* life attempting to please *me*. Or at least our army of servants shall."

"For God's sake," Fraser says in exasperation. "Weren't there any lads to wed back home wherever you lot are from?"

"Don't want one," says Ishbel.

"Me either," agrees Sorcha.

Fraser is so baffled by this reaction that he dismisses both responses as if the girls hadn't spoken. "Honestly, there's no reason for any of you to journey to the Isle of Skye. Wouldn't it have been easier to take a train into Inverness and pick up a suitor in the normal way?"

"Easier than taking my pick from Scotland's brightest, on an all-male campus with no competition?" Fiona flutters her eyelashes at him. "Present company excluded."

"Are you saying Fraser isn't one of Scotland's brightest, or that he's not in the running to be *anyone's* husband?" Ishbel asks.

"Both," Sorcha and Fiona respond in unison.

I can't hide my snicker.

Fraser glares at me as if *I* were the one who had made the jest. "You think you're worthy of being here?"

Without flinching, I answer, "Girls have the same aptitude as boys, and I appreciate this opportunity to prove it."

He scoffs in derision.

I know from arguments with my own brother not to engage further. I *am* clever, and I *do* have aptitude . . . but what I don't have is the advantage of the boys' prior education. I'll start at an undeniable disadvantage and may look quite silly indeed at the first lecture. I *am* out of my element.

As if sensing my thoughts, Ishbel gives my fingers a quick squeeze. My hand feels safe in hers. She murmurs, "Don't let him win, of all people."

"I've already won," snaps Fraser. "I've a post as permanent assistant to the headmaster awaiting me as soon as I complete fourth year. As for you all . . . you might as well practice cooking and cleaning, because you'll be lucky to land work as housemaid."

From first impressions alone, I know there's no chance of ephemeral beauty Fiona emptying chamber pots for work. I wager she *will* have lads salivating over her at first lecture. Truly, the only thing she's missing is a crown.

Fraser turns to me. "You must take the placement exam before you start classes tomorrow, so that the headmaster knows where to put you." He smirks. "My suggestion is to put you right back in the carriage you rode in on."

"Placement . . . exam?" I repeat in horror.

Apparently, the fairies didn't account for this.

6

"A three-hour placement test," Ishbel confirms. "The five of us each took our aptitude assessment long before being granted our scholarships. Out of thousands of girls, only half a dozen of us were chosen."

"The best of the best," Sorcha agrees without looking up from her knife.

There are two other girls in the room who haven't spoken up yet. But the quiet ones are never to be underestimated.

Fiona buffs her fingernails. "I could have afforded the tuition without the scholarship, but it was my high marks on the assessment exam that let me through the door at no cost. All those years of private tutoring paid off."

My chest feels hollow. Perhaps *they* are the most gifted female students from their respective cities, but my short time in a rural, one-room school only occasionally populated by children needed on their farms ended four years ago. The closest thing I've ever had to private tutors were the teachings of my grandmother and mother. Not that I expect old legends of beasts and fairies to be relevant at boarding school.

I *have* read any text I could get my hands on, which weren't many. I wasn't raised in a wealthy family like Fiona's. She probably has more books in her bedroom than I've ever seen in my life.

"Wh-when is my test?" I stammer.

"This afternoon," Fraser replies.

"Can't wait," I say.

"Then you'll be delighted to know it won't be your last. At the end of the school year, all six of you must take a new assessment exam."

"What? Again?" the other girls murmur in dismay.

Fraser looks smug. "In theory, if you lot have achieved more than anticipated, Headmaster MacKenzie can place you at higher levels. But in reality, we know it will prove that girls don't belong at a respected academy like this one. Those whose academics haven't progressed to required standards will be expelled from campus."

"What?" The girls gape at him.

"When all six of you are booted out, then the experiment is officially over, and Floodbane can get back to being the best all-male academy in Scotland," Fraser finishes with a self-satisfied smile.

"Why are you here 'helping' us settle in, if you hate us so much?" I demand.

He wrinkles his nose. "I did not volunteer. I was assigned to this odious task. I'm being paid to waste my time with you."

"But if no one wants us here, why did the administration bother to send you and organize all this to begin with?"

Fraser sighs. "You'll hear the rumors the moment you step on campus, so I might as well be the one to tell you. Headmaster MacKenzie is being forced to temporarily open the school to both sexes to receive a significant financial endowment from the parent of one of the students."

"Which student?" Ishbel asks.

"I don't know," Fraser says in exasperation. "They're maintaining his anonymity because the rest of us would thrash him in place of his father."

"Who says the student is a he?" Sorcha glances at Fiona. "Any chance your parents did this?"

She shakes her head. "Trust me, they'd boast about it if they shared any part."

The other girls also shake their heads. Whoever the wealthy parent might be, he isn't one of ours.

"Then I don't understand your animosity," says Ishbel. "Do you not like free money?"

"Oh, we'll get the money," Fraser assures her. "As long as you six leave because you choose to do so of your own free will, or because your academics don't progress to standard."

Sorcha twirls her knife. "So . . . you can't kick us out."

"We can if you break school rules or fail your assessment exams," he shoots back.

My stomach churns with acid at the reminder of the impending placement test.

"One year isn't terribly long to put up with this farce of

female education," Fraser says magnanimously. "*If* you last that long."

"You'll see what we're made of." One of the remaining two girls finally speaks and gazes coolly at Fraser from hooded, narrow black eyes. She has the palest skin and the longest, shiniest black hair I've ever seen in my life. The combination should be jarring, but she is elegance personified. Her eyes flick to me, and she smiles. "My name is Euphemia, and at least we won't starve. There's nothing I can't do in the kitchen." She turns to the girl next to her. "This is my roommate. Do you cook, too, Maisie?"

Maisie doesn't answer. She hasn't looked up once since I walked through the door. I *think* she has tawny skin like mine, but don't *know* because she's mostly hidden beneath thick gloves, a drab long-sleeved, floor-length dress, and a tumble of black curls shielding her face from view. She gives no sign that she's heard a single word of the conversation around her.

"Do the boys cook and clean for themselves, too?" I ask.

"Do the boys . . ." Fraser chokes on his initial response. "Of course we don't. Male housing has staff. Our focus is on our education."

"Are we supposed to grow potatoes out front?" I press. I've spent my whole life tending fields, but I'd hoped not to have to develop farmland out of nothing. All that's out front are two trees and a tangle of weeds.

Fraser rolls his eyes. "You'll receive weekly deliveries of basic food and supplies for as long as you remain on campus."

"You said we're not on campus," Ishbel points out. "Campus

is the white castle with unbroken windows and solid walls, a full mile's walk through the woods."

"And you'll see it when you attend your lessons, starting tomorrow morning at eight o'clock sharp. No tardiness. Crawl home to your mum if you can't arrive to lecture on time. Three infractions means automatic expulsion. Maps of the school are on your beds, along with your schedules." His eyes snap to me. "Except for yours. Report for your placement exam in two hours, or forfeit your scholarship."

Maisie's lips part beneath the curtain of black curls. Her voice is soft and hesitant. "Are we allowed to—"

"You've taken enough of my time," Fraser snaps. "Figure it out yourselves, since you're so clever. With luck, we'll never speak again."

Fortunate phrasing. If he'd made that last comment as a wish, we might all find our mouths sewn shut, or our bodies turned into rag dolls. I dash to open the door for him, not out of politeness, but to hurry his bad aura out.

As soon as the door shuts, a knife whistles through the air and lodges in the wood up to the hilt, at the exact height of Fraser's head.

"Good riddance," says Sorcha as she moves to yank her knife free. "And goodbye."

She turns toward the narrow, cobwebby stairs.

"Wait," I blurt out. "That wasn't much of an introduction to each other. Have you all broken your fast? We could—"

"Uninterested." Sorcha disappears up the stairs without bothering to wait for her roommate Fiona.

I turn toward Ishbel. "You said we're all in this together. I believe that, too. Individually, it would be each one of us against hundreds of boys who don't want us here. But if we unite—"

"Speak for yourself," says Fiona, smirking. "I won't have any trouble with the lads."

"Pity about these uniforms, though," Euphemia says. "Is yellow *anyone's* color? How can we thrive whilst dressed like lemons?"

"That's what corsets are for," Fiona assures her, plumping up her bosom. "The right tools will let me show off my considerable advantages. No matter how dreadful the uniform."

"How can you think about boys?" I ask. "Didn't you hear anything else Fraser said?"

"I wasn't listening. If you'll excuse me, I've less than twenty-four hours to select the perfect accoutrements with which to break hearts at eight o'clock tomorrow morning." Fiona pivots and dashes up the stairs after Sorcha.

Euphemia clutches her uniform and a cookbook to her chest. "I'd like to fit in. The rest of you may do as you please, but I don't intend to give these boys any reason to say a cross word against me. Come on, Maisie. We might as well unpack our things and settle in like the others."

Maisie, the shy wilting daisy, grabs her basket, head down, and scampers up the stairs after Euphemia.

The room is empty now, save for Ishbel and me.

"Well . . ." I mumble.

She waggles her eyebrows at me, unbothered. "No breakfast

for them means more for us, I say. Were those pudding pots I glimpsed in your basket?"

"Clootie dumpling and cranachan," I confirm with a smile. "I saved them from the carriage."

She fans her face and moans. "I *love* sweet raspberries."

Ishbel and I drop to the floor, picnic-style, and dig into my basket. We grin at each other with mouths filled with honey and spiced berries. She licks the honey from her lips, and I do the same.

"Do you think I'll pass the aptitude test?" I ask nervously.

It's not a fair question. We've just met, and Ishbel has no idea whether I can write my own name, much less do mathematics.

"Of course you'll pass," she replies without any hesitation. "Fraser said it himself—this one is a *placement* test. You may get dumped in with a bunch of first-years who are four years younger than you, but like Fraser said, they won't kick you out unless you fail the exam at the end of the school year."

She's right. The pudding stops curdling in my stomach. "What year are you?"

"Fourth, and I placed that way, much to Fraser's existential angst," she answers with a grin.

"He would have even more existential angst if he hears you use phrases like 'existential angst,'" I tease her.

"Oh, he will. I intend to use my extensive vocabulary, as well as my skills in philosophy and Latin and Greek . . ."

My jaw drops in wonder. "You know all that?"

"I've four older brothers, and I sat in on all their tutoring, until my father allowed me to have tutoring of my own. Are you worried about not keeping up with the academics?"

"I'm intelligent enough to learn, but I haven't had the same base. It's like everyone else is starting the race three steps from the finish line, and I'm forced to start six miles away."

"Then stop worrying. I'll help you," she promises. "You don't need fancy tutors. You've got me."

We grin at each other and pop honey-covered berries into our mouths.

Floodbane Academy's female housing may not be the picturesque boarding school quarters of my dreams, but at eight o'clock tomorrow morning, I'll begin a world-class education that will open the door for a much better future. I feel as though I've won a king's ransom.

Maybe wishes aren't so dangerous after all.

7

Wishes are the devil's plaything.

From the moment my housemates and I step past the grand iron gates and onto Floodbane Academy proper, a voice rings out, "Gardyloo!"

The attacks begin.

Rotten fruits and vegetables pelt us from all sides amidst a cacophony of whoops, whistles, and jeers.

It's hard to say whether the thunderous applause from the bystanders is to mock our ruined hair and clothing, or to reward our ill-wishers for their remarkable ability to aim a moldy tomato.

"Run!" Ishbel yells.

We run.

Our plan to arrive with the other students and stroll confidently up to the school doors hadn't factored in slipping on rancid blackberry slurry in front of the entire student body, many of whom are openly spitting in our direction.

Nonetheless, we hurry *toward* the school, not away. We

haven't come this far—personally, and as an entire gender—to be frightened off by insults.

Or bruises from the blows of whole apples hurled our way at lightning speed.

"Lads! *Lads!*"

A long whistle pierces the air as a short white man with round spectacles and a smart black bowler hat steps out of the school and onto the main step. He blows his whistle two more times, a short blow and then another long one.

To my surprise, the male students halt in their tracks, as if this long-short-long whistle pattern holds particular meaning for them.

"That's Headmaster MacKenzie," Ishbel pants, as she swipes rivulets of wild cherry juice from her cheeks.

"Lads!" The school's massive front garden is now as quiet as a graveyard. "I'm ashamed of the uncharitable greeting I witness before me. A demerit for each of you!"

At this, our persecutors roar in outrage, each shouting out flimsy lies, from "It wasn't me" to "I didn't see them standing there when I threw that old plum."

"Quick," I whisper to my housemates. "Let's get to our classrooms."

Sorcha cracks her knuckles. "I'd rather give them a reason to remember me."

"We can't go *in*," Euphemia protests. "Our clothes are ruined, and have you seen your hair?"

Fiona whimpers. "How are we to attract suitors when we look and smell like pig sties?"

"Oh, grow *up*," snaps Sorcha. "Not a boy in this school gives a flying fart about any of us. Catriona's right. We go to class and carry on. It's every lass for herself now."

"Tardy three times, and we're expelled," I remind Fiona. "I'd rather have cherry pits stuck in my hair."

"But we'll split up," stammers Maisie. It's the first time all day I've heard her finish a sentence. "We each have different morning classes."

Sorcha stares at her. "Did I not just say 'every lass for herself'?"

"That's all you ever say." Euphemia shoves her fists onto her hips. "I'm of the opinion that we—"

"If we shall each receive a demerit regardless, let's make it count, boys!" shouts a distant voice.

It's the only warning before we're pelted again—this time, by stones and sticks.

"Back to Ishbel's plan," I scream amidst the chaos. "Run!"

We dash across the littered grass to the front door as beleaguered Headmaster MacKenzie sounds his trio of whistles again. This time, we don't wait to see if he regains control of his pupils. Maps in hand, we scatter like mice deep into the building, in search of safe haven.

All we find are more cats with claws.

We keep our tails tucked in tight.

As impressive as a turreted white castle looks on the outside, precious little natural light filters through the arrow-slit windows. The high stone walls make me feel like a mouse trapped in a labyrinth. Students scurry to and fro, jostling me from all sides as if I'm invisible. Or perhaps I'm *too* visible, and the beasts cannot contain their urge to trample me.

I'm on my own. Sorcha and Maisie are in the same mathematics class. Fiona is surprisingly good at geography. Ishbel tested leagues higher than us all and is the only one in Latin and Greek.

I glance down at my map. The principal corridor runs the whole perimeter of the academy, with entrances to administrative offices and classrooms of varying sizes along both sides of the hallway. If I picked a direction and started walking, I would eventually end up back at the main entrance.

The center of the map contains the largest common areas. The refectory, where the boys take their meals. An auditorium that can fit the entire student body. A large, open-air courtyard divided into two sections: a spice and vegetable garden for the kitchen and an open grassy area where students can study with their friends.

Upstairs are the dormitories, which the girls and I are forbidden to enter—not that we'd be so foolish. There's no map of that floor for us, though logic suggests the lads must be housed in one wing and faculty in another.

My first class is Philosophy, at the rear of the building. I hurry, before our tormenters can corner me inside. I'm so focused on the map in my hand that I nearly crash into a large clump of boys who suddenly stop walking.

They're staring at a section of wall plastered with notices. The first one to catch my eye is an illustrated advertisement for next month's school play: *The Taming of the Shrew*.

I cannot help but suspect that the infamous drama about a

man taming a woman was chosen on purpose, to correspond with the unwelcome arrival of female students.

But the greatest horror is the series of pasted lists to the right: names and score results for the placement tests. My stomach sinks.

Marvelous. Now everyone knows how unprepared I am to be here.

Many of my roommates scored high for their ages, thanks to prior tutoring and schooling. Although I scored high marks in a few subjects, I failed several others. I'm to share those classes with students much younger than me, which will just reinforce the blasted supposition that girls have inferior brains.

Or at least, that this particular girl is inferior.

Because half of the boys are still outside, I'm able to find a seat close enough to the front of the hall to hear the philosophy lecture. Not so my second class, or any of the others. It's not that I'm late, it's that every vacant seat I walk to immediately becomes occupied.

In the mathematics hall, boys pile their coats and books atop any chairs that would otherwise have been empty, leaving me to stand at the rear of the room, trying to scribble notes without daring to let go of any of my belongings.

At that pitiful sight, the professor is forced to scold the class to make room for me, although he clearly sides with the students. Though he never bothers to meet my eyes, his nose wrinkles when he turns his face in my direction. Class is interrupted for a full ten minutes as we await a volunteer to free a spare chair. When at last one of the reluctant lads removes his coat, he's met with such vitriol, I doubt he will escape the day unscathed, either.

This would never happen at the Morrison Institute for Young Ladies. The tales my mother used to tell me about life there and beyond were likely spun whole cloth from her imagination, but whatever the reality of an all-girls school in Edinburgh is, it must be heaven on earth compared to this hellhole on the Isle of Skye. Nonetheless, I know Mother wants me to value education. I will do my best to make her proud.

In my composition class, blank surfaces fill with boys and coats and books. Once again, I find my tense shoulders pressed against the rear wall. This time, the professor doesn't make the smallest pretense to rescue me.

It may be ambitious, but I vow to learn two years' worth of education in this one school year. Especially if Fraser's right, and this year might be the only one that Floodbane gives me.

I need to squeeze every possible advantage out of this opportunity. Then I can move to a big city like Inverness or Edinburgh to educate and empower less fortunate girls just like me.

No matter how hard these boys try to keep me in my place, I *will* graduate with honors. If not from Floodbane, then elsewhere. A brilliant performance on my end-of-year exam is my path to transferring to a better place. The Morrison Institute for Young Ladies might be out of reach, but *some* all-girls school would likely welcome me . . .

If I survive my year at Floodbane and avoid a wedding to the butcher.

At lunchtime, the lads clamber out of the classroom and stream down the corridors toward the grand refectory, where a fully staffed kitchen has spent the entire morning preparing delicious foodstuffs for them to enjoy.

My five housemates and I are meant to traverse the woods back to our crumbling abode, cook up something edible from scratch, then hike back to the school. All without being late to the afternoon period.

I've no way to know what my housemates choose to do, but I'll not be easily defeated. So rather than make the trek back toward female housing—who knows what dangers lurk in those woods—I step out-of-doors long enough to gather handfuls of the least bruised fruit littering the lawn.

The groundskeeper gives me a grunt of acknowledgment before returning to his task of cleaning up after the lads. Which makes him the only male to greet me with anything but malice. I wave and hurry to my first afternoon class.

The lecture hall is empty. I have my pick of seats, front and center. I may be pelted by pebbles and spit-soaked wads of paper, but they shall not see me cower.

After I finish two apples and a plum, I take advantage of the quiet and open the book of short stories. There will be assigned readings all school year long. I may not have understood a word of the geometry lecture earlier, but books have long been my favorite escape. Reading is my happy place.

I finish the first two stories and am halfway through the third when the gong sounds, and boys file in. They make no attempt to hide their dismay at finding me safe and comfortable at the head of the class. I've not won the war, but I've bested them in this small battle. They shan't forgive me, but for the moment, I allow myself to revel in having achieved any victory at all.

"You don't belong here," one of them snarls, giving my chair a savage kick on the way to his own.

"You're wasting your time and ours," says another boy with a vicious tug of my hair.

"You're far too simple to learn," says a third, banging against the back of my chair hard enough to cause the book to fall from my hands. "Women belong in kitchens and bedrooms, not classrooms."

This introduces a new, vulgar strain of insults. A self-contradictory hodgepodge of all the ways a lad might choose to use the female body, mixed with vehement reminders that *I* and my housemates could never tempt them to touch us.

The tirade ends when the professor walks into the room. Suddenly, my classmates are perfect angels, sitting still and silent in their seats as though I'm no longer visible.

The chairs to my left and right are empty. None of the lads wished to give the mistaken impression of friendliness by sitting too close to me. But as the professor launches into his lecture, a boy skids into the classroom, sends a wild look about the otherwise full seats, then lets out a loud, aggrieved groan before slumping into the seat next to me.

"Late again, Angus," drones the professor.

Angus is more perturbed by his proximity to me than any impending threat of expulsion.

Unless there is no such policy? For the first time, it occurs to me to wonder if Fraser made up that rule—or if the strict three-tardy limit only applies to me and the other girls.

"You didn't miss anything," I whisper to Angus.

Catch more flies with honey, and all that.

"Shut up," he hisses back, his rage so venomous that spittle shoots from his lips and lands on my bodice.

I wipe away the spittle with the back of my hand, which rubs across the necklace my mother inherited from my grandmother. I tug the tiny iron cross free from under my high-necked muslin collar and worry its thin spokes between my trembling fingertips.

It's a good thing I read today's material before class, because my heart is beating too wildly to concentrate on the professor. His words sound like wind, howling across the open moors in the scant moments before a sudden downpour.

What the devil am I doing? Will *anyone* here allow me an education?

I think of my last conversation with my father and brother. Of Mary Somerville, the first female member of the Royal Astronomical Society. Honorary member, as my brother pointed out. She made it that far and remains powerless. Wings clipped, like the rest of us.

Eliza Wigham, an abolitionist and suffragist. Brilliant, dedicated, tireless. And as Hamish would say, ineffective. Women may never gain the right to vote.

Sophia Jex-Blake, the most relevant of my heroines. The first woman to study medicine at the University of Edinburgh. She *graduated*, as I'm hoping to do. But enough disgruntled men protested that the university repealed her degree.

At this negative self-talk, the iron cross between my fingers seems to grow warmer. As if the lingering essence of my mother and my grandmother and my great-grandmother are warning me not to let the naysayers win without putting up a fight.

8

I tuck my mother's cross back beneath the safety of my bodice and lift my chin. My future students are counting on me. I won't disintegrate like a dandelion at the first wet breeze.

The next time the professor asks the class a question, my hand is the first one to shoot into the air.

He doesn't call on me.

Twelve other students give wrong answers to a simple question I could have answered in my sleep. Not that I'm given a chance. For the rest of class, no matter how fast or how long my arm is in the air, it's as if I'm a ghost.

The professor isn't rude to me, but he makes no attempt to acknowledge my existence either. No one does.

Then, despite my arm being up, the professor calls on Angus, who's not even paying attention. He's whispering to the even burlier lad on his other side, with limbs like tree trunks. Startled, Angus jerks back toward the professor and stammers a few generic platitudes that could refer to almost any given story . . . but not the one we were supposed to have read.

His towering comrade jumps in to try to save him, though he hasn't any more clue than Angus does. Both boys talk over each other, throwing in a few big words as if it'll distract the rest of us from their small ideas.

"None of that makes any sense," I blurt out, despite not having been called on. "Obviously, the author's theme is the danger of extremism in anything. Much like Sir Walter Scott in *The Heart of Midlothian*, this passage highlights religion's role in moral behavior, superiority, and hypocrisy. In fact, one could interpret this text as . . ." I blather on for several minutes out of nervousness.

This is safe ground. The plot points and characterizations, from the obvious to the subtle, give more than enough fodder to make logical assumptions based on explicit points from key passages in the text.

Angus and his friend look as though they want to murder me.

The professor still doesn't acknowledge me. He calls on someone else, as if I hadn't even spoken. That boy regurgitates my answer, word for word, and reaps disproportionate praise from the professor and other students alike.

I hate all of them.

And then I hear it. From the tall, hulking boy on Angus's other side.

"Did you hear that girl try to best us?" he mutters to Angus. "I wish she—"

"*No!*" I snap in horror, my raised hand slapping down atop

my desk with enough force to cause my book and pencil to jump several inches. "Don't you dare finish that thought!"

The invisibility spell is broken. The entire class is staring at me.

"Did she shush *Roderick MacLeod*?" whispers a distant voice with a mixture of terror and awe.

I wasn't trying to make an enemy. I was trying to stop some peabrain from undoing everything that got me here or turning me into a dead chicken or worse.

"He said, 'I wi—' " I can't choke out the word. Not even in explanation. Too dangerous. "He was about to make a W-I-S-H."

This has the opposite effect of what I wanted. The word *wish* now reverberates around the classroom, along with loud chuckles and snorts of disbelief.

I start again. "You know as well as I do that where there's woods, there're fairies."

The rest of my defense is quickly drowned in disparaging comments.

"Are we *in* the woods, genius?" asks Angus.

"Fairies?!" Roderick throws back his head and laughs with a heartiness far more exaggerated than the moment calls for.

All the other lads join him in cackling.

"They don't need woods," I stammer. "That's just their highest concentration. They're wherever shadows are. Watching. Listening. Waiting for the dangerous word you just spoke. One never knows when they'll take action, but that's no reason to endanger—"

"*Now* you're in danger?" A distant male voice shrieks with laughter. "Have you *seen* your clothes and hair?"

The schoolboys that had no notes on the text we were meant to read bubble over with commentary on their backward, rural classmate and her quaint superstitions. Idle tales no more likely than being drowned by an aquatic horselike kelpie or having your boat gobbled whole by the beast of Loch Ness.

Nothing I say is going to change their minds.

"Oh, leave her alone," comes a smooth male voice from right behind me.

The others are as surprised as I am. The taunts vanish as open mouths turn toward this new interruption.

"You this chit's white knight, Dougal?" mocks Roderick. He's so wide and tall, he manages to loom over my entire row without even rising from his chair. Roughly six and a half feet and fifteen stone of pure muscle.

"Aren't we all supposed to be protectors of women?" Dougal's voice counters behind me, his smooth tone low and bland.

He's not picking a fight. He's reminding the class that if females have our approved role in society, so too do the males.

"That's enough," interjects the professor. Interrupting at long last, before Dougal can remind too many boys of their basic humanity. "We've ten more minutes. Let's return our tongues to discussing the lecture."

It is the longest ten minutes of my life.

I'm dying to turn and see what this Dougal person looks like. Why did he defend me? Will he get away with it? Or will the others lie in wait for him, the way they did to my housemates and me? What made him decide I was worth defending?

I know I shouldn't read much into two casual sentences,

but my mind is spinning tales far more fabulous than anything printed inside this book. I would love not to have the *entire* male student body hate me and my housemates. Where there's one ally, maybe there could be more.

When at last the professor dismisses us, I leap to my feet and spin around.

Dougal does not look as I imagined. Average height, average weight, average face. Brown hair, brown eyes, brown freckles. Around my age. He doesn't look as though he's been picked on a single day in his life, or like he regularly swaggers about rescuing fair maidens.

And I owe him the world.

"Thank you," I gush with feeling.

He neither blushes nor waves me away. Just smiles with the same calm, unbothered demeanor he'd been projecting during class, and shrugs.

"New here?" Dougal asks dryly.

I cringe. I do not have my best foot forward today. "Very new."

He motions for me to follow him out of the classroom before a new wave of students can flood in.

We fall into step together. My brain jumbles trying to reconcile his smile amidst everyone else's scorn. A boy? Interested in being friends? With me? Or at least not openly attacking me. Good Lord, is "surprising lack of physical assault" the level my expectations for human decency have sunk to?

In any case, I cannot allow anyone, including this nice lad, to lure me away from my goals. All I've ever wanted is to be a good person who makes a difference, even a small one.

Concentrating on my studies is my best chance to achieve that. When I've succeeded, *then* I can let my guard down and make room for distractions.

"A wee bit of advice," Dougal says. "Stay away from Roderick and his crew. They run this school. It's not just you girls. Some of the lads they bullied . . . We never saw them again."

"Students disappeared into thin air?" I say in disbelief.

"No. They disappeared in carriages or on horses or running as fast as they can. Some with visible bruises. All with their academic records in shambles."

"That's awful!"

Out in the busy corridor, we both receive plenty of malicious looks, but at least there are no rotting projectiles. We converse quietly as we walk.

"How can Roderick and his friends have so much power? I can see he's built like a wulver. Why doesn't anyone try to stop him? Don't the headmaster and the administration run Floodbane Academy?"

"You'd think so, wouldn't you?" Dougal shakes his head. "You really are new here. The answer is money. The answer is *always* money. Roderick's family is rich. He's the fifth generation to attend this school. What about you? Why did you choose Floodbane?"

"I . . . This location was chosen for me by someone else, who didn't explain much. I don't even know if there's some specific focus to this school, or why it's so prestigious."

Dougal's forehead lines with confusion. "Focus? The focus is on education."

“I mean, is this a religious institution? A military academy? Something else?” I hate that I’m feeding into the girls-are-dense stereotype, especially in front of dozens of witnesses passing in the corridor, but I know of no easier way to get quick answers.

“Historically, Floodbane caters to elites. Sons of the titled, the wealthy, and the well connected.”

“Which one are you?”

“Connected,” he answers without hesitation. “My family’s only half as rich as Roderick’s, but I’ve never wanted for anything in my life.”

Wow. Good for Dougal. That must be nice.

My eyes narrow. Why would Mr. Wealthy-and-Connected step in to save some upstart girl intruding upon his precious school? Nobody at Floodbane is nice for no reason. Dougal must want something. Even if it’s to toy with me for his own amusement.

“How do you like Floodbane so far?” he asks.

See? He cannot be serious. No one reasonable could *like* the violent reception we received.

“We’re only allowed to attend classes as day pupils,” I hedge.

“I heard you weren’t staying on campus,” he acknowledges. “Perhaps for the best.”

I want to argue, but . . . he’s right. I’d sleep with one eye open if I lived in the same building as these boys. And maybe a knife in my hand, like Sorcha.

“How do you like the female housing?” he asks.

I widen my eyes. “What’s not to love about a dilapidated, multistory, possibly haunted structure that may or may not still be standing when I get there after school?”

He gives a wry grin. "They were going to demolish it and put up a vegetable market. If it weren't for that abandoned house's strong bones, you wouldn't be here right now."

If it weren't for a lot of things, I wouldn't be here right now.

Because I don't trust Dougal, a part of me wants to be rid of him . . . but for as long as he's game to stand around talking to me, this might be my best opportunity to gather intelligence.

"What's Floodbane Academy like for lads?"

Dougal considers. "Well, this castle is massive, and in impeccable shape—"

"It really is a castle?" I exclaim.

"It used to be. The great hall is now a library, the bailey is where we practice sports and music, the keep contains dormitories and administrative offices. The chapel is still a chapel. We have regular assemblies for entertainment and fireworks every holiday."

"That sounds incredible," I breathe.

"Well, it's not for *you*," snaps an eavesdropping boy as he elbows past us. How long was he behind us, listening in? "Come on, Dougal, why are you telling her all this? She can't have any of it. They're not even supposed to be here."

"You're wrong. I was invited and accepted on scholarship!" My fingers curl into fists. They don't know my admission is due to my brother's wayward tongue and not any particular merit, and they don't need to. "I have a letter!"

Why isn't Dougal speaking up on my behalf this time? Isn't he trying to convince me he's my knight in shining armor?

As I turn to face him, the warning gong sounds.

Dougal steps in front of the boy who was harassing me,

blocking him from my view. "I must go. Shall I walk you home after school?"

Be alone with a boy, in the deep dark woods, on purpose? Dougal's kindness may end up being genuine, but we met mere moments ago.

"No, thank you. Your aid isn't necessary."

He frowns. "I hate to say this, but you shouldn't be alone."

"I won't be," I assure him. "My housemates and I look out for each other."

This is a slight overstatement, but we *do* live together, we did walk *here* together, and we'll walk back together, too. Probably.

He nods, rather than press further. "Good. Then I'll see you tomorrow."

The final gong sounds. All the remaining students in the corridors dash to our next classes, each disappearing through crowded doorways.

On to the next gauntlet.

9

Thanks to loitering with Dougal in the corridor, I must sit in the farthest corner of the classroom. The strap of my satchel bites into my collarbone, and my skirts snag on the cracked bench.

Unlike the other instructors, who all but ignored my presence, the religion professor goes out of his way to call on me first for every question, doing his best to trip me up by quizzing me on the most esoteric Bible passages and out-of-context quotes.

Clearly, he cannot fathom what it's like to grow up in a village with a population smaller than the number of students in this room. When I wasn't busy with chores, there was nothing else to do *but* read the same books over and over again. Including the Bible. And if he thinks a single villager would dare to not show their face at the church every Sabbath morn, then he vastly underestimates the social pressures of rural country life.

I answer easily, without hesitation. And by passing his

"test," I fail the real exam: The professor grows more perturbed with each correct reply. I also don't ingratiate myself to my classmates. Particularly Roderick and Angus, whose thick hands have shot up a fair few times, only for the professor to call on me instead.

When class ends, the two stalk past me, one on each side, knocking into my slender shoulders with their broader ones hard enough to send me stumbling. My belongings tumble to the floor, where they're trod upon by my gleeful classmates. In seconds, my pencil is in shards and splinters. The pages of my Bible, ripped from its spine by the careless weight of countless pairs of boys' booted feet, all muddy from the out-of-doors.

When I finally gather it all, the professor is glaring down at me. His arms are crossed, his face a formidable scowl.

"A demerit for you if a single scrap is left behind," he warns, as if this were my doing.

I nod and claw up even the most microscopic hints of detritus from my ruined school supplies.

By the time I've found a bin for the rubbish and make my way outside at last, the schoolyard is empty. No groundskeeper, no rotting fruit dotting the grass, no angry boys whatsoever.

Nor is there any sign of my housemates.

Maybe I *should* have asked Dougal to wait for me.

I stop walking halfway across the wide expanse of grass and glance over my shoulder at the school doors. What if my housemates were held up in their classes, too? Should I wait for them?

Or did they wait for me, only for me not to appear? Are

the girls already back at our housing, getting more and more concerned by my continued absence?

Come to think of it, did they even return to school after lunch? By eating mine in my classroom, I belatedly realize they've no idea what became of me. Perhaps they thought I gave up and went home to my mum, as Fraser had suggested we all do. Or perhaps *they're* the ones who packed up and left, and I'm the bunny rabbit twitching my nose all alone in a big clearing. Not sure which way to hop, because I detect a predator in every direction.

The school door bangs open, and I jump out of my skin.

It's Fraser, looking bored and sanctimonious as always. He leans against the open door. "Ugh, what are you doing here? Did no one explain to you that the gong means *go home*?"

He's not exactly the president of the academy welcoming committee, but I'd rather run into the headmaster's lackey than most of the other boys from my classes.

"Thanks," I mutter. "I'm going."

I turn my feet toward the woods.

"There isn't a bear," Fraser adds, apropos of nothing.

Damn it. I pause and swivel back around to glare at him. "What bear?"

"There isn't one," he repeats. "What did I just say?"

I know good and well that there's no bear in these woods. Scotland doesn't have bears. Fairies, yes, and far scarier magical beasties, but no *bears*. Why, then, would Fraser bring it up? Has one escaped from a traveling circus on the other side of the isle? Is he hoping the rabid creature will tear me limb from limb?

"If you're scared," Fraser drawls with a smile, "take the left at the fork in the trail, instead of the right. It's not marked, or well trod, but it's a shortcut to the female housing."

I narrow my eyes at him, my jaw moving in thought.

From somewhere behind him, deeper within the school, comes the grating echo of boys' laughter. The raucous sound is hauntingly familiar.

Fraser glances behind him, down the corridor. "Ah. Here come Roderick and Angus."

That settles it. I'll take my chances with the bear.

Skirts flying, I tear off over the grass to the sound of male laughter. My lungs burn and my legs tremble, but in no time, I'm out past the great iron gates and into the dark thicket of the woods.

Here, I must slow my pace. The sudden lack of sunshine leaves me momentarily blind, and I don't want to trip over sticks or tree roots.

As soon as my eyes adjust to the murkiness, I move forward. There is no fork in the trail. How clueless does Fraser think I am? I walked this same path eight hours ago, on my way to school. There was no fork then, and there's no fork—

There it is. Narrow, and grown over with vines. Impossible to spot when coming from the other direction. I wouldn't have seen it if I hadn't been warned to look out for it.

I stand there, staring at the overgrown crevice, indecisive. "Blast."

Would I be more foolish for taking Fraser's shortcut, or for ignoring it? He suggested all six of us girls go back where we belong, but he didn't call us names or throw wads of spittle-soaked paper at us. Frankly, he's as rude but not any crueler than the professors.

In fact, Fraser works for the headmaster. He's scant months away from a permanent role as assistant in the academy administration. No matter how deeply he doesn't want me here, he's not going to fling me into the mouth of a bear, for God's sake.

Nonetheless, I can't do it. The hidden fork may or may not lead to a viable passage, much less a shortcut. On the other path, I can still see the impressions of my housemates' boots imprinted in the fallen leaves.

I jog as fast as I dare, without making too much noise or risking a sprained ankle.

Deep within the forest, I'm an arm's length away from the protective rowan tree at the halfway point when I'm swept off the ground and hauled into the nettles, screaming.

The bear.

It got me.

10

A massive paw claps over my mouth, stifling my screams.

No, not a paw—a human hand. A big one, but furless and smooth. I'm not being mauled by a bear. I'm being abducted by a boy the *size* of a bear. A boy I've never seen before, with fetid breath and a grip as tight as an iron trap.

I kick and flail with all I have but only knock the bark off innocent trees. The boy has my spine smashed to his chest, one hand over my mouth, and the other arm trapping my arms to my sides. My feet don't touch the ground. I can kick all I want, but he might as well *be* a bear for all my pitiful boots do to slow him down.

He drags me through the brambles. We burst into a small clearing I've never seen before. I spot a narrow wooden table—rather, a carpenter's sawhorse—standing waist-high in the center of a circle of dead leaves. It cannot be here for anything good.

"Shut up," the boy hisses in my ear. He doesn't take his hand from my mouth.

I can no longer scream loudly, but whatever this is, I won't make it easy for him. I kick and buck as hard as I can. Soon, I succeed in butting the back of my head against his chin hard enough to make him cry out in pain. Good. I hope he bit through his tongue.

He gasps. "Bitch."

Rustling sounds in the forest. A mini stampede. It's probably too much to hope for an actual bear.

A different set of branches part, and two scoundrels I do recognize bound into the clearing with expectant, grinning faces.

Roderick and Angus. My biggest fans. Hulking over me like malevolent oak trees.

Seems I should've taken Fraser's shortcut after all.

I struggle like a wild thing, my efforts redoubling. If all three lads get their hands on me, there'll be no breaking free.

"Well done, Mungo," says Roderick, his eyes glittering. "You found a sweet treat for our afternoon tea."

"Not sweet." Mungo spits blood past my ear. Red droplets fall onto my bodice. "Cracked my lip open with her hard skull."

I buck backward and try to do it again.

"Feisty, I see." Roderick's smile widens. "We'll see how long it takes us to break this filly."

Stalking toward me, he loosens his cravat and slides the square of white linen free from his neck. With Mungo's aid, the disgusting sweat-stained cloth is tied fast across my mouth and behind my head as a gag.

I call the trio every swear word I've ever overheard.

All that comes out are angry muffled grunts, like the rooting of a pig.

"Angus?" Roderick prompts, as if expecting a lump of sugar for his tea.

"Right." Angus tugs off his own dirty cravat. This one ties my wrists together in front of my stomach.

Roderick inclines his head, pleased. "Mungo?"

Mungo drops me without warning.

Unable to break my fall with my bound hands, I tumble forward, landing face-first on dirt strewn with dead leaves. My teeth clack together hard enough for me to see stars.

That's all it takes for Mungo's cravat to tie my ankles together without resistance.

Angus frowns. "But how are we—"

"Not yet." Roderick flicks a hand. "Lift."

Mungo and Angus carry me to the sawhorse and lay me lengthwise along the thick wooden plank as though I'm an offering to the gods.

All three back up and admire their handiwork.

I'm now free to buck and thrash, but all it would accomplish is to send me crashing to the ground again. This time, I might lose a tooth or shatter my own nose.

I can only lie here, trembling. Hating.

Roderick tsks his tongue. "You caused demerits for the whole school this morning. Poor showing, lass."

I did no such thing! They earned their own bloody demerits by throwing projectiles at six unsuspecting girls.

But as before, my protests are no more eloquent than the buzzing of a fly.

"Mm." Roderick strokes his chin. "You want to talk?"

I nod furiously.

"Are you going to scream?" he asks.

Obviously, cretin.

"If you make a peep," Angus says idly, "we'll kill you."

"Slowly." Roderick's eyes sparkle.

Defeated, I shake my head. No, I won't scream.

Off comes his disgusting cravat, but it doesn't go far. Mungo keeps it and his thick palms at the ready, prepared to suffocate me at a moment's notice.

"You think you're clever, don't you?" asks Roderick.

My mouth is dry. "I think I'm lucky to be at Floodbane, given I've been out of school for the past several years."

"Oh, bragging now, are we?"

I blink at him. "What?"

He gestures at himself and his friends. "We've had tutors all our lives, and you flit in from some faraway farmland, showing me up without even trying. Is that what you're saying?"

"That's not what I was trying to say," I mutter. "But if you're capable of putting two and two together . . ."

Roderick shrugs off his coat like a snake shedding its skin and steps forward. "Do you want to know what other pieces I can fit together?"

"I'm sure you're as bright or even brighter than me," I blurt out, desperate to placate him. It hadn't been clever to poke the beast. "You just didn't have a childhood filled with the same few books to read, and nothing but time tilling fields in which to ruminate over the author's choices."

He tilts his head. "Be that as it may, you made me look bad in class, in front of my subjects."

I frown. "You mean . . . peers? Fellow students?"

"He means subjects," Angus corrects me. "Roderick is king of Floodbane. Even the faculty bows to him."

"Or did, until today." Roderick flashes his teeth. "Do you know what a king does to those who would usurp him?"

"Off with their heads," Mungo whispers against my cheek, his foul breath sending waves of gooseflesh beneath every layer of protective clothing I'm wearing.

"Can't let women who think for themselves roam free," Roderick agrees. He holds out his hand.

Angus places a knife in Roderick's palm.

Fear lances me. I imagine all the ways they really could kill me, right after whatever other atrocities they intend to commit to my body in the name of fun and perceived revenge.

After all, they can't let me go, can they? I could tell the whole world what they've done.

Then again, who would believe a silly girl?

"Sometimes," says Roderick, "royalty has to send a clear message to their subjects."

Bile rises in my throat. "You expect to get followers and loyalty from torturing and killing me?"

"I told you, I already have followers and loyalty," he replies with a smile. "With a small sacrifice, I expect to keep them. An offering, to the only god who matters. Myself."

"You're sick," I whisper. "You're mad."

He doesn't care in the least. "Do you think you belong here with us?"

Trick question, not that he knows it. "I was sent a scholarship."

"To observe your betters quietly, not run your mouth! Do you think you're smarter than us?"

"Can't we all be clever? Isn't that what we're here for? An education?"

"I'm here to rule, remember? Tonight, I'll make sure you don't forget that."

Mungo grunts. "What if you made her your queen and ruled together?"

Roderick jabs his blade in my direction. "Anyone with half a brain would know I'd never be attracted to this sentient cow."

"All cows are sentient," I murmur. "The living ones, anyway."

He glares at me.

"And some are quite pretty," I add.

He grinds his jaw.

"She's from the Highlands, ain't she?" says Mungo helpfully. "Those cows *are* rather fetching."

"Shut up, Mungo," Roderick grinds out through gritted teeth. "Some subjects serve best in silence."

"It's getting darker," Angus interrupts. Only the faintest light now trickles between the trees. "Should we get to the best part?"

Roderick caresses my cheek with the blade of his knife. "Absolutely."

"Hey!" cries an angry voice. "What are you doing?"

I flail, nicking my cheek with the knife, but in a glance, I recognize the face of the new arrival. Fraser, the headmaster's assistant.

Thank God!

"Fraser!" I gasp. "Help! They're trying to—"

"I said *not* to start without me," he snaps, pulling out a knife of his own.

The air vanishes from my lungs, and my elation dies with a whimper. Tears leak from my eyes as I realize the horrific truth:

No one is coming to save me.

"Hurry up, then," snaps Roderick. "We've got to be back in our dormitories before evening headcount."

A hysterical giggle splinters in my throat at the idea that what worries my attackers most is being scolded for not going to bed on time.

My head spins. The forest feels unreal. The knives, unreal. My own skin, unreal.

And yet I cannot deny the sting of blood dripping down my cheek.

All forests are full of fairies. I want to shout for them to save me, but I know better than to make a wish. They'd turn me into a chicken egg to spite me, and I'd find myself crushed under the nearest boot.

"She thinks she's better than us," Roderick tells Fraser.

I shake my head. "I never said—"

"Mungo?" prompts Roderick.

The neckerchief gag is back on in a flash.

"Fact number one," says Roderick. "You're not better than

anyone, least of all me. Fact number two. You don't belong here. To illustrate these points, we will now divest you of everything you don't deserve. Lads?"

Four knives fly at me all at once.

Hems rend. Buttons pop. My bodice is ripped open to my corset as the Floodbane coat of arms embroidered on my chest is torn away. My academy pelisse is sliced to ribbons, along with the layers of sleeves and skirts beneath it, piercing my skin in a thousand tiny gashes.

"Do you think you're one of us *now*?" Roderick snarls as his knife flashes down again and again. "Do you think you're perfect and pure *now*? Do you think you belong anywhere near polite society *now*?"

I continue to flail, but it's no use. Fighting back risks the knives cutting deeper.

Roderick laughs. "I'll keep going until I penetrate your brain."

Angus snorts. "And if she hasn't one?"

"Then we'll penetrate everything we can. We'll have fun, won't we, Catriona, my kitty cat?"

All of the boys curl their fingers like pretend claws and swipe their hands at me playfully, like kittens cornering a frightened mouse.

Angus's eyes brighten. "Know what Catriona would hate even worse?"

I cannot imagine hating anything worse than what's already in store for me.

Roderick guffaws, then pitches his voice to a high falsetto. "No, not the W-word! Anything but the W-word!"

Wishes. They're talking about making reckless *wishes.* On purpose!

He rasps the side of his blade along the whalebone of my exposed corset. "I bet you wish you were a fairy, so that you could fly away."

This is close enough to my great-great-granny's dying wish that I flinch.

He grins.

"I wish she *was* a magic fairy," says Mungo. "She could gift a lass to each of us."

Angus laughs. "I wish she was bonny, so that I'd want her."

"What are you going to wish for, Roderick?" asks Mungo.

"I have my wish." Roderick tosses his knife aside and tugs my bound hands around his neck.

Excruciating pain explodes through my . . . feet?

Agony so intense, so white-hot and all-consuming that, for a brief moment, I pass out.

"Wh-what did you do to her?" stammers Mungo. "Is she dead?"

Maybe I was unconscious for longer than I realized.

Roderick's chuckle rumbles against my ripped bodice. "Not yet, but I'd wager she'll wish for death soon enough."

I can feel more than his laughter. I can hear his heartbeat. All four of their heartbeats. The air whistling in and out of their lungs. The rushing of their blood in each individual vein. The wet flapping of each ventricle of their black hearts deep inside their chests.

"And now for the good part." Roderick's weight crushes down on my chest, his breath hot and sour.

Mungo's bulk pins my legs, while Angus's steely fingers dig into my wrists. Smirking, Fraser gestures for more action, as though directing a favorite scene of a play.

Abject terror sends a jolt of power through me. I yank my arms and legs apart. The cravats that had bound my limbs shred from the force, as if the tight knots had rotted apart at my wrists and my ankles.

A flicker of confusion lines Roderick's brow. "What the . . ."

I claw at his face, at Angus's, at Mungo's. I'm a tempest of elbows and sharp heels and torn fingernails. The boys pile back on, but I'll *not* let them win.

"What in Hades is going on here?" Heavy footsteps dash toward the fray. Thick arms fling Roderick off me as if he weighed no more than . . . a sack of rotten fruit?

The boys shrink back to reveal the groundskeeper, pale and horrified, with a hunting rifle in one hand. "What's the meaning of this, lads? Lass, are you all right? What have they done to you?"

I've never been further from all right as I am in this moment. What's left of my clothing hangs from me in tatters. Every exposed bit of skin, smeared with my own blood. I choke back a sob. They will not see me cry.

Rather than try to explain, I turn and run. Clomping off into the woods as fast as my legs will carry me.

"Wait!" the groundskeeper calls.

I don't wait. I know what he thinks he saw. The aftermath of a violent . . . Roderick will get his wish regardless. I realize with horror. Taking my purity, or even the impression of having done so, will ostracize *me*. I'll be expelled without a second thought. Sent home to the rural Highlands, where I'll become the village pariah. Even the butcher won't want me anymore.

Just as I wished. And not at all as I wished.

I duck branches and vault over tree roots with surprising agility, given I feel like a stranger inside my own body. I press my mother's delicate iron cross to my chest for safety and jerk my hand away when the skin burns where it touches. Those bastards have cut me in so many places, I can no longer even take comfort in my mother's love.

When at last I trot free from the forest, my feet burn with agonizing pain. I lift what's left of my skirts, half expecting to see two mangled stumps instead of human legs. My boots are still there. The little bows I'd tied into their knots as perfect as they were when I left the house this morning.

And yet deep within my marrow, I know nothing will ever be the same again.

11

Somehow, I bury my emotions until the horrors of the woods are behind me and the derelict female housing comes into sight.

The door is open. A gust of wind sends a plume of dead leaves into the air. Ishbel hovers at the threshold, one hand cupped over her eyes, although the sun has now set. As if she has been standing, right there, like that, since the moment she arrived from class to discover I'd not yet made it home.

At the sight of her, the backs of my eyes sting with the weight of unshed tears.

At the sight of me, her arms open wide. She rushes forward, her boots sending the dust of crushed leaves billowing behind her.

My legs are boneless, limp as overcooked carrots, disintegrating into a soggy mess beneath me. But I don't let that stop me. Somehow, I sprint faster, almost flying, until I am indeed airborne, launching myself into her outstretched arms with enough force to implode both our bodies on contact.

Ishbel holds as firm as the rowan tree beside the house. Her soft strong arms wrap around me tight, enveloping me in warmth and newfound friendship and safety. I don't remember sobbing into her neck, but the top of her bosom sticks to my cheek with salty wetness.

She strokes my back, my arms, my hair. I know she feels the frayed fabric scratching against her palms, the ripped edges stiff with my dried blood. The matted curls atop my head are full of eight hours' worth of the debris thrown at me. Wads of spittle-soaked paper, bits of rotten fruit, dirt and leaves from the forest. It all begins to come free as her clean, patient hand strokes away the confetti of compounding nightmares.

Ishbel asks no questions. Not yet, at least. She brushes sweaty tendrils from my temples and kisses my cheek. She is crying, too. One look at me was enough for her heart to break.

My first thought is neither self-pity nor thirst for revenge, but rather fierce protectiveness. I cannot allow what happened to me to happen to Ishbel and the others. We cannot live like this.

Suddenly, viscerally, I feel what my great-great-grandmother must have felt, standing before that open window, knowing that not a single tomorrow was going to be any better than the thousands of crushing yesterdays she had already endured.

Inverness has a railway. If I could get there, I wouldn't need wings. I could allow puffs of hot steam and the loud clang of rotating irons wheels to carry me somewhere else. Anywhere but here.

"Catriona," Ishbel murmurs.

I push her away, though it's the last thing I want to do. I'm not safe to be around. I'm broken.

I step past her. "Leave me alone."

Her soft hand slips into mine. "Not going to happen."

My throat closes. I do my best to swallow the hard lumps that form. My heart is no longer racing. My exposed bits of skin are cold and clammy. A gust of icy wind sends goosepimples rippling across my flesh, raking my tender skin against the tears in my clothing, and breaking open dozens of still-forming scabs.

"Let's get you cleaned up," Ishbel says softly.

No one sees me climb the stairs, a bloody ghost. The other girls are in their rooms behind closed doors, studying, sobbing. It has been a long day for all of us. I am glad for the privacy, though I still fear the morrow. Who knows what tales the four horsemen of hatred are spinning about me over at the school. The rumors will have passed through every ear and mouth by morning.

I don't really register Ishbel slicing off my ruined clothing with shears. Leading me to a large metal tub in the center of our bedroom. Making countless trips downstairs to the kitchen fire to trudge up the steps with pail after pail of clean hot water for my bath.

No one but my mother has ever seen me naked, but to my surprise, I'm not overcome with shyness. Perhaps I've already endured the maximum quantity of humiliation the Fates could inflict upon me in a single day.

The memory repeats without cease: Fraser's cold sneer, Angus's eyes scanning for weakness, Roderick's flexing muscles,

Mungo's ready fists. The sour taste of the gag. The panic of bound wrists. Four flashing blades at once.

I tremble uncontrollably, knees up, arms wrapped around my legs. Allowing my limbs to be manipulated as easily as a rag doll, whilst scented soap and Ishbel's light sweet touch erase every remnant of horror from my hair and my body.

"You have very few scratches," she says with astonishment. "I thought you'd been cut to ribbons."

"My dress . . ." The syllables come out garbled. "My pelisse . . ."

"We have spares," she reminds me. "You, more than most. A fresh round of supplies was delivered for you while we were at school."

Right. The fairies wouldn't want me to miss a single moment of this wish-come-true.

When I'm clean and dry and dressed in a long white cotton nightgown, Ishbel tucks me into my bed, then climbs in beside me.

Only then does she ask, "Do you want to tell me exactly what happened?"

No. I want to burn the memory to ashes.

But the words spill from my lips unbidden. How I'd found myself all alone. How they'd tricked me, trapped me, tied me up. How the sting of their words was nothing compared to the slice of the knife. How I'd lost consciousness for a moment, from fear or pain or both.

Ishbel is horrified. "They might have done *anything* to you if you couldn't fight back!"

"I *couldn't* fight back. From the moment Mungo caught me, I was helpless. They were going to kill me when they were done."

"What do you think they wanted from you?" she whispers.

I needn't answer. Ishbel already knows. She grabs my hand, and we shudder in unison.

Ishbel curses. "I could murder them. How did you get away?"

That part is murky. "The groundskeeper arrived. He had a hunting rifle."

"He should have shot them," Ishbel says vehemently.

"By then, I was free and running away. Running here. Running toward you."

She squeezes my hand. "I hate those boys."

"So do I."

"If I had the power to destroy them, I would."

They are the ones with the power. Was it pointless to dream of a better life? Should I give up now and crawl back to the butcher?

"We must stick together," Ishbel whispers, as if reading my mind.

My voice shakes. "Mother says, 'Sometimes, family is all that we've got.'"

Ishbel hikes herself up on one elbow to face me. "Family isn't all that you've got. Your mother may be far away, but I'm right here. If we don't have anyone else, we can at least count on each other."

I blink rapidly toward the ceiling, focusing as hard as I can on the planks of stained wood rather than the blurry shimmer coating my eyeballs. I miss my mother *so much.* I silently wish she were in this bed with us, hugging me. With my free hand, I loop her necklace around my wrist, letting the tiny iron cross dangle. With my other hand, I hold on to Ishbel.

We lie like that for several moments before her head turns to face me again. Lines crease her brow. "If the groundskeeper arrived after you were already free, how did you break loose?"

"I don't know." I uncurl my fingers from the cross, letting the talisman dangle from its loop of twine. "Maybe this protected me."

Ishbel nods. She thinks I mean God, not the enduring love of the brave women who came before me. I'm certain my mother's cross saved me from my attackers. I hadn't been wearing the talisman during Hamish's outburst, but now I don't go anywhere unprotected.

"We can't let the boys win," Ishbel announces. "No matter how hard they try to demoralize us. They're wrong. We belong here, too."

"Not completely wrong," I confess. "You were meant to be here, but I wasn't. My brother Hamish made an idle wish to shame me, and this is how the fairies chose to grant it."

"Good." Ishbel doesn't question this explanation. No doubt she too was raised with the same stories. Like mine, her family may have experienced the capriciousness of fairies firsthand.

"In the woods, the boys tried to make wishes at me out of cruelty. But nothing happened."

"Maybe the fairies weren't listening."

The fairies are always listening. Although they don't always choose to respond, one cannot count on their disinterest.

"Something peculiar did happen . . ." A memory bubbles back to the surface. "My feet hurt more than I ever thought possible."

"You walked farther than you normally do?" she guesses. "I had to stand in most of my classes. That's hard on your feet."

"Not like that. Unimaginable pain. As if every bone had been crushed with a hammer, and the bloody stumps had been lit aflame."

Ishbel's eyes widen. "You had it worse than me. Do your feet still hurt?"

I glance down at them, my toes poking up through the bedsheet. "They're sore, but the feeling was indescribable."

She throws the sheet aside and crawls down to the foot of the bed, lifting my feet into her lap.

"What are you doing?" I stammer in surprise.

"Something I learned from my mother. Tell me to stop if you don't like it."

Her thumbs start on the stiff arch of my foot, applying slow steady pressure upward and outward over and over with exquisite patience, until every last shadow of tension is rubbed away and my muscles are soft as moss.

I've never seen anyone do this, but now that I've experienced it for myself, I make a mental note to treat my own mother. And Ishbel too, as soon as I learn the trick.

She's right. Family needn't mean just my mother and our dead ancestors. We and our housemates could form a second family. Or at least choose to be friends.

If no one else on this small island wants to welcome us, then we shall welcome each other. We can even have a little ceremony to make it official. Us against the world, or at least versus the cruel lads of Floodbane.

Maybe together, we'll have a chance.

12

The next morning, it is Sorcha who grips her knife in her fist.

"I'll kill them," she snarls.

"That's what I said," agrees Ishbel.

"But in my case, I mean it." Sorcha glares out the door as though she can smite a path through the woods with the fieriness of her rage.

I'm less certain. Sorcha hasn't seen the way Roderick's shadow stretches across a room. The way Angus's grin never reaches his eyes. How Mungo's hulking form blocks the sun from sight. How Fraser's clipped accent and smug posture, knowing his ties to the administration, make him untouchable.

Feet dragging, I'm the last to leave the house. "We can't kill them."

Sorcha spins to face me, jaw dropping. "You, of all people—"

"I don't even like to kill chickens."

"Those lads *are* chickens!"

"Which I just said I don't want to kill. We're better than

them. Vengeance is never the answer." I clutch my new pelisse tighter around my chest. "One cannot respond to violence with violence."

"I can," Sorcha mutters.

Though I don't say so aloud, I share the sentiment. I cry every time livestock must be slaughtered, but when it comes to those four boys and what they did . . . what they wanted to do . . . Of *course* I'd love for them to get their comeuppance.

But I'd settle for preventing them from harming anyone else.

Euphemia pipes up, "You'll be tardy more than three times if you're locked up in gaol for murder."

"Worth it," Sorcha singsongs.

"No." We head toward the school together. "No boy is worth the loss of your dreams."

"My dream is to kill them," she says.

Euphemia sends me a look. "What's your dream, Catriona? You don't want to fight like Sorcha, and you're not fishing for suitors like Fiona . . ."

"I want an education," I reply in exasperation. "Is that such a peculiar thing to seek at a school?"

"She wants to move to Inverness or Edinburgh," says Ishbel. "And help girls like us avoid falling in with lads like Roderick and Angus and Mungo and Fraser."

"I hated Fraser on sight," mutters Sorcha.

"Floodbane is my first step in the right direction," I explain. "Those boys can try to make this experience as bad as they like, but they can't stop me."

I hope.

"They came close to ruining you," Ishbel says quietly.

"Well, now we stick together," says Euphemia.

Sorcha raises a pumped fist in solidarity.

Our steps aren't exactly buoyant. None of us fancies being in these woods a moment longer than necessary.

When we emerge, boys are everywhere. But there are no projectiles in sight. Just a teeming mass of adolescent males with identical haircuts and yellow suit coats with the academy crest upon the breast.

As we make our way forward, they part like the Red Sea. *No*, false analogy. They're not parting so much as lying in wait on two sides, creating a walkway. The way villagers crowd the pavements when a royal procession clomps through the middle of town.

"What's happening?" Maisie trembles as her head swivels left and right.

"I've no idea." Whatever this is, I can't imagine that it's a good thing.

Even Fiona inches forward awkwardly, instead of with her usual sway and swagger. She wanted the boys' attention, but not like this. And she's the first to realize what's really going on.

The moment we reach the school's front step, Fiona grabs my elbow and touches her lips to my ear. "They're not watching us. They're watching you."

Marvelous. I was right about the rumors.

My housemates and I exchange uneasy glances. None of

us have the same first class. Most of us won't see each other all day.

I croak, "Lunchtime?"

"I'll meet you right here," Euphemia says without any hesitation.

"We all will." Ishbel sends pointed looks from Fiona to Sorcha. "From now on, we come to school together, and we leave school together. Agreed?"

There is no argument. Everyone agrees so fast, you'd think we rehearsed synchronized nodding on the walk over.

Ishbel squeezes my hand. "Good luck."

Sorcha tries to slip me a knife, but I shoo her away.

I rethink that decision the moment I walk into class. Where out-of-doors, the crowd was hushed, in here it's not.

Slut is the first word I can pick out from the whispers. *Hussy. Tart. Slattern.*

Well, that's the first mystery solved, then. It's clear that my attackers' version of events made a few adjustments to matters of consent and who wanted what.

And they have the advantage of being the first to spread their tales. Roderick with his swagger, Mungo's threatening scowl, Angus with his cruel laugh. Fraser's icy stare.

Saw her me self, floats another whisper. *Teats hanging out, plain as day.*

Dozens chime in with their own lies about my slovenly appearance during an illicit rendezvous. If half the people who supposedly spied upon me had been present, there wouldn't have been any room in the forest for trees.

"I didn't lie with any of them!" I snap when I cannot take the unfair censure anymore. "Did you not see the scratch marks upon their faces?"

Their eyes shine with the eerie glow of the devout. "Of course we did. Bloody near got killed themselves, fighting off that kelpie for you, now didn't they? Big as a dragon, it was. Roderick and his boys fought it back to the water with their bare hands. Heroes, they are."

My mouth falls open, but not even a tiny gasp of outrage escapes. I've nothing left to give.

"If anyone could fight a kelpie and live to tell the tale, it would be Roderick," a first-year boy says, impressed.

Warm murmurs of approval and awe ripple through the ranks.

I want to vomit.

Yesterday, no one believed me about fairies. And today, it seems reasonable that the great bollocks-for-brains Roderick overpowered a shape-shifting water stallion the size of a dragon with nothing more than his fists and an overinflated sense of self-worth?

A boy digs his sharp elbow into my ribs. "Heard about your role in the matter. Out all alone to meet up with a lover, were you?"

The others erupt into a mix of high-pitched sounds somewhere between the squeal of hungry piglets and the whine of a bitch in heat.

Another boy smirks. "Shrieking and crying like a baby, until Roderick took matters into his own hands, weren't ye?"

Aye. I was indeed shrieking and crying like a baby. Thanks to Roderick and his gang.

"The most dangerous beasts are the ones within these school walls," I hiss.

The boys laugh. I'm hilarious. If all else fails, I've a future on stage in a comedy.

My voice shakes as it rises. "*They're* the monsters! If any part of my 'teats' were ever visible, it wasn't of my own volition!"

One of the lads rolls his eyes. "A likely story."

"Even if that were true," says another, "all that proves is that *you shouldn't be here.*"

I reach trembling hands to my mother's cross, which I've left on the outside of my high-necked bodice today for easier access. Somehow, I manage to catch the pad of my thumb on a surprisingly sharp corner, and I jerk my hand away to reveal a drop of blood.

One of the boys snorts. "Fragile, aren't you?"

"You'd like to think so," I snap. "Like it or not, my friends and I are here to receive the same education as you are."

At that, they all guffaw.

"Law and medicine?" cackles one lad. "Be serious."

"A waste of time," chortles another. "Go find a school teaching watercolor and sewing."

"Boys!" Our instructor enters the room, clapping his hands. "Take your seats."

After a disorienting moment, I realize I'm back to being invisible to this professor, who sees no point in acknowledging a female's presence.

Class after class, I'm given the same reception from the male students. Leering looks and lewd comments, mixed with passionate eulogies, glorifying the masculine strength and brave heroism of King Roderick and his faithful squires.

I nearly grind my teeth into nubs.

Was it not enough to paint me as the Floodbane whore? All four of them needed to become gods?

At lunchtime, the other girls fill me in. After I'd fled the scene of the crime, the groundskeeper demanded an explanation. In their panic, courageously saving me from a rabid kelpie was the first nonsense that shot out of the boys' mouths.

The groundskeeper knows our legends are based on facts. He told the boys that they were lucky to come across me when they did—a sentiment I'm sure they agreed with. To add insult to injury, the groundskeeper apparently told the headmaster that not only did my attackers not owe me an apology, but what was owed is me offering them my eternal thanks.

I'd rather sacrifice myself to a dragon.

In my literature class, Dougal is once again right behind me. I can feel his clear brown gaze boring a hole through the many extra layers I chose to wear today. If I knew where to find chain mail, I'd have thrown some of that on, too.

When class ends and everyone rises to their feet, I expect Dougal to shame me like the others. Or launch into a sanctimonious speech about the weakness of women and how I never should have come here and how the fault for any inconvenience suffered is all mine.

It nearly breaks me when he says quietly, "I should have been there, Catriona. I'm sorry."

I blink hard and look away fast.

"If only you had accepted my protection!" His voice wobbles. "And if only you hadn't needed it."

Damn it. I force myself to meet his eyes. "There was no kelpie."

He holds my gaze sorrowfully. "I assumed as much."

I swallow hard. I hadn't expected to be believed. To have a boy regret he had not been there to offer protection from other boys.

"It's not your fault," I mutter. Dougal would've been no more successful beating back four large lads at once than I was.

Even if Dougal had managed to foil their plans yesterday, I'd have been vulnerable some other moment instead.

It's a sad fact of life that, with some men, there's no way to avoid violence.

The best a girl like me can do is to postpone it.

"I'll try to be more vigilant in the future." He tilts his head. "Perhaps I can aid in other ways. Are you doing well in your classes?"

"Some of them," I hedge. "Unlike everyone else, I haven't had much formal schooling. Ishbel has promised to help me every night, but I hate to take up all of her time, when she needs to study for her own classes, too."

"I don't care about my classes," he says. "I'm here because my mother forced me to be. I'd rather be working in a field than taking exams. But I know better than to be anything less than perfect."

"I'm the one who wants me to be perfect," I admit. "I don't want good marks. I want the *best* marks, so that I can transfer somewhere that does want girls like me. I'm going to be an educator myself one day."

He tilts his head. "My mother always wished for a daughter like you, who would say things like that and mean them. Instead, she's stuck with me. Someone who can name more flowers than philosophers, and who would rather pick up a shovel than a pencil."

He looks so properly miserable that I cannot help but chuckle. "And yet you were going to offer to be my tutor?"

"Well, I wouldn't *like* it." His eyes sparkle with humor. "I was hoping you'd say it was your deepest dream to sow a field of bilberries, or to hear about the progression of wild cherry cultivation on the Isle of Skye. I would've happily bored you to death with useless facts about plants, history, and geography."

"I'd be grateful, and fascinated. I want to know everything, remember? As a future educator, I need to be well rounded. And if that means eating a field of bilberries—"

"*Sowing* a field," he scolds me. "You can eat the first harvest three years later."

"Good Lord. Then I guess I've time to study with you, learning about history and geography. Maybe once a week, after classes, if at least one of my friends is also staying late?"

"Still don't trust me to walk you home, do you?" He sighs. "I don't blame you. Being cautious speaks highly of your intelligence. My mother would eat you up."

"I've a mother of my own I'm hoping to return home to," I inform him. "Though, if you'd take my brother Hamish off my hands . . ."

"I'd be disinherited," Dougal says sorrowfully. "Apologies."

Ah, well. A girl can dream.

13

When walking with my housemates back to our housing after school, the mood is somber. None of them mentions the vicious gossip, but my mathematics professor smirked in my direction the entire hour. The religion instructor made the sign of the cross when I walked through the door.

I reach for my own cross as we make our way single file through the woods. The place where my mother's talisman rests itches, despite layers of muslin and cotton separating the cross from my décolletage. It isn't the sharp edges of the iron scratching me, then, but some other malady. Perhaps the brush of a poisonous leaf after the boys sliced open my clothing.

Just what I need: a growing rash of red, itchy welts covering my entire body.

For now, the area is small and out of sight above my bosom. The iron cross scratches my fingers, and I let it fall back to my chest. Despite the high-necked bodice, my sensitive skin beneath twitches with pain, as though I were being branded with scorching hot molten iron.

When we arrive at our dank, ugly housing—none of us think of it as *home*—most of my housemates scatter like autumn leaves. Euphemia to the kitchen for some restorative baking, Sorcha to her whetting stone, Fiona to her looking glass to plan for tomorrow, Maisie to burrow under her covers until dawn comes and we must start all over again.

"Have time for tutoring?" Ishbel asks as we enter our room.

"Yes," I answer with relief. "As much time as you'd like to give me."

This is both true and not true. After our hostile reception, I do want to prove myself. But my entire being also feels fragile, as though my skull might burst into pieces from trying so hard to keep it together.

Luckily, I needn't pretend with Ishbel. She won't judge me for my rage or determination.

The small shared nightstand in our room isn't large enough to spread out books and papers, so I drop to the warped wooden floor between our beds. It's narrow. If I fold my arms like chicken wings, my elbows can touch both our mattresses at the same time—but at least it gives us a surface to work with.

Ishbel wrinkles her nose. "What about the table downstairs?"

"Euphemia's using it to cook our supper," I remind her.

Ishbel sits on the edge of her bed and leans over to untie her boots. I watch as her nimble fingers make short work of the knotted cord, loosening it from the eye holes until she can slip one silk-stockinged foot free, then the other.

I almost blurt out, *You even have beautiful feet*, but stop myself. She is gorgeous from head to toe, though. Slender ankles, high arches, perfectly straight toes. My feet are nothing like that. Knobby toes of jagged lengths, warped as if I use them to hang upside-down from tree limbs like a bat. Luckily, she cannot see—my stockings are wool, and hide the evidence of my imperfections from view.

Rather than slide off her mattress to the floor to join me, Ishbel scoots backward until her spine touches the thin, wood-paneled wall. She pats an empty space next to her on the bed and lifts her eyebrows.

I scramble off the floor, gather up my books and papers, and join her.

We turn to face each other, with the papers in the middle. I'm sure her mattress and blanket are the same as in my bed, but it feels cozier on her side of the room. Maybe it's the warmth of her body so close to mine, our bent knees grazing each other as we peer forward at the open books between us.

I clear my throat. "Just philosophy and mathematics."

"You're doing well in the others?"

I nod. Dougal offered his services in geography, and I tested well ahead of my age in religion, literature, and composition. But I've had little exposure to geometry or the discipline once known as natural philosophy, which modern practitioners are beginning to call "science."

"All right." Ishbel folds a piece of paper into a triangle. "The Pythagorean theorem states . . ."

Her voice is like honey. I drink it in hungrily. I find myself trying to memorize her cadence and mannerisms as much as her melodic explanations. One day, when I'm a professor, I want to enthrall my pupils just as much.

Years from now, I suspect that I'll still reminisce about the year I spent on the Isle of Skye, hunched atop a thin mattress with Ishbel, our knees touching and our breath mingling as we bend our heads together and make do with the limited supplies provided in our school satchels.

Even her hair smells good. Not like the square cakes of cheap suet washing soap provided to us by Floodbane, but rather a gentler, sweeter scent. Almost floral enough to double as a light perfume. I want to ask if she's brought this from home, and whether it's a family recipe she'd be willing to part with. But I don't want her to think I'm not paying attention to her lectures.

"Quiz," Ishbel announces, sketching a few quick figures on a piece of scrap paper. She adds numbers to the first. "What is the length of this hypotenuse?"

The sensory side of my brain might have been distracted by toes and shampoo, but the part of me determined to become a future educator was paying close enough attention to her words.

"Eighty-one," I reply without hesitation.

"That's right!" Ishbel beams at me, as if she's never met anyone more intelligent.

My skin flushes with pleasure. I want to impress her as much our schoolmates or a future headmaster. Her approving smiles are as good a motivation as besting the others.

She pats my knee and gives my leg a little wiggle. "We're

ready to move on to natural philosophy for now. What are you studying this week?"

I fumble through my notes for the right page. "Something called a . . . periodic table of the elements?"

"Ah, yes." Ishbel nods as if it's an old friend. "There were several different arrangements floating about, but the Mendeleev version gained official status four years ago, when he won the Davy medal."

I stare at her. "Er . . . what's a Davy medal?"

"Royal recognition for outstanding contributions to the field. We can discuss my favorite winners later. First, let's look at this chart. What these columns of periodic elements purport to do is . . ."

The next half hour passes in a blur of lectures and quizzes and delighted smiles. Whilst I'm tucking my new sets of notes into my school satchel for tomorrow, our bedroom door opens with a bang.

Ishbel's head jerks up with annoyance. "Could you try knocking next time?"

I twist to look over my shoulder.

Fiona fills the doorway, one hand on a jutting hip and the other wrist pressed to her forehead in a dramatic pose.

"Sorry." She gives a full-body shudder. "I couldn't take it anymore."

"Can't take what anymore?" I ask. "If you're bored—"

"I've plenty to do," she says. "Too *much* to do, is the problem! We're supposed to be studying until our tiny feminine brains burst, but the oppressive gloom of this rickety structure makes me feel like I'm being buried alive in a dark, poorly built coffin. How are any of us supposed to stand the gloom?"

Ishbel and I meet eyes. Fiona's not wrong. We all hate this hideous house. But when I'm barefoot in Ishbel's bed, calling out *H* for hydrogen and *K* for potassium, it's like the ugliness around us cannot penetrate our little bubble.

Fiona shattered the illusion, however. Suddenly, I feel the dampness of the cold air again, and smell the dank *we-didn't-bother-to-clean-this-hellhole-before-dumping-you-here* staleness in the air.

"It's not fair," she wails. "The boys should live here, and *we* should get the castle!"

Well, that's not going to happen. Even if the lads could be talked into such a poor trade, only a fraction of them could fit inside this house before the walls crumbled to pieces.

But that doesn't mean there isn't room for improvement.

I swing my satchel onto my mattress, then slide off Ishbel's bed and onto my feet. "Stop what you're doing. I've an idea."

At the sight of me shoving my boots back on, Ishbel scrambles out of bed to do the same, before I even tell her my idea.

Fiona is less trusting. "What do you plan to do?"

"What I hope we *all* do, is spend an hour or two giving this place a scrubbing. We can't straighten the crooked beams or make the stairs stop creaking, but we can wash the dirt off the walls, sweep and mop the floors, and air out this stuffy, humid stench."

I expect her to balk. Fiona's idea of hard work is ordering about her future rich husband's cadre of servants.

But to my surprise, she brightens and chirps, "I'll tell the others!" before disappearing down the stairs.

Soon, every window is wide open, with the curtains drawn to allow a brisk cross-breeze of fresh woodsy air to waft through.

Downstairs already smells far better than upstairs. Whilst Ishbel and I were studying, Euphemia was busy making dozens of little spiced cakes, filling the air with the warm scent of nutmeg and cinnamon.

All six of us drag buckets of soap and water to every corner of the house, scrubbing from rafters to floorboards until our rags are gray and tattered, and our aching backs not much better.

The ground floor consists of a sparsely furnished parlor, the kitchen, and a cramped dining area, as well as a small pantry beneath the stairs, where the academy drops off supplies. On the upper floor are the three bedrooms, each big enough to fit two narrow cots, with a chamber pot apiece, one small nightstand, a tall mirror, and a skinny wardrobe in which to house our uniforms.

All of which is caked with dirt and moss and spiderwebs that have likely been growing unchecked for decades. It takes hours to clean. We cannot undo years of negligence armed with nothing more than brooms and buckets. But beneath the dirt hide surprisingly sturdy floorboards, which now sparkle in the sunlight.

Once the many bins of dust and dirt and buckets of slop water have been deposited outside, we collapse into the six hard spindly chairs surrounding our sole narrow table, and proceed to wolf down Euphemia's cakes as though we might never get another meal again.

"We make a good team," Ishbel says in pleased surprise.

All six of us grin at each other. Well, five of us smile. Sorcha gives a grunt I choose to interpret as the curmudgeonly equivalent of confetti.

"It reminded me of Sundays with my sisters at home," Maisie says in her soft voice.

"You come from a large family?" I ask.

She nods. "Seven."

"Not me." Fiona flutters her fingers toward her face. "I'm an only child. Manual labor reminds me of our *maids*."

"Quelle surprise," Sorcha mutters in disgust.

"Now we're like orphans at an orphanage," Euphemia says. "An accidental family."

Sorcha looks mortally offended. "You're not my siblings."

"Then you needn't be part of the sisterhood," I tell her.

The others' eyes widen, and they lean toward me with interest. "What sisterhood?"

"The Phoenix Sisterhood," I answer confidently, though I'm making it up as I go. "Ishbel's right—we'll get much farther as a team than on our own."

"Why a phoenix?" Maisie asks.

"Try as the lads might to keep us down, we'll keep rising again and again," I tell her. "If any one of us were all alone, it might be too hard to go on, but working together, we can defeat any foe."

"Does that mean I get to teach you all how to throw knives?" asks Sorcha.

She's in! Even if for bloodthirsty reasons. Uniting against a common enemy is a good rallying cry.

"What about you?" I ask Sorcha. "Do you come from a large family?"

"Three older brothers," she answers begrudgingly.

"Did any of them attend Floodbane?" Maisie asks.

"All three," Sorcha answers with obvious pride. "And now me, too."

Maisie nods. "My grandfather did, as well."

"Did you all attend other girls' schools before this?" I ask them.

"I took lessons at a convent," Maisie replies. "My mother used to be a nun."

"Used to be a nun!" we exclaim before peppering her with questions about her mother's religious fall from grace.

"She fell in love. My father was the local parson."

We shriek again at the scandal of it all, with Maisie dropping shocking revelations as if commenting on the day's rainy weather.

Euphemia shakes her head in awe. "I went to an ordinary local girls' school. My parents solicited admission at the Morrison Institute for Young Ladies, but my marks weren't high enough to be considered. Maybe next year."

"I'm hoping to transfer there, too," I blurt out, delighted by the idea that I might have a friend in the ranks already.

Less delightful is the realization that the institute turned down someone who'd had a lifetime of formal education. Can I really learn enough in one year to outperform Euphemia's many years of proper schooling?

I must. I *have* to. The only choice is forward.

"Where'd you go to school?" I ask Ishbel.

"I didn't. I'd have loved to attend a girls' academy," she says with feeling. "Unfortunately, I was stuck with tutors until the Floodbane scholarship was granted."

"I had tutors, too. Handsome ones, until my parents learned better." Fiona lets out a breathy, nostalgic sigh. "Two of them were sacked for stealing kisses."

"Did they do the stealing, or did you?" Sorcha asks dryly.

Fiona giggles. "Let's say I welcome a variety of lessons. When I meet my future husband, I don't want him to discount me as an option because I'm a poor kisser!"

Ishbel's eyes lock with mine. "Have you ever been kissed?"

My skin flames hot at the question—and scrutiny. I shake my head no. "Not . . . yet."

Her dark gaze doesn't leave mine.

"I hope never to kiss anyone," says Sorcha. "I'll stick a knife through the ribs of any boy who tries."

"If a lad tried to kiss me, I'd die of embarrassment," Maisie whispers.

Euphemia replies, "Honestly, you can just stand there, they don't care."

We all gape at her.

"Trust me. Ninety percent of the lads at Floodbane have 'lass who won't slap me' as their sole criterion. They don't know what they're doing either. I've had less sloppy kisses from a sheepdog than the slobbery disasters I endured back home."

"Ew!" Maisie covers her face with her hands.

Sorcha holds up her knife. "Maybe I should carry two of these."

"You're *supposed* to get some of their spittle," says Fiona. "When your tongues touch."

Maisie looks like she might retch.

Ishbel raises a brow at me. "I haven't tried that trick."

Does that mean she *has* been kissed before, in a manner less . . . slobbery? Do I want to know? Part of me is dying for every detail, while another part of me doesn't want to hear about her past conquests in the arms of neighborhood lads. I might retch like Maisie.

"So, who do you think is our mysterious benefactor?" asks Euphemia. Ostensibly, the question is directed at all of us, but she's looking right at Fiona.

"I told you," Fiona says. "My parents didn't do it."

"You said that," Euphemia agrees, "but rich people know other rich people. Maybe you got chosen because your parents are friends with whomever has promised the school this large endowment."

Fiona's jaw drops. "Are you suggesting I didn't *earn* my place here?"

Sorcha glances up from her knife. "Nobody's 'suggesting' anything. You're sixteen, yet all your classes are first-year level."

"Fine! I may have exaggerated how high my marks on the assessment exam were. I don't test well." Fiona's pout blossoms into a shameless grin. "Because I spent far more time kissing than studying. My future husband won't care if I know where to find France on a map. He wants me to birth babies. All I need to know is how to spend his money."

"I'm glad for an education and to meet all of you," Ishbel says slowly, "but it's otherwise not been a warm welcome. What happened to Catriona could happen to any of us. I don't feel safe here."

"Me neither," Maisie agrees with a shiver.

Euphemia makes a face. "It's awful. I don't know whether to thank our benefactor or throttle him."

"Those bullies should never have attacked Catriona, but I'm still happy to be here," Fiona says stubbornly. "This is the best thing that's ever happened to me. Maybe it'll be the best thing that's ever happened to any of us."

Ishbel gives a crooked smile. "Phoenix sisterhood forever?"

"Bloody right," Fiona answers. "Birds of a feather flock together and rise from the ashes as swans."

"That's . . . too many mixed metaphors," Sorcha mutters.

Euphemia shoves the crumb-speckled dishes to one side. She puts her hand palm down in the center of the table. "Phoenix Sisterhood, unite!"

The name was my idea, so I'm in. I place my hand on top of hers. "Phoenix Sisterhood."

Ishbel's soft, warm hand covers mine. "Phoenix Sisterhood."

Maisie's next, her mumble barely audible, but her hand right there atop the pile.

Fiona joins us. "Phoenix Sisterhood!"

Then nothing. We all turn our heads to raise our brows at Sorcha.

"Oh, whatever." She lets out a long-suffering sigh, stabs her knife into the scarred table, then brings her hand down onto the pile with a stinging slap. "Phoenixes aren't swans, Fiona, you featherbrain. Phoenixes are phoenixes."

"Just say 'sisterhood,'" I whisper.

She rolls her eyes. "Phoenix deuced Sisterhood, you harpies. Happy?"

Everyone shrieks and waves their arms about as if we six personally won every possible award in the name of Scotland.

Even Sorcha is smiling.

For a blissful moment, we all let ourselves believe that our troubles are over.

14

My idea from the night before rushes to mind. "We should have a friendship ceremony."

Ishbel repeats, "Ceremony?"

Sorcha snorts. "We already did the phoenix thing and cleaned the house together. I'm not doing a bloody handfasting with any of you next."

I sigh. "I didn't say we should get married."

Ishbel's hand touches mine. "I'll do whatever you need."

"It's not for me," I explain. "It's for all of us. They're trying to tear us apart. The stronger we are as a team, the better."

"You know what's better than a team?" Sorcha says. "Sharp blades."

"No, we don't need physical force. But we *do* need to be a force to be reckoned with. We won't have to fight these boys if they're too scared of us to come within arm's reach in the first place."

"And you think a ceremony will accomplish that?" Euphemia asks dubiously.

"If this is more magic like your fairies," says Fiona, "then it's about as real as Roderick's kelpie."

"Not magic. A short ceremony. Half an hour of your time at most. You needn't—"

"Of course we will join you." Ishbel's firm voice right behind me is far too loud and pointed to be meant just for my ears. "We're the Phoenix Sisterhood, after all. Right, girls?"

I'll take that as a yes. "Pluck any flowers that catch your eyes."

Soon, the six of us gather in the front garden, which isn't nearly as tidy as the newly cleaned house. I brush aside the dead leaves piling between the two big trees guarding our house. The girls and I arrange ourselves in a circle on the freshly cleared dirt.

Once we're all seated, Euphemia asks, "Now what?"

I gesture at the piles of flowers in their laps. "Now, we each make a crown for the lass to our right, as a symbol of welcome and friendship."

"But you said to pick the prettiest flowers," Fiona exclaims in horror. "I have to give mine to *Sorcha*? She probably prefers thorns."

"That's how this works. We each give our best to each other, and are the better for it, together. It's a solidarity ceremony."

"The fastest way to finish this charade is to start," Sorcha announces and begins to slice leaves off of stems with her knife.

"Maisie, what do you think?" asks Euphemia.

Maisie looks startled at being asked at all.

"I—I don't know," she stammers. "My opinion has never mattered."

Euphemia makes a face of commiseration. "My mother told

me I could have as many opinions as I wish, so long as I never voice them in public."

"You see?" I prod. "Here, amongst ourselves, we can share our thoughts and opinions freely, even if they aren't the same as each other's. That's an important piece of the sisterhood."

With a wide array of expressions from reluctance to open interest, the others bend their spines over their laps to start fashioning their own crowns.

"If you like, you can talk to your crown as you weave it," I tell them.

This suggestion earns five doubtful glances.

"What would I say?" asks Maisie.

"Remember, you're making this for the lass next to you. We're infusing these with positive energy. You can say things like, 'You're not alone' and 'I'm here for you,' and 'We'll get through this together.' "

All right, yes. Done correctly, there *is* magic in this ceremony.

I coax, "We must do our best and graduate with honor, so that other girls are given chances to follow in our footsteps."

"Wonderful," Sorcha mutters. "Now I've got to worry about girls in the future I don't even know?" But her hands are busy twisting bright green stems into a circle.

To my left, Ishbel scrambles to fetch more flowers for her crown.

It's working. My body feels light, and my heart fills with hope.

Euphemia's face lights up. "I understand now. We're crowning ourselves the queens of Floodbane."

Fiona glares at her. "*I* am queen. You are at best a lady-in-waiting."

Before I can put out that fire, Ishbel is back. Shyly, she hands me her finished crown. "This is for you."

I go to reach for it, then see what it's made of. Reflexively, I knock it to the ground.

Ishbel jerks back as if I'd slapped her.

"I'm sorry," I stammer. "You just—you can't use hawthorn and rowan."

"Because they're trees, not flowers?" asks Euphemia.

"Because it's hawthorn and rowan. Hawthorn trees belong to the fairies. Cutting any part of one invites great misfortune. Rowan is the tree of protection against malevolent forces. It shields us against bad luck and evil spirits. We must not allow any damage to either of them."

Everyone stops working on their crowns. They're looking at me and Ishbel's fallen offering in dismay.

The damage I should have been worried about was the effect my instinctive reaction would have against this group's very new, fragile bond.

"Forget it," Euphemia says, tossing her crown over her shoulder.

Maisie does the same. "I wasn't going to get it right anyway."

"No," I stammer. "That's not what I meant. You all—"

"Are done bonding for now," Sorcha finishes. She rises to her feet and grinds the delicate petals of the most beautiful crown of flowers I've ever seen in my life beneath the heels of her boots until it disappears into the dirt. She looks tempted to throw her knife into my heart.

Euphemia snatches Fiona's crown and runs off, with Fiona shrieking right on her heels.

Ignoring my outstretched palm, Ishbel stalks back to the house with Sorcha, leaving me seated alone in the dirt, surrounded by crumpled petals and the abandoned stalks of dying flowers.

15

"I'm sorry," I say for the hundredth time the next morning. "We need to stick together."

My pleas may as well have been in Welsh.

When I suggest getting to school early, everyone but Ishbel acts too busy to join me. I'd apologized profusely to her the night before. Ishbel forgave me five words in, but I sense a reticence that hadn't existed before. During our lonesome hike this morning, I appreciate the chance to be alone with her and recover the camaraderie from before.

We part ways once we arrive at school. Twenty minutes remain before the first class. My bones are restless. I still feel that strange new urge to assert myself. Roderick and his squires told their side of the story. Why shouldn't I?

The other boys don't care about the truth. The school administration, on the other hand . . . Aren't they paid to listen to their student body and resolve any problems? Roderick and friends might not be expelled for their horrific actions, but surely disciplinary measures are due.

I realize my error as soon as I enter the administrative office.

"May I help you?" a middle-aged man I'd never seen before asks. The secretary isn't the problem. The problem is the administrative junior assistant seated at the desk next to him.

Fraser. My attacker. The one who'd tried to trick me down a shortcut that likely would've led to my doom even faster.

Also known as Headmaster MacKenzie's head boy.

"Erm," I say eloquently.

Fraser crosses his arms over his chest, tilts backward in his wooden chair, and smirks at me.

The secretary rubs his face as though I'm wasting his time. "Is there a problem, Miss . . . What is your name?"

"Catriona Cameron." I expect my voice to shake, but it comes out steady. Perhaps a little deeper and stronger than ever. "And aye, there's a problem."

The secretary puts down his pen. "Would you like to tell me what it might be?"

"I'd rather tell Headmaster MacKenzie, if you don't mind."

"We do mind," Fraser says in the smarmiest tone possible. "Headmaster MacKenzie is a busy man. Too busy to speak to the likes of you."

"I didn't ask for your opinion," I murmur.

The secretary intervenes. "Headmaster MacKenzie is indeed a busy man. If you'd like to be considered for a future appointment, then fill out an incident report and an audience request. Mr. Fraser will see it reaches the proper hands."

Oh, I bet he will. If he even reads a single word that I write, the last person on earth he would hand it to is Headmaster MacKenzie.

There's no help for me here. There's no help for any lass in my position. This was a fool's errand.

I turn and walk away.

"Miss?" the secretary calls out behind me. "Did you change your mind? Miss . . . What was her name again?"

Fraser's mocking laughter fills the corridor like billows of black smoke.

I curse beneath my breath. *Damn it! Damn him! And damn me!* Why did I think it would be so easy? Just waltz in and say, "I thought you might like to know that these four boys hurt me and would've done far worse if not for the groundskeeper" and—poof!—Roderick et al. disappear into thin air, never to be seen again?

I'd be better off praying for them to be mauled by werewolves.

Stalking faster, I nudge my necklace aside to scratch at the scab forming above my bosom. I'm glad the high neck of my gown hides the wound from view. Luckily, the itchy rash hasn't spread anywhere else on my body. I can barely withstand the one small area. The inflamed red skin feels like it's burning a hole past my sternum and through every ventricle of my heart.

This talisman is a symbol of my mother's love, I repeat to myself with every step. My literal cross to bear. Even if the talisman exacerbates the rash beneath, I'll not remove it. Two tiny interlocking bars of purest iron are all that I have left to protect me against dark magic and malevolent creatures.

I'm so busy praying, I'm not watching where I'm going. I slam headlong into a tall, balding professor I've never seen before.

"Can I *help* you!" he exclaims in the same tone one might use to say, *Go throw yourself off the nearest cliff!*

"Er . . . the library," I blurt out. "Which way is it?"

I suspect he points the way out of irritation and habit, rather than any particular desire to make life easier.

Nonetheless, I thank him and pick up my pace. Only a quarter hour remains before I must be present in class. I push open the doors and stumble to a dead stop.

Floodbane Academy's library . . . is . . . *phenomenal.*

The soaring Baroque ceiling is three stories tall and covered with biblical frescoes adorned with gold leaf. Tall white columns wider than the trunk of our enormous hawthorn tree rise in fluted opulence. Portraits and busts of old, well-fed rich men are everywhere, hanging on walls between tall bookshelves, and adorning carved long wooden tables, lined with cushioned seats for study sessions.

I'm standing in the center of the room, craning my neck with my mouth hanging open, for so long that a short man with thick black hair rises from behind his desk to come check if I'm still breathing.

"Can I assist you?"

"Maybe." I try to focus on him instead of all the distracting majesty surrounding me. "You work here?"

"Yes. I am head librarian. What do you need?"

"Can I read any book I like?"

"While in this room? Yes, anything you please. If it's a volume authorized for external lending, however . . ." He plucks a random book off the closest shelf and flips the back cover open. "Then you'll need to sign your name on this card and hand it to me or one of my associates."

I gape at him. I can take these books home with me?

"Any damage incurred is your debt to pay," he warns me. "Lost books require mandatory replacement by the student who signed his or *her* name on the card."

I bobble my head in a brainless nod. "How many can I borrow at once? What is the maximum?"

He stares at me as if the sounds my mouth is making do not form real words.

"Maximum number of books?" he repeats, as though the concept is new to him. "As many as you can carry at once, I suppose. No wheelbarrows allowed in the library."

He chuckles at his own jest before going back to his desk.

I cannot chuckle. My brain is addled from the sight of so many books and so many gold-leaf frescoes. Read whatever I want? Take home as many books as I please? I didn't know a dream like that *could* come true.

The implications astound me back into speechlessness. This means I can learn *anything I want, anytime I want.* Not just the subjects in my classes. Anything. Everything.

"Miss Cameron?" comes a gruff male voice.

I spin around in shock, my surprise rising less from being recognized as from being referred to in a polite manner.

It's my fourth-hour literature professor. The class I share with Roderick and Angus and Dougal.

"Shouldn't you be in class, Miss Cameron?"

I point at the ornate tall clock behind him. "Not for five more minutes, sir."

"Very well." He glances over his shoulders as if fearful of

someone spotting him being a decent human to me. "You've a fine sense for literary themes, Miss Cameron. The ideas you share in class are good ones. You have potential."

I gape at him much like the head librarian had stared at me when asked what the maximum number of books was. The professor's words sound like a trout blowing bubbles beneath the ocean.

Yes, *I* know I sometimes have good ideas. *I* believe I have potential. But this is the opposite of how I was treated in class. I can scarcely reconcile that the same professor who could barely stand to skim his eyes in my general direction the first day has now gone out of his way to pay me a compliment.

"Th-thank you?" I stammer.

He smiles—*smiles!*—and heads off to teach his own first class, leaving me alone to goggle at my surroundings. I cannot wait to show the infinite shelves of books to my housemates. We can claim one of the study tables as our own, and we can *all* achieve the education of our dreams, ensconced within the library's oil-painted walls.

Assuming I don't ruin another good idea.

16

The gong sounds, and I jump out of my skin. What happened to my five minutes? I must run, or I'll be tardy to class.

I arrive in time to slide into an empty seat. Oddly, the spot I staked out yesterday is vacant, despite the late hour. By the time my pencil is in my hand, the lecture has already begun. Second and third periods fly by, as well.

When the lunch gong clangs, I step out of class only to be ambushed by Sorcha and Euphemia, who each grab one of my elbows.

"To the devil with these cads," Euphemia whispers into my ear. "We ladies don't have time to cook."

I frown in confusion. "What?"

Sorcha tugs me forward. "Come with us, you brainless tart. We're eating at the refectory!"

In minutes, we're strolling into a massive hall filled with long wooden tables of rowdy students. The boys perch on benches holding trays piled with delicious-smelling foodstuffs.

We slip into the queue. Me first, Sorcha second, and then Euphemia. The cook serves my tray before realizing we're girls. When he does, he refuses to serve Euphemia and Sorcha.

Luckily, the quantity on my plate is intended to fill the bottomless stomach of an adolescent boy, which means it'll do better than take the edge off for three young women.

We find an uninhabited table in the furthest corner of the hall. Its wobbly legs explain why it's empty, but we don't mind. The three of us tuck into the repast as if we've never been fed before.

It's a good thing we do. Less than ten minutes into our feeding frenzy, the boys around us notice our presence.

"Oy, you can't be here!"

"This is our food!"

"Get out!"

Each insult is accompanied by hurled food: warm fresh-baked biscuits, hot cross buns, a baked potato. My friends and I shove as much as we can into our satchels for later.

An angry trio of fourth-year lads comes swaggering up to our table to remove us by force. Er, most of us. The first boy grabs Euphemia by the armpits, the second grabs Sorcha, and the third yells . . . at Euphemia and Sorcha.

"If I ever see you two trollops in our refectory ever again—" he blathers.

I scramble out the door after them, bewildered.

As they straighten their wrinkled clothing, I frown at my friends. "I'm the one whose 'teats were hanging out' the other day and you two are the trollops?"

"All six of us," Sorcha replies with a roll of her eyes. "We share a reputation as well as a house."

Euphemia nods. "It started yesterday, as soon as we arrived at school. They called us tarts, hussies, you name it."

"Slattern," Sorcha supplies helpfully. "I like that one."

"Slattern," Euphemia confirms. "Apparently, we're all impure in the eyes of Floodbane Academy now."

My breath catches. No wonder tensions were high at my failed friendship ceremony last night. They'd all experienced the most humiliating day of their lives, through no fault of their own. Mere proximity to me was enough ammunition to be painted with the same insulting brush.

My eyes sting. "I'm so sorry. Please forgive me."

"For God's sake." Sorcha rolls her eyes. "We don't think what *they* say is *your* fault."

"Ladies!" Ishbel skids up to us.

We pass her a choice selection from our stolen buns and biscuits.

She tilts her head and gives me an odd look. "Are you wearing cosmetics?"

I blink at her. "I don't even own cosmetics."

With sarcasm, Euphemia repeats the faculty's warning, "Only 'lassies with loose morals' wear cosmetics."

Ishbel hasn't moved. "You look . . . prettier than usual. Your hair seems shinier, and your skin is incredibly smooth and clear. Even your eyelashes look longer."

"Eat a biscuit and stop measuring other people's eyelashes," says Sorcha.

"Or slip into the queue and see if you can get your own tray," Euphemia suggests. "We made it a good ten minutes before getting caught."

I'm not sure how true this is. *I* was the one who received a tray. *I* was the one who wasn't thrown out by her armpits.

Not that I know why. Even a sudden growth spurt of overnight eyelashes wouldn't explain whatever is happening.

"You can share my lunch." I slide my satchel closer to Ishbel, who has settled at my side. "Where were you?"

Her eyes widen. "I was *eavesdropping*."

We all lean toward her like flowers tilting toward the sun, school lunch forgotten at the promise of fresh gossip.

"What did you hear?"

She glances over her shoulders, then lowers her voice so as not to be overheard. "We're far from the only ones Roderick and his crew torture. Many of the lads who threw rotten fruit at us did so to avoid becoming targets themselves."

I nod. "Dougal told me stories about them bullying other boys into never returning."

"Did he tell you a few of them couldn't return because their bones had been broken?"

We all gasp. "What?"

"No one could prove Roderick and his friends were to blame. One of the victims was too frightened to name names, but the other two pointed fingers—and it didn't matter. It was the word of one lad against four others who not only gave each other alibis but also have frightened enough other students at this school to ensure corroboration of their innocence by 'witnesses' who weren't even present."

My lip curls. "Dastardly."

"And their loud stories, bragging about their many romantic conquests with the young ladies on the Isle of Skye? Fabricated, exaggerated, or twisted from reality."

"Obviously." Sorcha snorts. "I don't need to eavesdrop to know no sane woman would willingly invite their disgusting attention."

"It gets worse," Ishbel tells us. "Last year, a local girl was the first female allowed to take the Floodbane placement test, on the assumption she would fail miserably and put paid to the whole 'nonsense' of girls attending academies like this one."

"Let me guess," Euphemia says drolly. "She didn't fail?"

"Not a single question!" Ishbel crows with satisfaction. "She could've been headmistress instead of a fellow student."

"So they admitted her?" I ask in surprise. "I thought we were the first ones."

"We *are* the first ones. Floodbane was going to accept her based on scholastics alone—they had no choice, once the results were known. But then Roderick and his lackeys paid the lass a visit."

"What happened?"

Ishbel takes a deep breath. "Not only did the girl withdraw her application, but her entire family moved off the Isle of Skye."

Our jaws drop. "The whole family left?"

She nods. "No one knows what those boys said or did during

their visit, but every whispered rumor is worse than the last. I overheard five different theories that would make your skin crawl. We may never have that answer, but we already know the most important truth: There is no low that Roderick and his cronies won't sink to."

"Then that's it," Euphemia says hollowly. "No hope at all. They'll come for each of us. And they're probably not done with Catriona either."

My stomach sinks, and gooseflesh erupts across my skin.

Sorcha is outraged. "I don't accept that! We have the right to attend this school. Whether those lads want to accept our presence or not, they bloody well better get used to us."

"Foul language!" a passing instructor calls out. "Demerit!"

Sorcha bares her teeth at his back.

Ishbel turns to me. "Shall I walk you to your next class?"

"*I* was hoping to have that honor," comes a male voice behind us.

I spin around to find Dougal striding our way with a wide smile.

Ishbel doesn't smile back.

Of course not—she has no idea who this is, or whether it's safe to let her guard down in front of him. Quickly, I introduce my friends, and Dougal as the nice boy who stood up for me to Roderick and Angus.

That alone cements a place for him in their hearts.

"Don't tell Fiona that you're the first to land a suitor," Euphemia whispers.

I kick her. It's a good jest, but I don't want Dougal to hear.

"Don't run off with my girl, Romeo," Ishbel teases. "I expect her back in my possession right after school."

At least, I think she's teasing. Her brown eyes are dark and serious. I suppose she's wise to harbor reasonable suspicions about any boy, until proven not a monster.

"I promise to keep Catriona safe and sound." Dougal gives a self-effacing smile. "I must write my mother after school anyway. She's sent three letters since my last one home."

"Overbearing, is she?" asks Sorcha.

"Skilled at delegating," answers Dougal. "She dictates the contents to one of her secretaries while in the midst of other, more important tasks."

"One of her . . . secretaries?" repeats Ishbel.

My question exactly.

Dougal shrugs. "Mother owns the largest training and placement agency in Edinburgh for future female educators."

A tiny gasp of air escapes my throat. "You mean . . . similar to the Morrison Institute for Young Ladies?"

Dougal gives me an odd look, then points at his own chest. "Dougal Morrison. Don't you hear my name every day during attendance?"

"Yes, but I didn't think . . . I never connected . . ." No wonder he said his mother longed for a daughter . . . and would disinherit him if he brought home Hamish instead. His mother's influence—and wealth—are legendary. "What on earth are you doing *here*?"

"At Floodbane?" He taps his chest again with amusement as we head down the corridor. "Dougal Morrison. Male son, of the masculine persuasion. Was the bit about 'Institute for Young Ladies' unclear?"

I cover my face with my hands. "Obviously a boy cannot attend a girls' school. I wasn't thinking."

"I'll let you have that one." He gestures around us. "A year ago, I wouldn't have predicted female students at an all-boys school. But what Mother wants, Mother gets."

"Your mother was involved in the decision to open up the campus to both sexes?"

"Mother has campaigned for equal admittance since before I was born. She'll never forgive me for entering this world a boy instead of a girl, but in this one instance, I've proven myself useful. As a tool, anyway. A Trojan horse of sorts."

"Wasn't that trick used to sneak soldiers past enemy lines?"

"Exactly. My mother promised an obscenely large endowment to Floodbane Academy. But the money will only be deposited at the end of the school year—provided I and my female classmates are still in attendance."

I love this woman. "She *bribed* the headmaster of Floodbane Academy into allowing girls at his school?"

"Six girls and me. My academics are adequate only because my mother would have murdered me if I shamed her with a public display of ignorance. But as you know, I'd rather be out back gardening with the groundskeeper."

"Ah, yes, sowing a field of bilberries. She won't let you follow your dream?"

His eyes are sad. "Can anyone follow their dreams?"

I certainly intend to.

Only moments ago, I'd despaired of making any important connections at all, much less the right ones. And now the most impeccable of opportunities seems within reach.

The rash on my chest itches harder, but I push the pain away. Good things are starting to happen.

17

The week flashes by. Days full of lessons, evenings full of bonding time with friends, nights full of Ishbel's tutoring, then we whisper into the wee hours of the dark until one of us falls asleep.

Today is Sunday. At Floodbane Academy, the Sabbath is our one day without classes. I've convinced my housemates to spend our free hours exploring the academy's beautiful and well-stocked library after morning church service in the chapel.

"Are you certain the others want us to show up at their kirk?" frets Maisie.

"Do we care what boys want?" drawls Sorcha.

Fiona and Euphemia exchange sly looks.

"There are a few we can't wait to see in their Sunday best," says Euphemia.

"Or *out* of it," adds Fiona, with a fit of giggles.

I don't have a Sunday best. The school-provided wardrobe

is composed of ankle-length yellow pelisses to protect from the cold, along with identical thick, drab brown dresses with choking high necklines and scratchy sleeves that stretch down to my knuckles.

We head through the woods together. In my friends' company, I feel braver, and bring up the rear of the line today rather than ensconce myself in the middle.

But right when we pass the broken branches where Mungo snatched me off the trail, my feet once again explode with excruciating pain, as if the bones I'm walking on have shattered.

I stumble forward, knocking into Ishbel.

"Sorry," I gasp.

She shoots me a concerned look over her shoulder. "Are you all right?"

I grimace from the repeated jolts of shooting pain. "I . . . I can't . . ."

Her expression fills with empathy, and she lowers her voice. "Is it your menses?"

If it is, the monthly week of blood had never before brought with it a torture such as this.

Unable to formulate words, I wave her forward so that she doesn't trip and break a bone of her own on a stray tree root.

My feet now feel like crushed glass. I cannot keep walking. I hunch over, almost retching, and brace my hands on my knees. When I'm certain I'm not about to spill breakfast onto my skirts, I lift up my hems to make sure my poor booted feet are still there.

They are not.

I stare in stupefaction, unable to process what I'm seeing. My boots are gone. My *feet* are gone. In their place are the skinny, downy brown legs of a deer, each culminating in a large, jet-black, rock-hard hoof.

"What in the . . ." I whisper in disbelief. My heartbeat bangs in my ears.

Ishbel starts to turn around.

I drop my hems and jerk upright, wobbling on my two-toed cloven hooves with their unfamiliar thick black rigid toes poking out from where my feet ought to be.

"You're sure you're feeling well?" Ishbel asks.

I've never been less well in my entire life.

There's no way I can tell her what's going on, because I haven't any clue myself. All I know for certain is that I cannot show up in church with feet like Satan's hooves.

"Go on without me," I manage. "I'll meet you all in the library after kirk service."

I shan't go anywhere near the academy with legs like these. My knees are starting to bend the wrong way.

"You're going to walk back home by *yourself*?" Ishbel echoes in disbelief. "I'll come with you."

"No!" I cringe in remorse when she flinches back from me. "It's not you. It's me. I need to be alone for an hour or two to . . . cry, probably. You know how it is."

She nibbles her lower lip, unsure which path makes her the better friend. "You're certain you're all right?"

I will never again be all right.

"Everything's fine." I wave her forward. "Hurry up, or you'll lose the group. You can tell me later if I missed any lads worth looking at."

She wrinkles her nose, then blows me a kiss before turning and jogging around the corner to catch up with the others.

As soon as she's out of sight, I lift my hems again and see—

Stars. Colors. Swirling lights. A wave of nausea like nothing I've ever known twists me inside out, and then—

I'm behind Floodbane Academy. Stomach lurching, I stumble to regain my equilibrium. There are woods here, too. I'm less confused by the trees I don't recognize than I am by how I got here to begin with. The school is a tiny bull's-eye at the center of ring after ring of forest. It felt like I dispersed at a cellular level and reassembled half a mile away, but that cannot be right. Did I hit my head? Or sleepwalk across campus?

There are two boys in front of me. Unlike my friends, these lads are not in their Sunday best. Bare-chested, they lounge on the grass, their naked spines curved against large rocks. The excited heartbeat thrumming in my ears sounds off. As though I'm listening to *their* veins pumping with hot blood, rather than my own.

I recognize them as the two fourth-year boys who dragged Euphemia and Sorcha from the refectory by their armpits when we were trying to eat lunch.

Their voices are distorted and muffled, as if they are conversing deep under water.

"You swear to God you could feel her through her corset?" comes the slow voice of the boy on the right.

Unwelcome groping of a female classmate's breasts. Definitely the topic the good Lord was hoping to hear on His day.

"I wish a lass like that were here right now." The boy on the left sounds like he's talking through a mouthful of marbles. "I'd *show* you how best to handle her."

He bares his teeth and makes biting motions, shaking his head like a rabid animal.

I'd been frozen in place since I arrived out of nowhere. My heart nearly expired at their casual use of the word *wish.*

Suddenly, the scene before me seems to come alive. A breeze blows, leaves rustle, birds chirp overhead. The lads' vulgar comments become fluid and fast-paced. They interrupt each other in their quest to make even more shocking claims. I can smell the dirt on their feet and the sweat on their skin.

My feet are still deer hooves, and my previously nauseated stomach is now growling with sharp hunger. I could snatch a thousand birds from the trees, and they wouldn't fill this bottomless craving in my belly.

I blink in surprise at this disgusting thought. Me, who cannot bear to harm a chicken, salivating at the thought of wolfing down raw birds, flapping wings and bloody feathers and all.

Except that's not quite it. My eyes aren't on the birds. My sharp gaze hasn't once flickered away from the sight of the two half-naked boys before me. The hypnotic sound of their beating hearts and the rush of pumping blood has me too intoxicated to even think.

My stomach growls. Or perhaps that's me. My gnawing hunger claws at my stomach.

The unrelenting flood of senses is overwhelming. I hear everything, see everything, smell everything. The yearning to touch and taste is irresistible. I flex my fingers. My muscles twitch, ready for action. My body feels different, thicker, more powerful.

The two lads catch sight of me. Rather than startle or shout in alarm, they lick their lips as they leap to their feet and step toward me. Not another attack!

I turn and run.

Three steps in, I smack into an invisible wall and free-fall for a terrifying second. The world spins. Just as nausea threatens to overtake me, I pitch forward on wobbly hooves as I'm dropped right back in front of them where I started. Taller. Stronger. Hungrier.

The lads, too, are back on the grass, spines against the same large rocks, grinning.

"You swear to God you could feel her through her corset?" says the boy on the right, exactly as he'd done seconds before.

"I wish a lass like that were here right now," repeats the boy on the left. "I'd *show* you how best to handle her."

It's not just the same conversation, I realize in horror. It's the same *moment.*

How is this happening? I was trying to run away, not to run back in time to begin this nightmare all over again.

Frantic, I turn and sprint as fast as I can—only to be plopped right back, restarting the same moment, over and over again.

Each time, I materialize before them in time to hear my lewd classmates make the boasting wishes that summon me, again and again. Each time, the roar of their blood is louder, the scent of their skin more seductive.

There's no way out. At least, not for them. With nauseating clarity, I realize that the only way to break free is to satiate my unbearable hunger.

No. I can't do it.

I pray for the heavens to spare me. The fairies certainly won't help. I learned that from my grandmother. I hope with all my heart that she's not looking down on me from above, about to watch the horrific massacre fated to unfold.

That is what the fairies want. But there's no chance in hell I'm going to start slaughtering my classmates, no matter how much trouble they cause. I'm a schoolgirl, not a murderer.

The lads catch sight of me. Lick their lips, leap up, step toward me. Smiling. I am dizzy with anticipation.

They separate, approaching me from opposite sides, like hunters trapping a rabbit.

If only they knew.

I am the huntress, the bait, and the trap.

One of them lunges toward me.

I swat him away reflexively. One of my nails grazes his bare arm, drawing blood. Another surge of hunger rises within me, as well as a brief sway of vertigo as part of one deer hoof briefly turns back into a human toe.

The implication is clear. If I want to be human again . . . If I want to be *myself* again . . . I must first perform the most inhumane acts possible.

My hooves won't let me leave until the job is done.

Oh, shite. My grandmother's stories rush back to me. It's almost as if I've become . . .

A baobhan sith.

No.

I shake the thought out of my head, but I can't take myself out of these woods. I am drunk from the instinct to strike.

The first boy rubs at his injured arm. "Can I have her first?"

"You don't even know what you're doing. Watch me."

I recall the attack in the forest. Mungo wishing for me to be a magic fairy. Angus for me to be attractive. In the moment, I had despaired over my talisman's apparent inability to protect me from non-magical monsters.

In retrospect, I now see that the little iron cross indeed performed its duty. By allowing my attackers' cocky wishes to come true, I'd been granted the inhuman strength necessary to break free from the ties that bound me and flee from certain death to freedom.

My stomach growls. The sight of the bare-chested boys is too tempting to resist. Their venom-barbed words bring on a tidal wave of insatiable bloodlust. I want. I need. I hunger.

No matter how hard I try to hold still, my spry deer legs sprint toward them, launching me atop their startled bodies. I bite with teeth that have become a mouthful of razor-sharp incisors. I slash with fingernails that have turned into claws as hard as glass.

The more I try to withstand the primal urges overpowering my body, the more overwhelming and irresistible the desire becomes to kill and consume. I cannot control myself. Soon, all that's left is a godawful mess of teeth-torn muscles and half-gnawed bones with the marrows sucked dry.

And me, on my knees in a puddle of warm blood, sobbing into my soft human hands.

18

What yanks me out of my spiral of sorrow and self-pity is the stench of burning human flesh.

My flesh.

Which is apparently no longer so human.

I yank the protective cross from my bosom, snapping the thick twine instead of my neck. Smoke smolders up from my bodice in an elongated T shape. I unfasten enough buttons at the nape of my neck to shove the layers of itchy fabric free from my inflamed décolletage.

Red boils bubble and pop like tomato soup simmering in a cauldron. Before my eyes, the bursting boils turn into hives and welts, then smooth into an angry red rash, and ultimately dissolve into nothing at all.

A sob hitches in my throat. Careful not to let the iron touch my skin, I dangle the talisman from its broken twine until it disappears into my skirt pocket. This isn't a permanent solution. Though my skirts are layered and thick, the cross is still too close for comfort.

But there's no way in hell I'm leaving behind my last link to my mother's love.

I struggle to my feet, human once again, and do my best not to look at the carnage surrounding me. I rub my arms and shiver for an embarrassingly long time before I realize I'm not going to *poof* out of there the same way that I arrived.

That's a power beasts have, not ordinary girls.

Which is unfortunate, because it means I must forge a new path through the woods. I cannot saunter past the main campus wearing a bedraggled gown sodden with my classmates' blood.

I force myself to look at them. They're not boys anymore. Just scattered bones and chunks of teeth-ripped flesh. Only their dismembered heads remain untouched. Even in the deepest thralls of magically induced rage, I hadn't been monstrous enough to consume their brains and eyes.

In other words, despite the carnage, the two lads remain instantly identifiable. I glance in vain for something to bury them with. Unless I fancy spending the next five hours scraping at the root-knotted forest floor with a stick, I must leave them to the crows.

I really don't want to be caught here anyway.

Fists clenched and shoulders tight, I pick my way through the woods far from the school. There's a coppery taste in my mouth that I wish I didn't recognize. Bits of gristle stuck in my teeth. I try to spit them out but swallow them instead. Then retch.

When I reach home, my housemates are still at church

service. I'm thankful that the unwelcoming misogynists of Floodbane Academy neglected to provide the female housing facility with staff.

No one sees me peel off my blood-soaked clothes and burn them at the hearth. No one sees me scrub the sweet-smelling evidence from my trembling body right there in the kitchen. There's no point in carrying buckets of clean water up the stairs for a bath when it'll turn scarlet the moment my toes touch the water.

Once I'm clean and dressed—thank God for my infinite supply of identical clothes—I sweep the house and scrub the floor before heading out to meet my friends at the library, as planned.

At least, I hope it goes to plan. I don't fancy popping out of sight like a pricked bubble in the middle of a conversation about fractions or geography.

When I reach the giant wrought iron gate marking the entrance to Floodbane Academy, the groundskeeper is right next to the hinges, trimming the hedgerows.

His reflexive smile turns into a look of concern. "Are you all right, lass?"

Not in the slightest.

If I look like I've just survived the worst moments of my life, then that's accurate. Not that I can give him or anyone attached to Floodbane a truthful explanation.

But . . . perhaps there's someone I can talk to who isn't connected to my scholarship.

"Are you from Skye?" I ask.

"Aye, native, born and bred."

"Then you might know . . . Is there someone in a nearby village who knows about . . ."

Here my question falls apart. Fairy curses? Penniless girls who commit murder?

The groundskeeper's smile is open, his eyes expectant. "Aye?"

"I don't know . . . a town elder . . . of sorts?"

Really what I need is a cross between my grandmother and a witch. Someone who knows things and can help.

The groundskeeper frowns. "An elderman? Like a bailie or a provost?"

"Any respected women? Someone who knows about . . . the old ways?"

His face clears in sudden understanding. "Aye, a luckie. Goodwife MacAskill. Some say the widow is more than a century old herself, though she's as spry as my own mum."

The groundskeeper looks older than my father, so I'm not too sure how spry his mum could be. But Goodwife MacAskill sounds perfect.

"How do I find her?"

He points back the way I came. "Pass your lodging and follow the river through the woods to the main village. Head up the hill to your left. Keep to the trail until you reach a tiny house perched at the edge of the cliff. If it hasn't fallen into the sea, that is. The grounds may look overgrown, but those are all herbs she uses in her potions. Some folk go to her for healing."

I press my hand to my thundering heart. That's precisely what I need: *healing*.

“Thank you.” I dash into the forest.

By the time I stumble free from the other side of the woods, I’m sweating and struggling for air. I allow myself a deep breath before charging up the hill to my left, taking a slippery gravel path straight up to the edge of a cliff. There sways a house as rickety as our female lodging, teetering on the precipice of ruin. I needn’t peer over the edge to hear violent waves crash against the rocks far below.

I tap gently on the front door, lest the pressure of my hand knock the whole structure into the sea.

When no one comes, I call out, “Goodwife MacAskill?”

Belatedly, I realize there’s no guarantee she would even be at home. Perhaps her vocation as a healer means she spends her days down in the main village, attending to cases requiring her attention.

Yet I cannot give up. I knock again, risking ill fortune by banging a little louder. “Goodwife MacAskill? Are you in there?”

This time, the door eases open the tiniest crack . . . and then flings open wide.

An ancient little white lady, with a body about as big as a skeleton bleached in the sun, shoots out her arm and grabs my wrist in a viselike grip. Before I even have time to speak, she hauls me into the cottage and slams the door shut behind me.

The interior of the cottage is pitch-black, except for a single flickering candle down a corridor. Long moments pass until my eyes adjust enough to make out any features at all of the old woman before me.

"Goodwife M-MacAskill?" I stammer.

"Dear God." She clasps my shoulders hard enough to rattle my bones. "What have they done to you?"

I'm unsure how to answer, and I've no idea whom she's referring to. My father? Hamish? Roderick and his crew? Do I look as though I've been attacked in the forest? Or do I look like a monster who does the attacking?

"The fairies, girl," she says in exasperation. "You stink of fairy magic and death."

Wonderful. At least I won't have to try to convince her of the fantastical part.

"I was cursed," I blurt out.

She drops her hands from my shoulders, shaking her fingers as though they've been burnt.

Not a great sign.

"Can you cure me? I'll do whatever it takes to break the curse."

"Cursed," she repeats, as if tasting the words. "How did it start?"

"Four boys," I answer, my voice shaking. I can't believe I'm going to tell the story, and be believed. "They trapped me in the woods after school. They were going to—"

"Don't tell me what the lads were going to do. Tell me what they did."

"They made wishes! That I were bonny. That I were a magic fairy. That there was enough of me for every man."

She huffs. "Reckless. Ill-advised. Effective. And you, girl? What did you wish?"

"Nothing. I was raised to know better."

"Untrue."

"It is true! My grandmother—"

She grabs my chin. "What did you *wish*? If not aloud, then in your heart?"

"Can fairies hear that?" I ask in horror.

"Not thoughts, no. But if you're wishing while they're granting, even unspoken words can cause unexpected wrinkles. What was your wish?"

"To save myself," I whisper. "To be strong. Invincible. Capable of fighting off a pack of boys and making them regret they'd ever tried to attack me again."

"And then what? Any other symptoms?" she asks, as if I've come down with a touch of influenza. But she's right. There's one other element I haven't yet mentioned.

"My feet vanished. Suddenly, I had hooves and legs like a deer."

Her eyes light up. "There's only one creature that describes. You're a baobhan sith."

I stagger backward.

The hated syllables echo through the goodwife's shadowy sitting room: *Baa-van shee*. As legend has it, the baobhan sith is a vengeful fairy, happy to visit any man who deserves her wrath.

Her victims never live to tell their tale. Innocent bystanders have reported sightings of a beautiful woman in a long dress, with deer hooves. She appears out of nowhere to massacre men and gobble them whole. The bloody corpses of her targets tend to be left unrecognizable—or drained dry.

My gran always said that baobhan siths were women's avenging angels. And that all women are worthy of rescue.

I never expected to become an instrument of death myself.

Goodwife MacAskill lights a candle and peers into my face. "I don't come across many of your kind."

"I don't *want* to be this kind! I want to be human."

"Why? Many a woman would prefer to have allies protecting and defending them."

"You don't understand. This will ruin my life. And other people's. The curse makes me . . ." I swallow hard. The flame of her candle flutters, sending shadows dancing around the dark, narrow room. The murky gloom and single chair before an unlit fire are far from welcoming, but I'd rather be here than back in the woods, surrounded by my own carnage. "Today, I . . . That is, I didn't want to, but I . . ."

"Ah, your first kill. Went well, did it?"

"Abominable!" I gag at the memory. "The worst moments I've ever experienced!"

"You'll get used to it in time."

"Who told you this? Is there someone else I could speak to?"

"My great-grandmother. Most of her bones are in the graveyard, though I did keep a finger." She gestures to an ominous row of mismatched jars atop the fireplace mantel.

I shiver. I cannot contact the dead, no matter how much I'd like to. "I lost my gran a few years ago. She told me baobhan siths appear when men make foul wishes to harm women."

"Yes. There are many ways to be summoned. As you get more powerful, you'll find yourself drawn to situations where a spoken intent to do immediate harm is enough to summon you, even without an explicit wish."

"I don't want to be summoned. Please, I don't want to kill anyone else."

The candlelight flickers in her eyes. "Even if they deserve it?"

"That's not up to me," I protest.

"Not before, but there is only one way a summons can end. Once called, you must obey your instincts."

"I don't have free will?"

"If you attempt to leave without fulfilling your destiny, the summons will bring you right back where you started."

Then I was right about what was happening to me. Being a baobhan sith means being transported against my will into a sliver of time from which there is no escape until I destroy those who would harm others. Even my grandmother hadn't known about the wrinkles in time. Incongruously, I half hysterically wish Gran were still alive so I could tell her.

Maybe she would know how to break the curse.

Goodwife MacAskill peers into my ears and up my nose. "You may often find yourself alone with cruel and aggressive men, but this is no coincidence. It's the result of their own actions. Their violence invokes you. Once called, a sith cannot be unsummoned. You must stop them."

"That's it?" My voice cracks. "There's no hope?"

With her free hand, the goodwife strokes her narrow chin. "Killing is compulsory, but there's room for creativity. You can play with your food, perhaps dance with it as some like to do. But if you dally for too long, instinct will take over. Either drain their blood daintily, or you'll rip into them like a rabid beast. Your choice."

"That's no choice! I want to break the curse. Please. Can't you help me? I'll do anything. Anything at all."

She purses her lips and closes her eyes, as if mentally reviewing every grimoire she's ever encountered. "I've never heard of a sith becoming human."

My shoulders crumple.

"However . . ." She opens her eyes. "There *are* spells to break curses."

Elation rushes through me. "I'll try it! I'll do it! Tell me how."

"Find a private space free from negativity. Cleanse the area by burning sage. Take a looking glass with you. Lay it face up toward the heavens. Surround it with an unbroken border of black salt. Place an object representing the person or persons who cast the spell onto the looking glass. Its reflection will cast the curse back onto them."

I blink. "I can't break my curse without cursing all four boys? Wait . . . will *they* become siths? I thought baobhan siths were women."

"Baobhan siths appear as women, yes. I cannot know what this spell will do. Usually, it's employed to disrupt the evil eye, not to turn a magical creature human."

"You're saying it may not work at all?"

"It might, and it might not. But it's the only spell I know of with any chance of success."

"Then I'll do it. I have a looking glass . . . Where would I find black salt?"

"A small shop on the mainland, thirty-five miles southeast."

Thirty-five . . . She might as well have said *on the moon*. My heart breaks.

She squints at me. "I'm due to pay a visit in about a fortnight. Shall I pick up some black salt for you?"

I nearly crumple to her feet. "Yes! Please! I'll pay any price."

No idea how, but I'll figure that out later. Along with how to hide my transition from my housemates—and how to resist killing anyone else for two long weeks while I await the cure.

She shoos me toward the door. "You'll hear from me again when I have the salt."

"Wait!" I stumble across the threshold backward, and flinch at the bright sunlight overhead. "Don't you want to know my name, or how to get in contact with me?"

She cackles. "Oh, I can find you."

Then she slams her front door in my face.

19

When I finally arrive at the school library, Ishbel is relieved to see me. "Are you feeling better? You look . . . stunning."

The others nod their agreement.

I feel like an exhausted, sweaty, panicked, post-murder-frenzy mess, who just learned my only hope is a magic spell I don't have the ingredients for.

Ishbel pats the empty seat next to her. "What is your literature class reading? Mine has selected . . ."

I sit and allow the warmth of her ordinary, nonproblematic prattle to wash over me. Slowly, my tight muscles relax, and I find myself nodding along with her and the others as we discuss Scottish writers Rabbie Burns, Sir Walter Scott, and the debut novel from newcomer Robert Louis Stevenson, *Treasure Island*.

"Do you think the Isle of Skye has treasure?" asks Ishbel.

Fiona and Euphemia exchange mischievous grins as they scoot their chairs closer to us.

"Not boys with inheritances," Sorcha snaps. "Ishbel means something of value."

"I'd settle for adventure," Maisie offers.

Ishbel's eyes meet mine. "I think we're in the midst of one."

She's referring to us being the first cohort of women at a previously all-male boarding school, but she doesn't know I've topped that. I've accidentally run headlong into more adventure here at Floodbane than I ever feared possible.

And more *friends* than I ever thought possible. The six of us gather around a long ornate table piled with dozens of invaluable books, in a library the size of a cathedral whose walls are painted with literal leaves of gold . . .

"This year doesn't seem real," I confess aloud. "Any of it."

"Wait for this." Sorcha passes me a newspaper that's been folded to reveal a two-column article.

"The Morrison Institute for Young Ladies really is Dougal's mother's school!" Euphemia blurts out before I can scan the headline. "He was telling the truth. We found dozens of articles about her. A few mention him, too. The year it opened, she won special recognition for making an outsized positive impact in her community."

I skim the article. "Did you think Dougal was lying?"

"Always assume boys are lying," Sorcha says dryly.

"Not Dougal. He's . . ." I don't know how I feel about him. I like him, no matter what Sorcha says. But I'm not overwhelmed with romantic passion. I'm not sure he is, either. Are we meant to be friends, or something else? I think about his mother and her elite agency for educating girls and placing them in gainful employment. Maybe she's the treasure I came here to find.

I will not only squeeze the best bloody education out of Floodbane but also wrangle an introduction to a woman who trains girls like me to perform the exact career I spent my entire life dreaming about. I really will be able to provide my mother with a better life.

But there's one wee, teeny-tiny caveat: I cannot simultaneously have that future and spend unpredictable afternoons murdering our fellow countrymen. My stomach lurches.

In the cavernous library's oppressive silence, images of the boys I killed flicker in my brain. Before. After. Before. After.

It's driving me mad.

I'm not sure how much time I have before the bodies are discovered, or what steps the authorities will take once they're notified. I hope to hell I haven't left a trail of bloody footprints straight to our door.

I have to survive until the black salt arrives a fortnight from now. Unless . . . there's a way to break the curse even faster? I don't want to put all my eggs in the goodwife's basket. What if she can't find black salt? Or a vendor demands a price that I cannot pay?

I push back my chair. While my friends study for their various classes, I hunt through the shelves for any tome that might give me hope.

My fingers pause on the spine of a guidebook to ornithology. Birds make me think of chickens, and chickens make me think of my grandmother's grandmother. Now more than ever, I'm certain I was right. It wasn't just Davina who'd been plucked and roasted for supper. The family coop is full of cousins whose squawks of warning fall on deaf ears before their boiled little bodies find their way to our supper table.

The Cameron clan has been slaughtering and eating their own relatives for generations.

My head jerks up when I overhear low voices on the other side of the shelves I'm browsing. Four lads at an oblong table, rhapsodizing about the bravery and invincibility of Roderick and his lackeys, who are across the library, copying other people's schoolwork.

"Roderick is like the reincarnation of Braveheart," one of them says.

The others nod their agreement. "He's our King Arthur and his valiant friends, the Knights of the Round Table."

Please. Roderick and his crew have never even *heard* of chivalry.

One of the students shudders. "I would have run screaming from a kelpie."

"And he fought it back with his bare hands!" His friend shakes his head in awe. "That girl is so lucky Floodbane has lads like Roderick around."

It's enough to make me vomit. Those blackguards did the worst things possible, and it only bollocks up *my* life, not theirs. My friends and I are ostracized and called cruel names, whilst Roderick & Co. get hoisted about on boys' shoulders and lauded as royalty.

An uncharacteristically bloodthirsty vision flashes through

me as swift and bright as lightning. My four attackers staring sightlessly at their former schoolmates from four lifeless heads impaled on matching spikes.

I shake myself out of the daydream, unsettled. I've never imagined anything like that before, much less with an involuntary smile upon my face. I'm disturbed that I haven't fully shaken off this morning's bloodlust. I'm not even in monster form.

"Hey, there, love," coos a male voice, as if trying to gentle a wild foal. "Want to come over here and sit with us?"

I blink the appalling imagery away to find the table of all four boys gazing at me with open expressions of interest.

"You're pretty," says one.

"Are you taken?" asks another.

"I'll take her," says a third.

The fourth turns to snarl at him. "She's mine."

I back away from the rack of ornithology books. Being pretty suddenly feels . . . dangerous. I need to break this curse soon.

Tilting my head forward to hide my face as much as possible, I grab a random book from the closest shelf and pretend to be engrossed in its contents as I make my way toward Roderick and his lackeys. I have to be ready when the black salt arrives.

Luckily, they are surrounded by so many adoring fans that no one notices when I quickly crouch below eye level to collect items from each of them. A yellow thread clinging to Mungo's uniform. A brown hair from Fraser's. A surreptitious scraping from the back of Angus's boot—

Just as I touch his heel, he turns around and catches me

in the act, his eyes widening with surprise and cruelty. "Look what we've got here, lads. A troll under the bridge!"

I scramble away, dropping my book in the process.

Roderick scoops it up, rips a corner from a page, and shoves the paper into his mouth. I know what's coming. Before I can make it back to the safety of my roommates' table, he launches the spitball through the air. The sticky wad lodges in my curly hair, and they all laugh uproariously.

The jest is on them. He just inadvertently handed me the final ingredient for the spell—saliva. Now all I need is the black salt, and my days of being a baobhan sith will be over.

I scurry back to the safety of my five housemates. The boys do not follow. As if out of sight, I'm once again out of mind.

"We have to stick together," I whisper to the others.

"Don't go near those boys," Ishbel scolds me. "It's not safe."

"None of us are safe around here," Euphemia agrees. "You were brutally attacked walking home from class."

"To be fair, that could've happened anywhere," puts in Sorcha. "Don't trust boys just because they're not from Floodbane."

I rub my face. "If any lad makes any of us the slightest bit uncomfortable, we must share their names and descriptions. Then we'll all know who to beware of, and who to trust."

Sorcha snorts. "Is any boy trustworthy?"

Fiona's feathers are immediately ruffled. "I can name ten or twenty fine, upstanding—"

"What about Catriona's beau?" interrupts Euphemia. "Dougal seems all right."

Sorcha glares at them for contradicting her rant, then sighs. "Fine. Not all boys are complete rubbish."

Ishbel looks mulish. "I don't know about Dougal."

Really? I also held sensible doubts at first, but he's been consistently great. And his mother! One of the most marvelous women in Scotland! She raised her son to respect young ladies.

"Dougal would protect anyone in the Phoenix Sisterhood," I tell Ishbel.

She mutters under her breath, "I don't think of you as a sister."

The words punch through my ribs. I know we're not a real family, but of all my housemates, I never doubted my connection with Ishbel was real. When we study together, our breaths and mannerisms synchronize. I can sense her moods without looking at her face. We fall asleep every night whispering to each other in the dark.

I don't know what has changed, but I don't like it.

She's no longer looking at me. The others are still chattering about the boys in their classes, and which ones are best kept at a distance.

"Dougal can't be everywhere," Euphemia warns. "Stay alert."

"Forewarned is forearmed?" Maisie asks nervously.

Sorcha holds up her knife. "Armed is forearmed."

"Information is power," I assure Maisie, with a quelling look in Sorcha's direction. "I'm sure there's more we can do, and we ought to think about that. Aside from carrying knives—which I'm not convinced is the answer—how do you all feel about us banding together to . . ."

No one is listening to me. All five pairs of eyes are aimed over my left shoulder.

The police have come to arrest me? Already?

My gut gurgles in protest. “What is it?”

Maisie points.

I suck in a deep breath and spring to my feet to accept full responsibility for any charges the authorities brand me with.

But it’s not the police. It’s Dougal.

Holding a single yellow rose.

20

"I thought I might find you here." Dougal gives me a crooked smile. "Missed you at kirk service."

"You were supposed to be thinking about God," Sorcha reproaches him.

He makes a boyish expression. "Not a goddess?"

My face heats. Euphemia whistles. Ishbel glares.

"Excellent retort," Fiona whispers to Maisie.

Even Sorcha doesn't have a clever response.

Dougal's eyes are back on me. "You look extraordinarily beautiful today. This gorgeous afternoon may not be your match, but might I invite you to have a walk with me anyway?"

"We'll chaperone!" Three of my five housemates grin and elbow each other. The fourth sharpens her knife. The fifth—Ishbel—just scowls.

"We'll stay in the front garden," Dougal tells them. "In full sight of the whole school."

"It's all right," I assure them.

Sorcha points with her knife. "We'll be watching from the window."

In moments, Dougal and I amble across the trampled grass that one short week ago had been strewn with thousands of rotten fruits. It smells clean and fresh today, however. Like summer flowers, and the first hint of fall. A handful of bees buzz between patches of clover.

"I heard a few of your friends are on the hunt for suitors," Dougal says at last.

I'm surprised enough to stumble. "If you're interested in Fiona or Euphemia—"

"I'm not. If I were, I'd have invited *them* for a walk."

"Oh. I mean . . . I'm not currently in a position to consider courtship . . ."

"I'm not ready for that, either. Though my mother wishes I were. To keep her happy, would it be so dreadful if I told her I've my eye on a nice lass?"

"There's . . . You . . . I'd be flattered."

"Mother may request to meet you," he warns. "She sends a secretary to fetch me home for Christmas holiday, but I wager she'll come herself if she thinks I've found a lass I fancy settling down with. She can be intense."

"I would love to meet your mother!" I flame with heat when I realize how odd it sounds to be more eager to meet the mother of a classmate than interested in the boy himself. "Intense is no problem. My parents can't afford to send anyone to fetch me, so I'd be stuck here doing nothing anyway."

Dougal looks horrified. "All alone for Christmastide?

Unacceptable. You *must* come to Edinburgh with us. We've loads of guest chambers, and it shan't be any bother."

"It's a deal." I hold out a trembling hand to shake on it.

Part of me wilts at the thought of not spending the holiday with my own mother. The other half of me says once I'm an instructor with pupils and a salary of my own, I can rescue Mother, and ensure the second half of her life is much safer and happier than anything she's experienced up until now.

"When you visit, I can show you our map room and answer pretty much any question you might have. Not because geography is my passion, mind you. It was simply drilled into me since birth. Plus, we've a hideous library with rolling ladders and soaring shelves filled with nothing but books. It's ghastly."

I laugh. "However did you survive such a chamber of horrors?"

"Out of the pot and into the fire." He pulls a face. "I cannot overstate how nonbookish I am. I wouldn't be at Floodbane if my mother weren't paying my way in."

"Well, that, and your placement test results," I chide him.

"They didn't even make me take one. I *could* have passed. My mother ensured I was at fourth-year level by age twelve. She was afraid I'd fail on purpose to stay home. And Headmaster MacKenzie wants her money too much to fuss about the details."

I slant him an incredulous look.

He grimaces. "I know how privileged that sounds. It's unfair to everyone involved. I took a spot away from a student who deserves it more. Who *wants* it more. But I swear it's not by choice. I'd rather be digging in the dirt."

Before I can ask another question, muffled shouts sound from the woods beside us.

Dougal stops walking, his eyes huge. "The kelpie!"

"There is no kelpie," I snap, though I cannot explain how I know. "But that doesn't mean someone isn't in danger. We have to help."

"Won't that put *us* in danger?"

I ignore him and inch between the trees. I'm not foolish enough to charge into a fray without knowing what I'm up against, but I could never forgive myself if boys were attacking another girl and I chose to do nothing.

Dougal follows behind me. Snapping twigs prevent us from being perfectly silent, but the brawl up ahead drowns out our movements.

It's the royal four, though this time they've trapped a clearly frightened boy. Mungo pushes the trembling lad to Angus, who pushes him to Fraser, who pushes him to Roderick, who punches him in the belly.

"I'm sorry!" gasps the boy. "I shouldn't have tried out!"

"Rugby?" I whisper to Dougal.

He shakes his head. "*The Taming of the Shrew*. That lad has the starring role."

"Roderick hates school plays? Does he have a grievance against actors?"

"The opposite. He's the understudy. Roderick would be the one on stage if he hadn't lost the part to this boy."

Naturally, Roderick would want to play a man who torments a woman physically and psychologically until she cows to his wishes.

"We can't let him beat up another student over it," I insist.

"You and me against the four of them? We should sneak away while we still can." Dougal tries to pull me back from the trees.

I cannot decide if he is cowardly or wise. It's true that we're unlikely to win a fistfight against four much larger boys, but I hate the thought of choosing not to stand up for someone else.

"All right," I whisper. "But we have to tell the headmaster."

"We can try," Dougal says in a tone that implies he doesn't believe any consequences will come of it.

Right. All complaints to the headmaster must first be filed through Fraser. My fists clench. These bullies will continue getting away with murder.

When we emerge from the woods back into the relative safety of the school lawn, Dougal's expression is grim as we turn back toward the library. "Yet another reason why I'd rather be back home in my peaceful garden."

"If you hate school so much, why are you here? And why would you be willing to introduce me to your mother, who runs the very institute I've dreamed of attending my entire life?"

His eyebrows raise. "Have you really?"

I nod. "My mother told me stories about it ever since I was small. She tried to convince my father to let me have a proper education, but there was never any hope of him agreeing to that."

"Well, I'm glad you're here now. If Mother believes girls like you should have equal education and opportunities, then it's the truth."

"You do realize you're the only boy on this whole campus who feels that way?"

"Perhaps the only one who says so openly. Mother warned me that 'everyone' would behave abhorrently to a female co-hort. Me helping you would make her proud." He lowers his voice. "Besides, now that I've come to know you, I've a personal investment."

I frown. "I've heard the stories about Roderick and his fellow bullies beating up other lads. Aren't you afraid of retribution?"

"Oh, they could absolutely trounce me if they tried," Dougal admits without hesitation. "Four to one are terrible odds in a fight. But they know better than to risk angering the headmaster. My presence ensures a significant percentage of the school's budget. Money that funds activities Roderick and his friends care about."

"Ugh. Tell your mother to forbid all sporting activities."

He chuckles. "She'd rather fight for girls to join the teams. In any case, bringing home a clever girl who loves to learn and wants to be a teacher will make a perfect holiday for all three of us. You two can haunt the map room and the library, while I sneak out to resume my apprenticeship with our gardener."

"It sounds wonderful," I say dreamily. "My mother would love to see me in such an environment."

"Tell her all about it in your letters home."

I decline to admit that my mother cannot read. "If only there were schools for grown women like her."

"Who says there's not? Is that true? If I tell my mother you said so, she'll probably have a new program in place by next year."

"If anyone could, it's your mum. Also, Dougal . . . I'm not sure the other students do know you're the reason for the big donation—and the unwanted presence of girls." I gnaw my lip, then add, "Please be careful."

He nods and drops me off at the library with a deep bow. I head back to the study table with my brain buzzing with all the ways a true friendship with him would be a godsend.

That is, until the cold claws of reality slice through the curtain of dreams. Dougal may be the answer to my prayers, but my beastly new double life is both of our worst nightmares. I *have* to get rid of this curse.

Whatever it takes.

21

Everywhere I go, my schoolmates' gazes follow me. Not as if I'm an eyesore with sweat-stained armpits and dirt-caked hems, but as though I'd been crowned this year's May queen at Beltane. I always knew prettier girls were treated differently, but it's dizzying to experience firsthand.

After eight hours of admiring glances, I practically jog home to see my reflection for myself.

Ishbel is right on my heels as I shudder to a stop in front of our shared looking glass.

"What's wrong?" she asks.

I'm too baffled by the question to even formulate a response. Stained underarms and dirty hems are the least of my problems. I'm dusted head to toe in the crumbs of rotting autumn leaves, and there is a broken twig hanging from the tangled knot of hair at the back of my head.

Ishbel watches me, not the mirror. Her eyes soften. "How do you manage to look prettier every day?"

I stare at her. *She's* the one whose beauty took my breath away at first sight. On a good day, I'm at best average-looking. This has been a horrid day, and I look like a literal goblin.

"I need a bath before bed," I mutter.

I'm too tired to do more than the minimum, but after supper, I clean myself up from the detritus of the day.

Ishbel is already tucked beneath her covers when I blow out the candle and crawl into mine. Moonlight slithers through the cracks between the wooden paneled walls and splatters strange shadows about the room.

"Ready?" Ishbel whispers.

I grin in the darkness. "Ready."

We are the first to bed, but the last to sleep, because we spend an hour or two every night scaring each other senseless with the legends and ghost stories handed down through our families.

"What's one we haven't done yet?" Her voice is trembling already.

I think fast. "Culzean Castle?"

"Ooh, that's a good one. So many ghosts."

I can't see her, but I know she just shuddered. I did, too.

"There once was a wicked laird," I begin.

"Sir Archibald Kennedy."

"Shh, let me tell it. A laird so selfish and so odious, he forced his tenants to sign over their lands to him. A man so rotten, he hanged his enemies and neighbors alike from the dour tree in his garden. A man so evil, fishermen couldn't distinguish between Hell and Culzean. Then one day—"

"At his funeral!"

"—the hearse stood still, and the horses refused to move. A crow had settled atop the primary gelding."

"Not just any crow!"

"That's right. It was the Devil himself, come to witness the passing of one of his own."

"Sir Archibald the Wicked wasn't the only demon of Culzean," Ishbel adds, taking over the tale. "Two centuries earlier, his direct ancestor coveted the lands of Crossraguel Abbey. But these lands belong to God, and not the wicked earl. In a fit of rage, he captures an abbot to blackmail him into signing over his lands."

"Then blackmail turns to torture."

"The earl roasts the poor abbot alive until—"

Loud banging erupts on my side of the wall. "Shut up, both of you! We can all hear, and you're scaring the stuffing out of us!"

Ishbel and I burst into muffled giggles.

"Come here," she whispers. "They can't hear us if we keep our voices down."

Stomach fluttering, I throw back my covers and pad barefoot across the wooden floor to crawl into bed with Ishbel.

We face each other, our cheeks on the same pillow and our hems tangled at our ankles.

"That wasn't even a proper ghost story," she whispers. "Those things really happened."

"Fairy stories are true too," I whisper back.

"Have you ever seen one?"

"No. But I know for a fact they're real."

She hesitates, then nods. “I believe in magic, too.”

“You’d be foolish not to. This is Scotland.”

“No, I mean . . .” Her voice lowers so much, her next words are almost inaudible. “My grandmother was a witch.”

My heart stops, then explodes against my ribs like fireworks. Might this be how I break the curse?

“Do you still talk to her? Can I meet her? Or write her a letter?”

Ishbel’s voice cracks. “She’s dead. I didn’t get to meet her. I just heard the tales my mother tells.”

Oh. Bitter disappointment rushes through me. I reach forward in the dark to find Ishbel’s hand. “I’m sorry about your grandmother.”

She twines her fingers with mine. “Gran told my mother many stories about where you live.”

I smile in the dark. “The Highlands?”

“Yes. She said forty years ago, when she was a young newlywed and expecting my mother, the Highland potato blight nearly killed our entire family when famine swept Scotland.”

Oh. My proud smile falls. I can only offer another soft, “I’m sorry.”

“It’s not your fault. Or any human’s.” Ishbel’s hand grips mine tighter, as if the words alone are dangerous, and our clasped hands are the sole bond keeping us safe from harm. “Gran said it was the Nuckelavee who caused it.”

I shiver despite myself. “My grandmother spoke of that demon, too. An enormous, skinless centaur from the Northern

Isles, whose fetid breath fells crops and livestock alike. She told me never to voice its name without making a quick prayer to repent."

Ishbel gasps, and her palm turns clammy. "I hope my careless words didn't call it back this way."

"No, you're safe with me," I assure her quickly, stroking my thumb across the soft skin of her hand to calm her nerves. "Magical creatures are . . ."

What, exactly? Imaginary? I know that to be a lie. If I can materialize across the isle to slurp the blood of a stranger, there's no reason why the Nuckelavee isn't also gallivanting around, causing its own brand of destruction.

Ishbel shudders beside me. "Not magical. *Monstrous.* I hope to never cross paths with anything so vile."

Acid churns in my stomach. Perhaps the Nuckelavee was once just like me. Perhaps he doesn't *want* the air from his lungs to blight crops and massacre livestock and cause the deaths of a quarter million people, but he has to *breathe.* Even if he's despised for it. Perhaps there is no lonelier creature in Scotland than a monstrous one.

Ishbel falls asleep long before I do, her fingers still curled trustingly in mine.

My thoughts are too plagued with memories of what I've done and nightmares about killing. I ease out of Ishbel's bed and cross over to my own, but sleep doesn't come any easier there. I toss restlessly, fighting fears not just of punishment for my crimes, but of being snatched out of Ishbel's arms by a summons. To show up somewhere with claws and hooves, in my nightgown, without any idea where I am. All I'll know is that I've been placed there to kill.

In the morning, I try to act normal, for Ishbel's sake. Which is the absolute worst possible way to look like a normal human. I second-guess how I'm standing, how I'm talking, whether my facial expressions seem ordinary and unpanicked.

I manage to be mostly convincing until I reach for my mother's talisman. I keep it in the pocket of my dress. The charm means safety, familiarity, my mother's love.

When the little iron cross touches my palm, however, it sears deep into my suddenly burning flesh with the sizzle of fresh sausages.

I let out a shocked hiss, drop the necklace onto the oak-paneled floor, then hop around the tiny, shared bedroom whilst howling in agony, shaking my steaming palm as though I'm trying to make my floppy hand fly off at the wrist.

You know, like a normal person.

"Are you all right?" asks Ishbel, peering up from stuffing school supplies into her satchel. "What's wrong with your hand?"

"Nothing," I gasp, angling my palm so she cannot see. "I'm fine. I nicked myself on a sharp corner and overreacted."

She pushes her satchel aside and rises to her feet. "Do you want me to look at it?"

"No! I . . . I'm embarrassed you caught me being such a baby, is all."

Ishbel's gaze softens. "I don't mind babying you."

Oh, God. She's a good person and wants to help, but I can't let her.

"My goodness, dear me!" I feign sudden surprise. I probably look and sound like a demented old granny. "I've gone and dropped my mother's necklace! Ishbel, would you be a saint and toss that into the armoire for me?"

She shoots me a well-deserved odd expression—my scholarship to Floodbane was definitely not for my acting skills. But she scoops up the fallen cross with good humor and no ill effects. In seconds, it's tucked into a shadowed corner of our shared tall cedar armoire.

There. Crisis averted. My lungs can breathe again.

Ishbel leaps across the small bedroom like a squirrel after a nut and grabs the wrist I'm unsuspiciously hiding behind my back. She jerks my wounded hand toward her bosom and forces my tender palm to face up.

To our surprise, there's nothing there.

We both stare in silence at my unblemished palm. My injury healed as fast as it appeared.

"You really are a baby." Ishbel shakes her head, her amused voice more fond than disgusted. She gives my palm a curative kiss anyway, then drops my hand back to my side. "Hurry up, or we'll be late for school."

I gaze after her for a moment, transfixed. Then I grab my own satchel and hurry down the stairs to catch up with her and the others.

Although I take the rear again, in case I grow deer legs and vanish, I'm in a much sunnier mood now that I'm not curled in a fetal position in the dark.

Or maybe it's the close proximity to Ishbel and our friends that renews my spirit and gives me strength. The power of unity amongst indomitable women whose bond tightens every day.

I chatter at the others about a new idea I've come up with to divide the household chores in such a way that everyone has tasks befitting their best abilities, and also days off in which to rest without responsibilities.

They're receptive to this plan, and the conversation drifts off to other themes with fluidity. It is I who marvels at my newfound assertiveness—you'd never have caught me drawing up to-do lists for Hamish and Father—and the ease with which my suggestion was accepted.

Rather than head straight to class, I first slip into the school library. There are no convenient guides about breaking fairy curses, but there are plenty of tomes on Scottish folklore. I find a slim volume about siths and press it to my chest with glee.

The gong sounds while I approach the librarian to borrow the book. To my confusion, he smiles and waves me away rather than have me sign my name to the list of loans.

Although I hurry, I'm late to my first class. My professor whirls toward me with obvious anger. Chagrined, I flash an embarrassed smile and open my mouth to give an apology.

Before I can say a word, his ire vanishes, and he motions me to a seat up front. A seat that already has a boy sitting in it. I shake my head at the lad. There are seats in the back where I can—

But the boy is already on his feet, all but genuflecting to the newly emptied chair like a squire to a queen's throne.

I make my way forward and wait until three dozen eyes are no longer hot on my neck before I ease a thin book entitled *Siths of Scotland* inside the philosophy tome I'm supposed to be reading.

Sith is a synonym for fairy. There are many kinds, with similarities and differences. There's the Cù Sith—a shaggy green hound with a terrifying howl—and the Cat Sith that haunts the Highlands. All very interesting, but not the reason I selected this book. I page past all the animal siths with haste, until I reach the phrase I've been looking for:

Baobhan sith.

I skim the chapter quickly. The text largely notes what Goodwife MacAskill told me in the village. Men's careless wishes or violent intentions trigger the summoning. Upon arrival, the baobhan sometimes seduces her prey or dances with him prior to draining his blood or consuming him whole. When she casts her full attention upon her victim, he's powerless to resist. The presence of a baobhan sith is a death warrant.

No mention whatsoever about becoming human. The book doesn't even mention how anyone becomes a sith. *I* always thought they were just . . . their own native creatures, like rabbits or otter. I didn't know ordinary girls could become baobhan siths. Maybe the writers of this volume didn't know either.

Disappointed, I thumb through other sections. None of the chapters mention anything about humans turning into fairies, but buried at the end of the book is a casual reference to what to do if you're cursed by a witch.

I snatch up my pencil and a scrap of paper to take notes. The chapter suggests a purifying bath steeped with a dizzying list of herbs, ranging from hyssop to mugwort to wormwood. Aggravatingly, it doesn't specify the quantities of each ingredient—not that we happen to have "root of vetiver" back home in the shared pantry.

It doesn't matter. I'll find the ingredients, and I'll make the magical bath, and I'll sit my arse inside it until I drown this bloody curse.

I'm so focused on scribbling notes, I don't even notice the gong has sounded and class has emptied, until I glance up to find a new wave of students streaming into the lecture hall.

Shite! Why didn't anyone yell at me to get going? I shove all my books and papers back into my satchel and race toward the door, where my face smacks into a familiar chest.

Dougal looks at me in surprise. "Did you get transferred into my philosophy class?"

"No, I'm late leaving mine." I feel so foolish even admitting it.

"What's your next subject? I'll walk you there before Roderick arrives."

I hurry with him down the corridor reflexively, though I cannot help but wonder if Roderick will still hate me now that I'm a sith. Technically, my powers of seduction are only guaranteed to work on the prey who summon me, but clearly vestiges of that spell are leaking out and affecting innocent men in the real world.

"You know," I muse to Dougal, "I'm surprised a bully like Roderick could make a friend at all, much less three of them."

"He got lucky. As a first-year, Angus was bullied himself, and came to Roderick for protection. When Angus grew taller and wider in his second year, he stuck by Roderick."

"Was Mungo bullied, too?"

"Not at all. Mungo learned cruelty watching his father the magistrate, whom he respects—and therefore gives Roderick that same respect. To Mungo, violence is power."

"And Fraser? He's the headmaster's assistant. He should defend students like us."

"Fraser will do whatever is best for Fraser. He's loyal to Roderick because the alternative is to be against him. A proposition no one can win."

"So Roderick means safety and leadership to them, and hell on earth to the rest of us."

"Welcome to Floodbane. At least my mother's institute has no such problems. Oh! I've just remembered." Dougal brightens and bounces next to me like a puppy. "She wrote back and loves your idea."

"My . . . idea?"

"Of creating opportunities for older women as well. Thus far, Mother approves of you wholeheartedly, sight unseen. And she says your mother could be considered for the first cohort of adult women to be educated at the institute."

My jaw falls open. Mrs. Morrison took my idea seriously, and intends to potentially include my mother on day one?

Indescribable joy vibrates through me. I've long dreamt of providing a better life for my mother, but assumed I'd need to marry well or study hard to put myself into a position where I could offer her sanctuary. This would be nothing short of a miracle.

Neither Dougal nor his mother have guaranteed admission to my mother and I, but last month there was no hope, and today there is a very real possibility . . . *if* I can break this bloody curse.

The unbidden memory of my summoning in the woods turns my stomach.

I *cannot* kill again.

22

At school, I keep my ears perked, but I hear no rumors about the missing boys. Instead of relieving my worry, the lack of a manhunt makes me more on edge than ever. Is the administration concealing a tragedy they've decided shouldn't become public? Or is no one surprised those two roguish lads would miss so many lessons?

In class, my morning instructors call on me repeatedly, even though I haven't raised my hand once. Because I'm unprepared to speak, my answers are halting. A stuttered sentence or two, blurting the first plausible nonsense that comes to mind.

Everyone stares back at me, rapt, as though I were giving an acceptance speech to become the next Queen of Scotland.

At the lunch gong, I race out of the classroom straight into Ishbel's surprised arms. She grabs me to keep us both from tumbling into our housemates.

"Cut your finger again?" Ishbel teases.

Sorcha swivels her head. "What's wrong?"

"Nothing," I assure them. "I'm just hungry. Let's go to the refectory."

Euphemia looks unconvinced. "They dragged us out of there, last time."

"Let me try." I can almost guarantee it won't happen again today. At least not because of the same two boys.

My ducklings fall into line. Soon, there are six of us in a row, with me leading the pack this time.

"Why, good morning, beautiful," a lecherous male server my father's age drawls, when it's my turn at the lunch line.

Perfect. I pin him with my full attention, willing my sith senses to imbue the air between us with maximum seductive persuasiveness.

"I, and all five of my friends, would like the best servings of everything you've got."

"Anything for you, poppet." He smiles at us. My wish is his command. We can barely carry the heavy trays he filled for us over to the nearest table.

"How did you *do* that?" Maisie asks in awe.

"I told you," Ishbel answers. "It's the eyelashes. Who can resist them?"

"No one cares about Catriona's eyelashes," Sorcha says with a roll of her eyes. But then she gives me a second glance, frowning as she inspects me. "Although you do look . . ."

I try not to squirm beneath so much focused attention. It's fabulous to use my powers for good, but I don't want my friends to suspect the dark side lurking beneath.

The girls aren't the only ones staring at me. Every boy in the refectory is gazing in my direction. Not with anger at us having infiltrated their private space again, but as if the morsel they most want to eat is the tatty lass from the Highlands sweating her way through two petticoats and a muslin dress.

"Are *all* the boys in love with you?" grouses Fiona.

"Teach me," begs Euphemia.

We all laugh, breaking the tension.

"She can't teach you to grow eyelashes." Fiona has added kohl to her own, despite the no-cosmetics rule. She tosses her head. "There's no accounting for taste, you know."

I hold up my palms in surrender. "I'm not trying to steal suitors from you."

"You don't have to try, do you?" Fiona mutters.

"Dougal is more than enough distraction for me, I swear."

This time, Ishbel smolders.

We pick at our food in silence. The other girls leave the table one by one, rather than sticking together as a group. Soon, all that's left is Ishbel and me, and she's not happy.

"It was a joke. Dougal is only a friend."

She shrugs. "Forget it."

I cannot wait to break this curse. I'll get no more special treatment at school, but at least I won't have to murder anyone. And maybe I can keep my friends. Ishbel matters more to me than fleeting popularity at an academy I hope to transfer away from next year anyway. I'm not even certain I can fall asleep alone anymore. Not after getting used to whispering in the dark with Ishbel, then drifting off to the comforting sigh of her slow, even breaths.

"Are you vexed with me, too?" I ask her.

"Over boys? I couldn't care less what lads think." She tilts her head, her dark eyes intense. "Do you care about them?"

"Not like Fiona. I prefer being tolerated to being pelted with rotten fruit, but I'm not ready for a suitor. I only have time for friends."

Her gaze shutters, as if this was the wrong thing to say. "You're not interested in romance at all?"

I suppose her question comes from the incongruity of every boy in the school suddenly panting after me.

"It's not personal to the boys. I mean, it is. Most of them were ghastly to us. But that's not the only factor. Dougal has been perfect, but I don't feel any burning ardor toward him, or whatever the poets say."

Her eyes are intense again. "Have you ever felt a burning ardor?"

"I'm not sure," I confess. "I find certain people attractive, and prefer the company of some more than others. I've always been too busy to search for a grand passion. Or knew I couldn't have it. My father wants to arrange a marriage to the butcher. Our wedding would be happening now, if I hadn't received a scholarship for Floodbane instead."

"I'll never wed," Ishbel says with absolute certainty.

"You can't know that. Perhaps you'll meet someone who lights a burning passion inside you—"

"Oh, I have. I'm just not interested in anyone I could marry." She hesitates. "You remember when I said I always yearned to attend an all-girls school?"

I nod. "We'd all rather have won a scholarship to one of those. Well, not Fiona."

"Right. Because she wants romance. Well, so do I." Ishbel rolls her shoulders back, as if gathering strength. "I'm not interested in boys. If I'm to find love, it will be with another girl."

I stare at her. A hundred different pieces click into place as I reinterpret countless moments together. I'd been so hurt when Ishbel said *I don't think of you as a sister*. Her words made me feel unimportant, when in fact, she might have been trying to tell me the opposite.

"I've shocked you." Her face falls, and she bites her lip. "Do you hate me now?"

On the contrary. I'm forced to reevaluate my own actions and feelings.

The moment I met her, I was overwhelmed by Ishbel's beauty. Her warm softness, as she enveloped me in her embrace. Since that day, I've gazed at her or shared her space whenever I can. Going so far as to crawl in bed with her every night, ostensibly so our whispers don't wake up our housemates.

But is that really why I've been doing so?

Although I always assumed I'd one day marry a man, all my instincts and actions indicate I'd rather be curled up next to Ishbel than sneak kisses with Dougal. He's sweet, handsome, and could provide a far better future than the butcher, but it's Ishbel who puts butterflies in my stomach. I do like boys, but . . . apparently I like girls, too. What would it be like to act on such feelings?

"Catriona?" Ishbel looks miserable. "Forget I said anything."

I take a deep breath. "I don't think of you as a sister, either."

Her eyes widen. She drops her spoon next to her plate, and slides her hand to touch the tips of her fingers to mine.

"I meant what I said about not having time for romance right now," I tell her quickly. "I've some important things to figure out first, but please know, I'm not hesitant because of any aversion to you."

She slides her hand back into her lap and nods without meeting my eyes.

I long to tell her all the strange and glorious ways she makes me feel, but it would help neither of us at the moment. I cannot consider any future until I've broken this curse.

And then what? Most women, even those who prefer men, don't marry for love. Ishbel herself admitted there can be no wedded bliss for us. The wisest way to secure my future—to ensure a life of ease for myself and my mother—would be to accept Dougal's advances, even if my heart thinks of him as second-best.

But I cannot make promises to him, either. Not while I'm a sith.

One of the boys at the table next to ours is staring so hard that his elbow knocks over a bowl of grapes, one of which rolls all the way beneath our table.

Ishbel bends down to retrieve it. She takes an inordinately long time before sitting back up.

"Everything all right?" I ask her.

"You tell me." Her expression is troubled. "There're smears of what looks like blood on the bottom of your boot. Did you get attacked again? Is that why you're so twitchy?"

"I . . . No . . . I . . ." My brain fails to conjure an innocent explanation.

I burned the clothes I'd been wearing during the massacre, because the school provides an infinite supply of uniforms. Boots, however, aren't part of that menu. I scrubbed mine as best I could, but blood stains are remarkably resilient.

"I lived on a farm," I blurt out at last. "My father and brother were always slaughtering animals. I've stepped through butchery you'd never be able to scrub from your eyes."

Three true sentences that in no way address the fresh stains on my shoes.

She doesn't seem convinced. "You're saying you came to school with boots spotted like that?"

Shite, I don't want to lie to her. Still, I force myself to nod. "Farm girl. That's what our shoes always look like."

Ishbel shakes her head. "Your boots were scuffed but unstained on Sunday before we left for church."

"You must be misremembering."

This is worse than a lie. Ishbel is one hundred percent right, and yet I'm trying to convince her that she can't believe her own eyes. This curse keeps getting worse.

Ishbel appears deeply hurt by my blatant mistruths.

"If you don't trust me . . ." She jerks to her feet and stalks away before I can call her back.

I'm now alone at a long empty table, with eight hundred hungry male eyes pointed in my direction. I leap to my feet and scurry away before they decide to pounce. Keeping my distance for their sake, as well as mine.

Who knows which of us would survive?

23

Ten minutes before the gong sounds for afternoon classes, I sprint out of the school, and into the woods. Not the deep side of the forest, where peckish woodland creatures may or may not be leaving the two lads' dismembered faces as pristine as I left them. The opposite side, where hopefully nothing monstrous lies in wait.

I try not to think about the effects of birds' sharp little beaks on distended human eyeballs, but once imagined, the picture is impossible to erase.

As soon as I'm far enough from the school not to be overheard by anyone within its walls, I throw back my head and arms and scream up at the heavens until I'm hoarse.

It doesn't fix anything, but the release makes me feel a little better.

"I know you're out there," I croak to the silent shrubbery encircling me. "I *wish* to be an ordinary human, do you hear me? I *wish* to be my old self again, seventeen-year-old Catriona

Cameron, the same lass who arrived here nine days ago. I *wish* for my friends and I to never suffer again or be scared another moment for the rest of our lives. And I want it right now!"

The only response is the distant laugh of a woodpecker.

Or maybe that's how fairies laugh, too. Openly, and from high above, with no remorse whatsoever.

I know they hear me. They're always listening. Either they're choosing to ignore my pleas . . . or wishes are only for humans, and I no longer meet the criteria.

My chance to make grantable wishes has come and gone. I'm a beast. A baobhan sith. Avenging angel—or unfettered monster—is my new identity now.

A fate foisted upon me with neither my consent nor conversation. The result of idle, impulsive wishes by greedy, self-important young men who already possessed all the advantages.

Those soulless rotters. I hate them.

When my brother Hamish wished for me to know how hard boarding school could be, he never imagined the chain of horrific events his careless words would unleash. Angus's and Mungo's wishes for me went even worse. Being more attractive stopped most of the bullying, but it also made me into a murderous monster. The reprieve isn't worth the cost of other people's lives. Or turning my own future into a nightmare.

From the fairies' point of view, perhaps what they've done to me changes nothing of substance. Humans hurting or killing other humans is perhaps the most human trait of all. My shoulders cave.

I trudge back to Floodbane.

Because the lunch break has not yet ended, boys are milling

everywhere in the front garden. Most glance at me with admiration, but leave me alone as I pass between them.

But before I can reach the entrance doors, I find my path blocked by Roderick and two of his henchmen. Angus and Mungo.

My voice is hoarse from all the screaming, but I do my best to summon what seductive powers of persuasion I have left. "Let me pass."

They act as though they don't hear me.

Or rather, as if they *wish* they couldn't hear me. Roderick's scowl appears permanent, but Mungo's gaze briefly softens and he struggles to keep his sneer in place.

A baobhan sith is meant to incapacitate her specific prey, not every man in the world. Victims tend to be complete strangers, so it would make sense for my powers to be strongest against those with neutral feelings toward me. These boys aren't neutral at all.

With my full attention, I might be able to compel some or most men to behave with kindness, but none of the literature indicates memory loss accompanies the symptoms. Mungo's lips may smile at me, but his brain knows he hates me.

Angus, meanwhile, keeps flickering like a candle. His face beams at me, then frowns. Beams, frowns. Between each alternating grimace, he steals long glances at Roderick for guidance.

"Go back to your little farm," Roderick commands me. "I doubt you're wanted there either, but at least you'll be out of my sight."

I gaze coolly at him.

"Aye," pipes up Mungo. "No one wants you here."

I turn to face him. "As if anyone wants you three around."

"Go on, then." Angus gives my shoulder a push.

I spin to snarl at him, and he freezes with his arm in the air. Slowly, his hand floats back to my shoulder, this time to give it a soft caress, like a child wondering at the fur of his first kitten.

"What the devil is wrong with you?" Roderick snaps.

Angus and I both glance at him, and the spell is broken—the fingers caressing me now give my upper arm a vicious pinch sure to leave a horrible bruise.

But at least this answers the question. For those with no reason to despise me, my sith seductiveness is effortless. For those who actively dislike me, my full attention is required to temporarily bend them to my will.

And for those who hate me, who see me as an enemy who must be destroyed at all costs . . . Roderick may find me attractive, but he's still out for my blood. Even if my direct gaze makes him uncurl his fists, he won't forget his goals or the fact that I'm in his way.

Such single-minded intensity makes me wonder if being "king" of Floodbane Academy is all that Roderick has. Perhaps his forebears were as awful to him as he is to others. Maybe going home means becoming nobody again. That could explain why he's trying so hard to make the most of his four years at the school.

Or maybe he's just a terrible person.

I focus every ounce of my will on Roderick, while trying to keep Mungo and Angus at the edge of my vision. "I said, *let me pass.*"

Mungo and Angus fall back. Roderick bares his teeth,

trembling with the effort of trying to resist. Finally, he flings his arms out, his movements as jerky as a marionette.

"Fine. Go. We don't want to look at your beaut—at your ugly face anyway."

I shoulder past him and sprint into the school for safety before he can change his mind. If they had snuck up on me from behind . . .

My desperate pleas to the fairies didn't work, but I can't stand around waiting for black salt to arrive. Just because the fairies won't help me doesn't mean there's no one who can.

I head not to class, but to the chapel.

The large chamber is empty. I drop to my knees before the giant wooden cross with its painted Jesus statue and clasp my hands in supplication. Head bowed, eyes closed tight, I beg God again and again to undo what the fairies have done.

Outside the chapel, someone sounds the gong for afternoon lessons. I don't move. I pray, over and over, growing more and more frantic, until my knees threaten to shatter beneath me from bearing my unmoving weight for so long on unyielding marble.

As before, there is no sign of having been heard. I tell myself this doesn't mean that my plea *wasn't* granted. The only way I'll know if I'm human for good is if my legs never sprout hooves again.

I don't wait for the minister to return to the chapel. Not because I fear he won't believe my claims, but because confessing that "my mother's cross burns my flesh on contact" is unlikely to take me anywhere I want to go.

My legs feel leaden as I walk to class. As if kneeling there praying for so long made each bone and muscle weigh ten times more than before.

Everyone turns to look at me when I enter the lecture hall.

"Sorry I'm tardy," I mumble.

The eyes continue to stare, as if mesmerized. Frozen in place like dozens of startled deer.

This alone tells me I'm still not human. Before becoming a sith, I'd never left a boy transfixed.

My seat is waiting for me, so I take it. The professor neither reprimands me, nor makes any notation in his notebook. After a pause in which I can detect each individual racing heartbeat return to its normal rhythm, the lecture continues as if I'd been seated in my place the entire time.

I rub my face with my hands. I've read the assigned anthology, so I'm able to give coherent answers when called upon.

My mind, however, is elsewhere.

All I've ever wanted is to be a good person. Trite, but true. For years, I thought this meant moving to a big city where I could help other women. With Dougal's help, this fantasy could actually happen.

But I can't think about next year yet. If I intend to be a good person, what steps can I take *today*? How can I prove who I truly am, and who I strive to be?

I don't like the methods of the baobhan siths, but I reluctantly admit I agree with the motivation: protect women at all costs. Hasn't that always been my aim? To improve the lives of lasses like me?

That's the true north I must keep marching toward.

In the following class, my pencil flies across my paper. This time, I'm not writing drafts of the assigned composition, but creating handbills to pass around before and after classes. Campaigning for female students' equal access to all amenities. Not just the refectory and the library, but also the laboratories, the arts and music rooms, the sporting events, the academic and social clubs.

I borrow spare sheets of paper from everyone around me, then place dozens of copies in each lad's hand as he exits the classroom, influencing them to pass the handbills to other friends and faculty.

They agree with the goofiest faces, bounding off like puppies to spread the revolution into every corner of Floodbane.

Riding high from this success, I decide I might as well be tardy to my final class. Instead of heading straight to Geography, I slip through the corridors to the headmaster's office.

As before, the secretary is seated behind the large desk in the reception area.

Fraser's smaller desk is unoccupied. An early Christmas miracle.

The secretary sees me staring. "If you need Fraser, I don't know when he'll be back. He's gone with the others to hunt for the missing . . . That is, he's attending to duties assigned to him by the headmaster."

That brings me back down to Earth. While I was busy championing for the rights of women, I'd forgotten about the two male classmates whose corpses I'd abandoned to be picked clean by foxes and buzzards.

The search is apparently on, though the staff does not yet wish to alarm the students.

They'll be alarmed soon enough.

"Might I speak to Headmaster MacKenzie?" I make myself look as innocent and audience-worthy as possible. "It's about an incident perpetrated by four male students."

"That sounds serious. Fraser handles such requests. He knows the procedures to follow."

"Please, could you help me?" I flutter my unnaturally long eyelashes.

The secretary relents and pushes to his feet. "I'll see if the headmaster is receiving."

He ducks into Mr. MacKenzie's office and shuts the door behind him.

I clasp my hands tight in front of my corset. "Please please please please please."

I'm not even sure who I'm praying to, but I mean it with every particle of my being. Justice, done the right way.

The secretary steps out of the headmaster's office with a smile, leaving the door open. "Good news. Mr. MacKenzie is very busy, but he can spare a brief moment to—"

I don't hear the rest. Pain explodes through my legs and feet, shattering my human bones and rebuilding them into sticklike, furry deer legs with enormous two-toed black hooves.

Oh God, not now!

"Erm . . ." I flatten my palms against my skirts, holding the hems down toward the floor as far as they'll go. "Maybe next time."

The secretary frowns. "There won't be a next time. Mr. MacKenzie has three minutes right now, in which he's willing to—"

"I'm sorry." I gasp as my knees buckle the wrong way. "Tell him . . . Tell him . . . Wee girlie problems?"

I race out the door to the sound of the secretary's shocked intake of breath.

A lady would *never* mention ordinary female bodily functions to another person, but in my panic and desperation, I could think of nothing else that would explain a mad dash down the corridor and out the front door.

Last time, the hooves came two or three minutes before I vanished into thin air. If I run as fast as humanly—beastily—possible, I might make it to the tree line before I disappear.

Damn those boys and their cursed wishes! The one chance I had to make them face consequences through proper channels, and even that's denied to me.

I run faster, furious that no help will be coming for me.

And with claws sprouting from my fingers, nor will there be any help for whomever just summoned me.

24

Mid-step, I'm yanked from the trail, turned inside out in a soup of colors and clouds, then deposited deep within . . . the same woods I was walking in? I hope?

There are three men standing before me. They look vaguely familiar, as though I've seen them at Floodbane. Professors, perhaps. I cannot think about that.

It's disorienting to be expected to kill a trio of grown men. Not just because it's three adults against one exhausted girl, but because young women aren't even supposed to speak to men, save for family members, authority figures, and clergy.

Then again, I haven't been summoned here to have a chat. Already, my fingernails have been replaced by claws, and my stomach is rumbling with disturbing insistence.

The man standing a bit further back in the trees has his hands cupped over his mouth. He's calling out for Niall and Kenneth. Presumably the boys I killed. I don't recognize the specific trees around us, but for all I know, these men are a few steps away from stumbling over a pair of disembodied heads.

The other two men hide muffled guffaws. As before, the distortion of the first few minutes stretches out their syllables. I understand enough to gather that these heroes are bragging to each other about the heartless ways they mistreat tavern prostitutes too desperate to decline their business.

A distant shout echoes through the trees. These woods must be crawling with men. The groundskeeper or refectory cook could step up behind me and witness my impending cruelty. Fraser is out here somewhere, too.

My stomach gives a vicious growl as if to say, *What is your point? Kill, eat, and be done with it.*

"Hey, brèagha," says the shorter of the closest two men, a smile widening across his face.

Brèagha means beautiful. It isn't how an older member of faculty ought to be greeting an adolescent female student.

I estimate thirty seconds, maximum, before they take their first predatory step in my direction.

Time is no longer stretchy, so I think as fast as I can. During the first traumatizing summoning, the more I resisted, the more overwhelming and irresistible the urge to kill and consume became, until I made a godawful mess out of two human boys because I could no longer control myself.

I don't want to repeat that experience.

"Don't be shy," says the second man, sliding one of his boots closer toward me. "We won't bite. Unless you ask us to."

His friend grins even bigger.

I learned last time that there's no escaping fate. If I can't run away, then perhaps the wisest move is to run toward it? Maybe the best way is to kill as quickly and cleanly as I can manage.

Just like Father and Hamish do with wild rabbits.

"Hey!" shouts the third man, turning toward us with a surprised expression on his face. "What's going on over here?"

"Not *now*, MacLeod," growls the first man.

"Go find the beast attacking our lads!" yells the second.

My heart races a thousand beats a second. Thank God I dithered like a schoolgirl instead of leaping forward like a hunter. The third man isn't part of this.

Concerned, Mr. MacLeod jogs in my direction. "Miss, do you need help?"

Because there's no reasonable response, I turn and run.

Whoosh, arse-over-teakettle in treacly colorful nothingness, then *thunk,* wobbly hooves back on solid ground. It's five minutes ago again.

"Niall! Kenneth!" from the innocent man in the distance, as before.

Whispers and cackles come from my targets a few feet ahead.

Dash forward this time. Just do it before the curse makes *you do it.*

Alas, my feet—er, hooves—do not move.

"Hey, brèagha," singsongs one of the men when they spot me.

I lift my hems in preparation to sprint toward them. His eyes widen. Hooves! Of course! I hike my skirts above my backward-bending deer legs to give them a hint of what's coming.

Rather than scream, they give appreciative whistles. This is unexpected enough that I drop my hems back to the grass and stare at them in confusion.

"What's going on over here? Miss, do you need help?" Mr. MacLeod asks again.

I grimace and hold up a finger before the first man growls. "I'll be back."

I turn and run. I'll keep starting over until I figure out what to do.

Last time, my vengeful new baobhan sith instincts took over. But if I use my powers mindfully, maybe there's a merciful way to do this without turning into an animal myself.

I may no longer be human, but I can be humane.

Or can I? My stomach's rumbles sound like the thunder of an imminent storm. The accompanying pangs of hunger make me dizzy with greed. I can't postpone the inevitable any longer. This curse comes with a built-in mechanism to ensure the job gets done: bloodlust.

"Mr. MacLeod," I call out to the good man. "Run!"

I don't want him to get caught in the mayhem.

He doesn't run. He steps through the brush toward me. "What's wrong, miss? Do you need help?"

I point in a random direction. "I saw the two lads that way! Quick, tell the others!"

This time, he takes off like a shot.

And I . . . belatedly realize my stupid mistake. Mr. MacLeod is now a material witness. He saw me loitering a few feet from two soon-to-be-dead men. Either I'm wrong about what direction the prior corpses lie, and he'll recognize my gambit as an obvious act of misdirection. Or else I'm *right* about where the boys' bodies are, which will make it all the more suspicious when two more corpses turn up right here.

"Shite," I mutter, then turn and run, restarting the moment five minutes earlier.

This time, when my hooves touch back down, the hunger is almost too sharp to tamp down.

What's my plan exactly? Be fast and merciful, then . . . beg Mr. MacLeod not to tell? Hit him over the head with a stick so he's struck with amnesia?

The hunger keeps rising. Whatever I'm going to do, I've got to do it fast. Or else the baobhan sith within me will take all choice away.

With a shaky breath, I roll back my shoulders and fix the men with my best seductive stare. Unlike Fiona, I've never practiced the art of flirtation, so my best attempt at seducing more probably looks like a squirrel squinting in the sunlight.

Somehow, it works anyway. The men go glassy-eyed and slack-jawed.

Good God, I wish I had my mother's cross with me. I deserve to be punished for what's about to happen.

My hand touches my chest, where the talisman ought to be, and I whisper, "May we women always be protected from evil."

"Hey there, my sweet brèag—" is all the first man manages before I'm climbing atop him, jerking at his head in hopes of snapping his neck with a clean break.

It's harder than you'd think.

My jaws close on his jugular. As I'm draining the blood from his broken neck, his friend takes a step backward. "What in the . . ."

Lord, I can't have *him* running off, too. I swipe a clawed hand after him and jerk him toward me by the breeches. He tumbles into the other's lap, and then I'm on both of them.

Biting. Tearing. Disemboweling.

"Miss, do you . . ." Mr. MacLeod's voice catches in shock, from somewhere between the trees. "Lord above."

"Close your eyes," I tell him around a mouthful of fatty flesh. Rivulets of fresh blood course down my cheeks. "This isn't me. I'm sorry."

He backs away, then runs.

I don't chase after him. Instead, I suck down blood and shove fistfuls of flayed tendon and juicy muscle into my mouth as fast as I can rip each fleshy glob from the men's fallen bones.

I don't stop until my fingers lose their ability to tear. My claws are gone. My hooves are feet.

Once again, I'm as human as I'll ever be.

25

I scramble up out of the mess I've made, and back away in horror. I'd meant to perform a civilized mercy killing, but once I smelled the blood, I slid straight into a feeding frenzy.

And now there's a witness. Mr. MacLeod. He heard my voice. He saw my face. I might as well have handed him a calling card that reads, "Catriona Cameron, crazed killer."

I scoop up my fallen school satchel and trudge away from the school toward the house. A large part of me expects at least a few of the men to beat me home. Nonetheless, when I arrive, the house is empty.

I go through the motions because there's nothing else to do but wash away the gore. Burn the bloody clothes. Scrub my boots better this time.

Where are the authorities? This is worse than a quick arrest. Mr. MacLeod must have told the others that *I* am the beast in the woods. They won't ask me to come along nicely. There will be torches and pitchforks.

Upstairs in my shared bedchamber, I dump my books and supplies onto Ishbel's bed. She'll make better use of them than I will, wherever I'm headed. I turn to the armoire to shove every meager item I own into the now-empty satchel. Unfortunately, I'm faced with the sobering realization that I don't actually own anything . . . save for my mother's protective iron cross.

A talisman I can't even touch.

Should I try to run away? Where would I go? I've no money with which to support myself. All my clothing is in school colors, with the Floodbane Academy insignia embroidered upon it, so I cannot sell it.

If I make my way home, what awaits me there? Marriage to the butcher? I understand his work more viscerally than ever, but we're not the same. He loves to slaughter and chose his life's work on purpose.

I shove my books aside and crawl into Ishbel's bed, pressing my face into her pillow to inhale her sweet scent. I'm not ready to give up on my dreams. They were so close to being possible. To being real.

I slam my fist into the pillow. Where was the local baobhan sith when *I* needed one?

At the very least, couldn't the Fates have foisted me upon Roderick, Angus, Mungo, and Fraser, instead of dropping me down, disoriented, in front of total strangers? Tigers like Roderick don't change their stripes. The lesson the lads learned from their aggression was that wishes and thrusting knives lead to even greater popularity. Which I guess is why they haven't needed to bully any girls other than me lately.

I squeeze the pillow in rage and frustration.

Goose feathers fly in every direction.

I drop Ishbel's pillow and jerk up into a sitting position, staring at my hands with stupefaction. Claws. *Claws.* Another bloody summoning, already?

A sob of frustration escapes my throat. Bitterly, I acknowledge that it has never been the fairies' intention to save me. They amuse themselves by granting unwise wishes in the most dramatic ways possible.

All in good fun. A fine jest. Hilarious.

I hug myself, mindful of my sharp claws, as I brace myself for the nauseating tumble through colorful swirls of fog.

Nothing happens.

My feet stay feet. There is no summons.

I unwind my arms from about my ribs and gaze down at my fingers. Aye, *fingers,* not claws. They were here, and then disappeared. Why? How? I'd been raging against the unfairness of being saved from certain death only to be delivered to an even worse life, when—

Ouch! Razorblades rip through my fingertips. The claws are back.

I wiggle them, willing my heart rate to settle. As my blood pressure calms, the claws retract, dissolving into nothing. I clench my jaw and focus, willing my claws back.

"What shall I do with you?" I murmur to the deadly, steely points.

Is the ability to generate claws on command good news or bad? I can defend myself better, when the cavalry comes to lock me up. Then again, there'll be no denying the monster I've become.

Once they realize I'm a baobhan sith, and not an ordinary murderess, my future will be iron chains and an iron box, until all that's left of me is an inch or two of bubbling flesh and a bit of black smoke.

A knock sounds at the front door. The authorities have come!

My claws fade as I scramble over to the bedroom window to see. There's the rowan tree, and the hawthorn tree, and the path leading into the woods . . .

And nothing else. There's no one out there. Just the wind.

Why would Mr. MacLeod not share the identity of the forest creature? Or did he do so, only for big strong men not to believe for a second that a slip of a girl could cause so much destruction?

Wait. A burlap bag the size of my fist slumps at the corner of our front step.

I race down the stairs and scoop up the little sack. It feels like sand. A little note is attached to the twine tying the neck closed:

> Short supply.
> No more black salt until winter solstice.
> Use this gift wisely.

Gift? Goodwife MacAskill is *giving* me the means to break the curse, free of charge! I cannot believe my good fortune.

There's no time to waste. I've already killed twice, and the cavalry could arrive at any moment. It would behoove me to be a human girl before their arrival.

I dash upstairs. I've prepared for this moment. In a tattered woolen stocking beneath my folded petticoats, I've hidden four small waxen effigies shaped to represent Roderick, Mungo, Angus, and Fraser.

There isn't enough salt to build a perimeter around the tall looking glass Ishbel and I share. Since my housemates are still on campus, I slip into Fiona's room to borrow her pearlescent hand mirror. Thus armed, I gather my supplies and hurry into a protective thicket of trees behind the house to perform the spell. Close to home, but out of sight from the authorities.

As I work the spell, I repeat the steps aloud.

"Find a private space free from negativity."

This one will have to do.

"Cleanse the area with burning sage."

This was easy enough to obtain from Floodbane's sprawling herb garden. I light it in a little dish I tucked into the wool stocking for this purpose. I'm careful not to move a muscle until every bit of sage is gone, and only ashes remain.

"Face the looking glass toward the heavens."

I place Fiona's fancy hand mirror on the grass. Its shiny surface reflects the fluttering leaves all around, and snatches of darkening sky overhead.

"Surround it with an unbroken border of black salt."

This is the trickiest step. The instructions didn't mention how thick the line should be. Black salt flows easily from the small sachet, but there is barely enough of it to encircle the mirror.

"Upon placing the objects representing the persons who cast the spell onto the looking glass, the reflection will cast their curse back onto them."

I waver at the final step. Will Roderick and the others become baobhan siths? Or will it curse them with something worse? Four vengeful kelpies? If I turn human while they become literal monsters, how will I protect myself then?

It doesn't matter. I can't live with myself as a sith. I'm no killer. If this is my only way out, I have no choice but to risk the consequences.

I reach into the woolen stocking and pull out the first effigy. It is the size of my thumb. I molded these tiny figures out of candle drippings over the past several days, and pressed into each soft chest a token of each bully it stands for.

A strand of Fraser's hair. A stray thread from Mungo's uniform. Mud, fallen from Angus's boot. A spitball, delivered to my hair from Roderick's own mouth.

One by one, I place them atop the looking glass, then sit back on my haunches to wait.

I expect thunder to sound, or lightning to strike, as it did when Hamish's wish came true. But nothing happens, other than pins and needles in my cramped legs from crouching for too long.

Then again, how would I know if the curse has migrated to its originators? They're not here to tell me, but I've other ways to test.

I cup my hands and curl my fingers so that I can see my fingernails.

"Claws," I whisper to my hands.

They oblige, ripping my tender skin apart as razor-sharp claws erupt in place of fingernails.

It didn't work. *It didn't work.*

I topple over onto the grass, in the fetal position. Tears stream down my cheeks. My legs twitch and tremble. Sharp claws rip into my sleeves as I hug myself tight and rock in place.

I was counting on this working, with all my heart. It was the best lead I had. The *only* lead. And I cannot expect Goodwife MacAskill to provide expensive ingredients free of charge a second time.

My throat is raw, and my eyes blurry. Was the border of black salt not thick enough? Was this clearing insufficiently peaceful? Did my candle-dripping effigies fail to properly represent those who cursed me?

Or would the spell never work against Roderick and his crew because technically, they just . . . wished. Fairies decided to grant the wish and curse me. I wouldn't have the least idea how to create figurines in the tricksters' images.

The woods rustles with movement. Footsteps. Voices.

I tense, every muscle ready to bolt. The noise is coming from around the other edge of the woods, on the other side of the house.

I haul myself to my feet, swiping the sticky tracks of hot tears from my mottled cheeks in order to peer through the branches. If it's the magistrate, perhaps it's best that I'm not in the house.

I scoop up Fiona's hand mirror. Is it a weapon? An item of

value to barter for sustenance during a long life on the run? I turn back to watch the path on the other side of the house.

The leaves part and spill forth five obviously worried young women.

School is over. My housemates are home. Life is moving on.

I rush out to greet them.

"There you are!" Ishbel throws her arms around me and breathes me in, nearly squeezing hard enough to crack a rib.

The others let this stand for the scantest of seconds, before ripping her aside to take their own turns hugging me and patting my cheeks with relief.

"You're safe," they repeat over and over. "We were so worried!"

"Wh-what?" is all I manage.

"There's been a terrible accident," says Maisie.

"Not an accident, dunce," Sorcha corrects her. "A monster is on the loose."

"The kelpie is back," Ishbel says with a shudder.

I stare at them. "The . . . kelpie?"

"They're evil water spirits that lurk in lochs and shapeshift into horses to lure lonesome wanderers straight to their deaths," Euphemia explains, as if I hadn't heard every one of these stories since I was a babe.

"There's water all around us," Maisie whispers.

"Are you carrying my pearl mirror?" Fiona asks in outrage. "Why is it dirty?"

"Here, take it." I shove the looking glass into her hands, then ask with as much innocence as I can muster, "Evil spirits on the rampage? Was there a death?"

"Four of them," Ishbel answers. "Two lads from school Sunday and two members of faculty today."

"It wasn't a kelpie." I should shut my bloody mouth, but I can't stand for the legends to be told incorrectly. "Kelpies target women, not men. And you said yourself, they live in lochs and rivers, not the woods."

Christ, now I've done it. No one said anything about woods.

To my surprise, no one notices. They're still arguing amongst themselves.

"There's a river in the woods," Ishbel points out.

"Catriona's right," Euphemia says. "Everyone knows kelpies shape-shift into horses, not statuesque blond goddesses."

I blink at her. "Into . . . what's that you said?"

"There was a witness," Sorcha explains. "The rugby coach saw the creature."

"A tall, *blond* woman?" I repeat, baffled.

"In a green gown," Ishbel confirms. "Someone not from these parts."

None of these traits describe me. Mr. MacLeod saw a short, brown-skinned, black-haired schoolgirl in an instantly recognizable bright yellow Floodbane pelisse, complete with the school's coat of arms.

Unless . . . he didn't?

I replay the massacre in my mind. Not the grisly part, but the moments leading up to the murders.

Did the men literally not see who they were up against? I recall the odd reaction when I lifted my skirt to show off my deer legs. Licked lips and a low whistle. I'd found that response deeply unsettling. It would make a lot more sense if what they'd seen was whatever Mr. MacLeod had described.

"Roderick and the others are insufferable," Euphemia informs me. "Telling anyone who will listen that they were the first to report a rabid kelpie on the loose and bragging that it failed to kill *them* because they're the perfect specimens of manhood."

"Perfect specks of shite," Sorcha mutters.

Ishbel grimaces. "They're more popular than ever. Some are calling them the Masters of the Hunt. Soon their inflated heads won't even fit inside the building."

I'm still stuck on Mr. MacLeod looking right at me and failing to see me for who I am. In my panic, I forgot the finer details of my own legend. Baobhan siths have always appeared before men as the most beautiful woman in the world. Mr. MacLeod's idea of beauty must be a statuesque blond. Whatever the other men saw, it wasn't a monster. Not until it was too late.

At least today there won't be any cavalry riding to my door.

"All right, ladies," says Euphemia. "Let's get back on schedule, shall we? Some of us have to study before supper."

I turn and follow them into the house. With a sinking sensation, I realize I've nothing to study *for*.

My bright future as an instructress in Edinburgh? I now see it for the impossible fantasy it has always been.

As much as I would love to dedicate the rest of my life to helping other lasses find success and safety . . . As much as my scholarship to Floodbane would seem to put me on that path . . . As much as my burgeoning romance with the son of the exact person who could make all that possible looks finally within my grasp . . .

It's a mirage. My heart falls. I can't even hold down a post as a scullery maid if I'm going to sprout hooves and vanish into thin air at the drop of a hat.

Even if somehow no one ever notices me leaving, at some point the walking back bathed in blood is bound to raise a few eyebrows.

The life of a baobhan sith is one of subterfuge and solitude. Never allowing anyone close, lest they glimpse the real me.

Before long, I *will* be living in the forest as the animal I truly am.

26

Indoors, this time I do pack everything I own in my empty school satchel. Which only consists of my mother's cross. I hold the necklace by the sturdy knot at the other end of the twine and drop it into the canvas.

Ishbel frowns at the state of the room. "Are those your books on my bed?"

"Throw them onto mine. I'll be back in a minute."

Careful to hold the bag far away from my body, I make my way down the stairs and out the door. Before I can disappear into the woods, however, a brown-haired young man steps out onto the grass.

"Dougal." I close my eyes. "How lovely to see you."

"Oh, thank God." He rushes forward, a blur of yellow in his crisp school uniform against the wide swath of dark green forest. He smells of damp grass and clean earth. "I've been so worried about you. Everyone else who's gone missing has turned up dead. Did you hear about—"

"I heard. Dougal, listen." I open my eyes.

His gaze is as kind and gentle as always. But is his kindness genuine?

Does Dougal like me for me? Or because this godawful curse makes him see me as someone far more desirable than I could ever be?

His brows lift in question.

I take a deep breath. "I can't go home with you for the Christmas holiday."

He looks crestfallen, then shakes it off. "That's all right. If you'll have a brief moment to meet my mum, that would be splendid, but we can postpone a visit until whenever is most convenient for you."

"It'll never be convenient. I can't be your intended, or even your *intended* intended. I can't be your anything. The best thing you can do is forget me. Or at least ignore me."

"I can't do that. I don't *want* to do that. And not because I sit right behind you. I like you, Catriona. I thought it might help us both if we were to . . . Was it something I said? Something I did?"

"Dougal, no. You're a good person. I like you, too. But there is no future for us of any kind. No tutoring. I don't even think we can be friends."

His pale face looks shocked.

I hate that I've hurt him. But I'd rather his heart be broken by a girl than torn to pieces by a monster, even if by accident.

He stammers, "But . . . if working with my mother was your dream . . ."

Tears fill my eyes. "It *is* my dream. It will always be my dream. But I've been cursed by fairies, and all my dreams are gone!"

He blinks. "Cursed by . . . fairies?"

He doesn't believe me. I shouldn't have said it. "You don't have to understand. But if my circumstances change, which I hope they do, I swear I'll run to you with open arms and beg to holiday with your mother."

He rakes a hand through his hair. "What curse? When did it happen?"

"Er . . ." I shift my weight. "It doesn't matter. I mean, it *does* matter. Right now, it's the only thing that matters. Trust me, Dougal. You don't want the details, and I don't want to share them. Leave it at that."

He crosses his arms, unconvinced. "Maybe I could help, if I knew what the problem was."

I hesitate. "Do you know anything about magic?"

He rubs the back of his neck. "No, sadly. Mother only permitted 'practical' subject matter in our home. No fairy stories allowed. When Roderick's rumors about you first started flying, I didn't even know what a kelpie *was*."

My hopes sink. "Do you happen to have wormwood? Or mugwort? Or black salt?"

He looks chagrined. "Practical spices only. Black salt? Is it mixed with tar or coal or something?"

"Dougal, listen to yourself. I appreciate your kind heart so much, but you can't help."

His expression turns mulish. "I don't have answers at the

moment, but I'm phenomenal at research. If my mother's upbringing taught me anything, it's how to learn. If there's an answer out there, I can find it."

"Well, if you do stumble across precise instructions for breaking a fairy curse, please let me know straightaway. Otherwise, just . . . keep being such a good-hearted lad. It's more important than you think."

He frowns. "Catriona—"

"Please. Until I break this curse, you're safest if you stay far away from me."

I walk past him into the woods, careful not to slow my stride, or do anything so foolish as to glance over my shoulder. I must be resolute. I *am* resolute. The best thing for Dougal—or any man who wishes for a long life—is to keep his distance.

The trees will hide me. The forest may have once failed to keep me safe, but it's now everyone else who must stay a safe distance away from me.

As soon as I'm out of Dougal's eyesight, I cut away from the path and into the brush. I can't seem to conjure up deer legs at will, but I slip deeper and deeper into the woods without leaving any trace visible to the human eye. I meant to hide, but instead my feet turn toward where this nightmare began.

Distantly, I hear Dougal reenter the forest. Calling out for me, jogging faster, in the mistaken belief he need only catch up to me to change my mind. He'll arrive at the school soon enough, and I'll be nowhere to be found.

The surprise of rejection will sting at first but fade over time. There will be better choices for him than me.

At least, that's what I tell myself, as I step into the small clearing where the boys trapped and attacked me. I smash my fist against my mouth to muffle a scream of rage. How is any of this fair?

Damn Roderick, and Angus, and Mungo, and Fraser! Damn their greedy, selfish wishes and this bloody eternal curse they've inflicted upon me! It's bad enough that part of me is now a monster. But to also peel away the last bits of me that were human . . . My chance to be a friend, a wife, a daughter . . .

The sawhorse they tied me atop is gone, but I don't need it present to know the exact place where they carved away my humanity. My boots head to the spot unerringly. I drop to my knees over the blood-flecked weeds where less than a fortnight ago, I pled for my life.

My mother's love saved me from dying. A trick her talisman cannot perform twice.

I set my canvas satchel on the leaf-covered ground before me, and peel back the opening to reveal the treasure tucked inside. A broken-and-mended loop of twine. A tiny iron cross, handed down from mother to daughter for generations.

"Those boys took this from me," I growl, my voice shaking.

Their cruel wishes broke the strongest ties I had: the cherished link to the women who came before me. My mother. My ancestors. My former self.

"This was meant to keep me safe from harm." The worn iron cross winks as the spinning bars tumble to the ground. "Now, it marks the spot where I died."

Looping the satchel across my chest, I rise to my feet and back away. As I brush the crumbling leaves from my skirt, my gaze doesn't stray from the necklace lying there in the dirt.

It was forged in love and left behind as a gravestone. X marks the spot. Symbolizing a locked door to a happier place to which I can never return.

Claws sprout from my fingers, underscoring the proof that my old self died the day that wish was spoken.

Continuing a long, sad, family tradition.

I stare down at the abandoned cross I can no longer bear to touch and wonder how much of that old story was true.

Did my great-great-grandmother make a wish for wings, while all alone in the kitchen? If she had done so, how would anyone even know?

Perhaps all women are cursed to be subjected to the whims of men.

Isn't it more likely that the person who made the ill-fated wish was her husband? Coming across her in the midst of a rare peaceful daydream, perhaps. Irritable that his supper wasn't yet on the table. Wishing that *she* were a perfectly cooked chicken, so that he could gobble her up.

How else would he have been able to tell the tale?

27

At the school library after lessons, I drum my fingers atop my legs beneath the table. My housemates are beside me, studying their books with intense concentration. Another thick tome of old legends is open before me, but I haven't turned a page in half an hour.

It's hard to concentrate. Yesterday's grief and anger have sunk back beneath the surface, hiding deep within my tense muscles. I feel . . . powerful. Strong. Restless. I don't want to sit and study. I want to be in motion.

My ears prick up at whispered conversations around me. It's easier to hear heartbeats and rushing blood and uneven breaths, but if I try, I can make out hushed words.

"It *must* be a wild animal."

"It's not a wild animal."

"Nothing else is capable of tearing down men that size!"

"There are no large predators in Scotland."

"Oh, there are. You both heard Roderick say it was a kelpie."

“Aye, and Mr. MacLeod said he saw an ordinary woman.”

“A *bonny* woman.”

“Well, whose tale do you believe?”

“A woman can’t rip apart a fellow human with her bare hands!”

“Of course not.”

“That’s five witnesses. One that saw a woman, and four that saw a kelpie.”

“Same thing, I say. Everyone knows kelpies can shape-shift. I’d wager my left bollock that the bonny lass is the same creature Roderick and the others scared away.”

“I’d be careful. Even if you’re right, that creature isn’t frightened of us.”

“A butterfly wouldn’t be scared of you, you half-wit. My sister could trounce you, and she’s eight years old.”

“Your sister—”

I shake my head to break the connection. I already know there’s something unnatural out there.

Or rather, in here. Sitting with her friends in the far corner. Extending and retracting my claws under the table over and over, until I can deploy each one separately, with precise control over length and speed.

I’ve either increased my tolerance to the pain or built up protective scars. It no longer hurts. It feels . . . natural.

The doors on the other side of the library open, and pure evil struts in.

“It’s them!” one of the boys whispers with excitement. “Roderick, Angus, Mungo, and Fraser!”

As if rising to bow before kings, the male students leap up from their seats, chairs clattering behind them. They rush over to laud the four swaggering fuds who deserve none of this brainless, sycophantic devotion.

Soon, my assailants are surrounded by so many fawning classmates that all four of them are hidden from my view.

I can still smell their blood. Hear it rushing through quickening ventricles in pleasure at having achieved such exalted status. Reveling in the glory of being celebrated everywhere they go.

"I hate how popular they are," Euphemia whispers.

"They don't deserve to breathe the same oxygen as Catriona." Sorcha sneers in the direction of the adoring crowd. No one is even glancing our way. "I hope all four of them fall off the closest cliff and drown in a bottomless bog."

Ishbel's big brown eyes flash with vexation. "Catriona is the one who fought *them* off, and *they're* the ones who reap fame and fortune?"

"I have to hear about their fake heroics everywhere I go," Euphemia agrees bitterly. "Fraser this, Angus that. Did you hear they're calling him King Roderick now?"

"Who hasn't heard?" Fiona mimes vomiting. "He's the one who gave himself that nickname."

I grit my teeth. "In Religion class today, when the instructor praised my essay, Roderick shouted out that I wouldn't have written a word of it if he hadn't saved my life, and everyone cheered *him*."

"I'm sorry, Catriona," Ishbel says softly.

I shrug and pretend not to care. Those boys may not have succeeded in destroying my body or soul, but they took something else, even more precious than academic recognition: my humanity. Just the scent of their male flesh makes my claws extend thick and sharp.

How I'd love to rip them apart.

My swinging, booted feet toy with the satchel tucked beneath my chair. Instead of just notebooks and pencils, I now carry a fresh change of clothing wherever I go. In case I won't have the woods for cover the next time I'm summoned.

My housemates breathe a collective sigh of relief when the King Roderick quartet finally parade away after copying other lads' schoolwork. Then the library goes back to normal. Everyone retakes their seats, and once again the enormous Baroque chamber is as quiet as a chapel.

With a declawed hand, I close the book of folklore before me. Ever since the attack, I've been searching for a way to undo what was done. But perhaps there's no hurry. Maybe I'll break the curse after I've cleaned up this campus.

I rise to my feet to return the heavy tome to its spot on a far shelf.

Every male eye in the library swivels toward me to watch my progress.

I smile to myself and add an extra swing to my hips. The boys' gazes don't feel predatory anymore. Their rapt attention feels worshipful. Like something I deserve to have.

All week, I've been using it to my advantage. Every professor knows my name. Every boy in this room has offered to be my private tutor. Sometimes I let them, for a minute or two, so that they can feel strong and important. Then I remind them to help my housemates, too. That any act of service to one of my friends is welcomed as though it were performed for me.

Fiona revels in all the new attention. She feigns confusion at counting to ten or writing the alphabet just so a queue of young men will form at her sides, ready and eager to help however they can.

Sometimes, the boys bring me little offerings. A freshly sharpened pencil. A brand-new notebook. A biscuit or a bit of chocolate.

One would think it would distract me from my studies, but my mind is oddly absorbent to new ideas now. I remember every word of every lecture. In natural philosophy and mathematics, my brain seems to work faster than ever before.

At this rate, I won't just go up a grade level by Christmas—I may be ready to graduate by June.

The library door opens again. Dougal. His eyes light up at the sight of me, and he hurries over.

"Catriona, listen. Just give me a moment."

I cannot bear to hurt him again. "What is it?"

He takes a deep breath, then plucks a folded paper from his breast pocket, like a magician unveiling a playing card. "I've a letter from my mother."

"How nice."

I've no letter from my own, not that I expected one. Even if my mother could read and write, without me there to help with her chores, she has no time to sleep, much less pen pages of correspondence. My father wouldn't post it for her anyway.

"I talk about you to Mother all the time," Dougal blurts out.

"She knows everything I know. About you, I mean. She knows loads more than I do. Her head holds more information than this entire library."

"She sounds incredible."

"I think she'll feel the same way about you. If you make a strong enough impression, she could arrange a placement for you when you graduate. And perhaps one for your mother as well."

I suck in a covetous breath. Quality schooling and paid posts awaiting my mother and I in Edinburgh! I want this so much it saps the marrow from my bones. My lungs hitch as I try to control the runaway beating of my greedy heart.

Father would never *let* Mother leave, even temporarily, but given Mother's lifelong dreams and her reaction to Hamish's wish, I'm fairly certain she would leap at an opportunity for freedom. With or without permission.

There is nothing I desire more than her safety and happiness. Even if Dougal is only arranging all this to get me to agree to a future courtship with him. I would marry him tonight in the school chapel if it ensured a better life for my mother and me.

But I cannot have it. This is another of life's cruel jests.

Dougal's face lines with concern. Who knows what anguished expression I've been making.

"Catriona? What's wrong? Is it the curse?"

"I need a moment. Some fresh air." I sidestep past him and rush out through the doors and into the empty school corridor.

I don't actually want to be outside right now. I want to be

somewhere comforting. Ishbel's bed springs to mind, but that's too far away. I'd settle for raiding whichever pantry in the school refectory hides all the best cakes and pastries. Nothing lifts a sour mood quite like too much sugar. I wish—

My nose cracks painfully on a thick glass door. I shake my aching head and back up half a step, at first unable to parse what I'm seeing.

I'm not in the empty corridor outside the library anymore. I'm in a narrow room, twice as long and half as wide as my bedchamber, lined with glassware and serving dishes. This must be the area where the refectory staff prepares our food onto artful platters.

And stores the baked goods. My breath steams the noseprint I made on a glass-protected cabinet filled to the brim with a mouthwatering variety of uncut cakes.

Dizziness assails me. I can *appear* wherever I'd like now? At the mere thought of wherever I want to go?

My head swims at the possibilities. If an answer on how to break my curse exists somewhere in the world, maybe I *will* be able to find it!

The pantry door swings open, and a startled cook lets out a mouse-worthy squeak at the sight of me.

"How did you get in here, young lady?"

Behind him, through the open door, I can see and hear the hustle and bustle of the kitchen. There is no way into or out of this pantry, except past two dozen white-aproned men.

The chef's wide eyes stare at me, expecting me to explain the inexplicable.

"I got lost?" I offer weakly. I cannot be the first one to try to sneak a biscuit or two after hours. Though I'd wager I'm the first one to appear out of thin air. But while I'm here . . . I give him my sunniest smile. "Do you have any fresh biscuits?"

"We just pulled hot bilberry cakes from the oven," he says, transfixed.

"Then I'll take three."

I walk back to class with my belly full.

28

The afternoon of the Sabbath, my housemates and I take a post-study session afternoon tea out on our front garden. We clear away the dead leaves and set out a pair of picnic blankets between the rowan tree and the hawthorn tree.

"Remind me," comes Maisie's soft voice. "Which tree does what?"

"Rowan trees guard homes and their inhabitants from misfortune and evil spirits," I begin, happy to see them interested in the old stories, and more inclined to believe me now, in a way they hadn't been before.

My friends know Roderick's original kelpie tales were lies, but nonetheless, anyone can sense the deep magic lurking in the woods right behind us, seeping out of the forest like fog across the nearby moorland.

And *something* has been killing the men and boys of Floodbane.

"But didn't you say hawthorn trees have to do with fairies

and other beasts?" Sorcha interrupts, her forehead creasing. "Why would we want them around? Wouldn't the trees cancel each other out?"

"It's not *fractions*," Fiona mutters. "Thank God."

"Just for that, I'm eating three-fifths of our pan pudding," Euphemia teases her. "You won't know if that's fair or not!"

Sorcha's curious gaze hasn't left mine, so I jump back in to answer her question. "No, the trees don't cancel each other out. They're complementary. Hawthorn trees only attract fairy magic and bad luck if they're struck down."

"Ah." Sorcha's face clears. "So, we protect them, and they protect us?"

I nod with a mouthful of pudding. "Exactly."

Maisie runs over to the hawthorn tree and throws her arms about its curving trunk. "Thank you, tree, for keeping us safe."

No one seems to find this impulsive embrace peculiar. Ishbel even blows a kiss at the rowan tree opposite so that it doesn't feel less loved.

"Cuttings of any part of a hawthorn tree are considered unlucky," I tell her apologetically. "That's why, when you snipped those flowers—"

She waves her hand to silence my explanation. "I'm glad you stopped me when you did. We need all the good fortune we can get."

"One of us already has more good fortune than she can handle." Euphemia wiggles her brows.

Fiona goes as red as her hair.

Whistles and gasps sound from around the picnic blankets.

"Fiona!" Maisie claps her hands, eyes shining. "Have you got an honest-to-God suitor?"

"It—it hasn't come to that point yet," Fiona stutters, casting a how-dare-you look at Euphemia. "Tavish has been helping me with my lessons and walking me to my classes this week."

"Tavish!" everyone singsongs, flapping our hands to fan our bosoms, as if overcome from the sudden heat.

Fiona shakes her head. "He's been a perfect gentleman the entire time."

"Much to Fiona's dismay," adds Euphemia, grinning.

"Don't be jealous," Fiona retorts. "Most of you said there were no good sorts to be had at Floodbane, but I found one!"

"Or at least one of the least bad," Ishbel murmurs.

Sorcha doesn't seem convinced, either. "A lad isn't a good man just because he's wise enough not to paw at you in front of everyone the first week he meets you."

Fiona's jaw locks. "Say whatever you like. You don't understand. Tavish is my way out from under my parents' thumbs."

I don't know Fiona's personal situation, but I *do* understand needing to grasp any way out possible with both hands.

"Congratulations." I meet her eyes, so she knows I mean it. "I hope he's everything you need him to be."

She smiles. "Thank you."

"Now that I know not to break the branches of a hawthorn tree," Ishbel says loudly, clearly attempting to defuse the tension with a swift change in subject. "Shall we try the crown-of-flowers ceremony again?"

No one jumps up and down in excitement, but nor do they stomp away from the picnic in disgust.

"As it happens," I put in, "I've been thinking about the Flood-bane Academy coat of arms. Invented by boys, for boys, yes? Not for us."

"Nobody consulted with me about that jaundiced yellow," Fiona confirms. "Have you seen how it clashes with the red of my hair?"

Euphemia appears doubtful. "You want us to redesign the school crest?"

"No . . . We could design our own. Something we choose that stands for *us*. The Phoenix Sisterhood."

Eyes begin to sparkle. "We pick the symbols and the colors?"

"I can embroider," Fiona offers.

"Every girl can embroider," Euphemia says dryly. "We're taught at age five, right after our first darning lesson."

"So that's a yes?" I prompt.

Enthusiasm bubbles up from the group like the frothiest champagne.

We agree to have three symbols on our crest, because *trì* stands for unity in Scottish culture. Like the interlocking leaves of the triquetra, dating back to runestones even older than its appearance in medieval texts and jewelry.

As for which three symbols themselves, that debate starts out heated and lively before simmering down into a trio the entire group agrees on:

A red berry from the rowan tree for good fortune.

A green leaf from the hawthorn tree for protection.

And a phoenix, because nothing can snuff our light out for good.

"How will we wear these?" Maisie asks with excitement.

"Sashes?" Euphemia suggests. "We can wear our uniforms as stipulated, then loop our Phoenix Sisterhood sash over our chest and shoulder. If anyone complains, we can say they're special scarves."

"Too bold," says Ishbel. "Even if the handbook has no written rule against wearing protective outerwear, they can still make us remove them."

"Then we sew the crests on something we cannot take off," I interject. "Like our collars. No one will be able to discern what designs we've embroidered there without bringing their faces improperly close. But *we* will know, and that's what matters."

"All right." Sorcha tucks her knife away. "Let's do this."

A frisson of excitement tickles up my spine. If *Sorcha* is eager to participate in a group bonding activity, then this is the greatest idea I've ever had.

We decide to replace white collars with new Phoenix Sisterhood colors. Shades and fabric are debated, discarded, refined. We decide on gorm, a lush Scottish blue evocative of both sea and sky, to symbolize that we shall not be held back in any direction.

I jump to my feet. "I'll go get supplies."

Euphemia blinks. "You have gorm muslin up in your room?"

"I always pack too much for trips," I mutter. "Stay right here."

Before anyone asks more questions, I race into the house and shut the door behind me. Rather than head upstairs, I blink out of our kitchen and flash into the academy's private haberdashery.

Being the Sabbath, there's no one here. I dash about the storage shelves, filling my arms with yards of blue fabric, plus needles and metal shears and colored thread.

Back in my bedchamber, I dump the new supplies into one of the empty baskets left over from my original carriage ride to Skye, and hurry down the stairs and out the door to the others.

"That was fast," Sorcha says in surprise.

She has no idea.

"I knew right where everything was," I demur. "It's no problem."

As soon as I start handing out supplies, all questions of where they might have come from are forgotten.

We work together as smoothly and as comfortably as if we were six sisters, who've been darning stockings at our mother's knee since we were old enough to crawl.

This time, I don't tell them that we have to stick together. They know. They *want* to. We're doing it. The proof is in our industrious little hands.

"What do you think is in the forest?" Maisie asks quietly while she stitches.

"Not a kelpie," Sorcha replies without hesitation.

"No, but something." Ishbel squints into the distance. "A wulver?"

Euphemia shakes her head. "They're from Shetland Islands, not the Isle of Skye."

"And no one said anything about a man with a wolf's head," adds Fiona.

"Pictish Beast?" Sorcha guesses.

Euphemia stares at her. "You don't think someone might have mentioned a single giant horn spiraling out of its forehead?"

"What about Benandonner?" suggests Fiona.

Sorcha makes a face. "Too far away."

"But he's a giant! Something that huge could stride here and back in no time."

Ishbel tosses out, "Have you heard of the baobhan—"

"What about selkies?" I blurt out. The last thing I need is for my housemates to notice similarities between me and the baobhan sith.

"Selkies can shape-shift," Euphemia agrees. "But I haven't heard of any being murderous."

"Me either," Fiona agrees. "Aren't they damned souls trapped in seal's bodies, who transform back into human form once every seven years?"

"I heard the every-seven-years limitation is a myth," Sorcha says.

"Seals don't kill people," says Fiona. "Kelpies are at least known to target humans."

"Niall and Kenneth were awful to everyone they came in contact with," Ishbel says. "Especially to first-year lads."

"The two dead instructors weren't any better behaved," Euphemia tells us. "They kept Fiona and me after class one day to reprimand us for flirting, but instead tried to get us to . . ."

"We slapped them and ran out of there," Fiona confirms.

"The cads!" Ishbel is outraged. "They're *faculty*. They're meant to protect us."

"I told you," Sorcha says. "Most men are rubbish."

"The ones on campus, anyway," Ishbel agrees. "I'm not sorry they got what they deserved."

Euphemia and Fiona nod. "We wanted to kill them ourselves."

"Violence is never the answer," Maisie's soft voice scolds them.

The conversation turns to other topics. Places mentioned in geography classes that we would like to visit. Food in the refectory. How our experience at Floodbane is both better and worse than any of us had expected.

By the time the first set of collars are finished, no one is thinking about the four grisly corpses found in the woods behind us.

No one but me, whose claws are itching to come out and play.

Sometimes violence is the *only* answer.

29

Five more days pass without incident. Then, in the early morning hours before my philosophy exam, I jolt awake to excruciating agony as the bones in my feet crush together to form hooves.

It's never a good time for pain this intense, but Ishbel and I stayed up far too late. She tutored me for hours, never losing her patience as she coaxed philosophy and geometry lessons into my distracted head. But if I don't manage a few solid hours of quality sleep, all that work will be for nothing. I need to be somewhat coherent to pass the exam.

But forty-five minutes into my hard-won slumber comes . . . *this*.

The shooting pain brings tears to my bleary eyes.

Wincing, I roll out of bed and snatch up my canvas satchel. There's no time to shuck my nightgown and struggle into petticoats and a high-necked dress with a hundred buttons down the back.

I'm halfway down the stairs when my bare foot—er, hoof—lands on nothingness. I pitch forward into the topsy-turvy murk of colorful clouds, and then I'm deposited, with all the grace of a falling sack of potatoes, outside what appears to be a public house.

Now I know I can be summoned outside the school grounds. Though I haven't the least notion whether the pub before me is one mile away or one hundred.

At least I won't have to use my legs to walk back home.

I rub my eyes and glare at the row of seasoned men lounging against the side of the pub, ales in hand. One of them has just pinched the rear of a barmaid, who yelps and scurries back inside with a stricken expression.

Laughing riotously, the drunkards slap each other's backs so hard that ale sloshes out of mugs and onto their clothing. None of them notices the mess . . . or me.

I glare at them as I lean my head from side to side to crack my neck. After this, I'll never get back to sleep. So much for having a fighting chance on my exams today.

Fury burbles within me. All men do is snatch away from me the things I cherish most. My innocence. My sense of safety. My ability to make the most of my education. My one chance at getting a few measly hours of sleep.

They don't deserve a single minute more of my time.

I dart forward, claws out, intending to dispatch all four reprobates at once with a quick slash across their jugulars.

I'm inches away from the first exposed throat when I realize I'm still holding my open satchel. The whole point of carrying around a change of clothes is to have something clean to don afterward, not to spray it down with arterial blood, too.

I jerk my hand back just in time. My nail barely nicks the first man, drawing only a single drop of blood.

He drops his ale, and the tin cup clatters. "What in the—"

"Be right back," I mutter, and take off running.

And running.

And running.

For some reason, the summoning isn't restarting. I'm dashing down a dim road, with four big, burly drunks lumbering right behind me. Given their size and intoxication, my targets are surprisingly swift.

I take that back. *I'm* the target.

One of them grabs me by the back of my hair and whips me around hard enough for clumps of curls to break free from my scalp. I yelp as much at the pain as from the sickening ripping sound.

It's the man whose throat I scratched. The single drop of blood now stains his neckcloth.

Blood! That must be why I couldn't go back to the beginning. Once begun, there's no stopping until it's done.

"Where you going, pet?" A gale-force of fetid breath steams my face.

This time, I needn't try to be seductive. Existing in this man's presence is all it took to gain his undivided attention. He's looking at me like he might gobble me whole.

The man behind him hands his own ale to one of their friends. "I'll hold her arms back for you."

The devil he will.

That's all it takes to remind me that these aren't innocent chickens whose necks I've been sent to break. These are the dregs of humanity, who ought to be down at the bottom of the bog with the rest of Scotland's most useless muck.

This time, I don't wait for the hunger to overtake me.

I go in for the kill.

With lightning speed, I jerk my arms from the second man's grasp, ejecting my claws right as my fingertips graze over his palms.

I slice through his tender flesh to the bone, leaving his tendons flayed and his fingers useless.

He howls and hops in a circle.

"Let's see you try to grab a woman now," I growl, tossing my satchel aside.

As if this statement were a personal challenge, the man holding the extra ale and his friend drop their half-full mugs to the dirt road. They spring at me in unison.

They're also incredibly sozzled. They might believe themselves to be mighty lions, but they move with the finesse of newborn kittens.

I bring both hands up and slice out to my sides, one-two, bifurcating their jugulars.

A spray of hot arterial blood shoots across my face, filling my mouth with the taste of copper.

Aye, the hunger is back.

The two remaining men take off running in opposite directions.

Clever lads, but it won't matter. Not because my deer legs

are faster than human feet. But because I don't even need to use my hooves.

Poof. I materialize in front of the man who started it all. He shrieks and jumps out of his skin. I help that process along, divesting him of every layer down to the bone.

The final man is screaming at the top of his lungs. We're far from the pub, whose own din drowns out any sound from the streets, but I can't be risking dozens of unplanned witnesses. Not when they all might try to rush at me at once. I don't want to hurt a single person more than I have to.

Unfortunately for him, the drunken assailant before me doesn't count as a person.

I leap onto his back, knocking us both to the ground. My tongue tells me my mouth is full of nothing but sharp incisors. I open wide and tear a hunk of flesh the size of my fist from the back of the blackguard's neck.

His cries stop as suddenly as they began.

I drain his blood and allow myself a few gratuitous mouthfuls of juicy muscle tissue before springing back to my feet. Wiping my bloodstained mouth with one hand, I scoop up my fallen satchel with the other. I sprint over to the protective shadow of trees to change out of my soiled clothes.

Now that the summoning is over, I'm no longer a beast. I'm recognizable as ordinary seventeen-year-old Catriona Cameron from the rural Highlands, whose thin muslin nightgown is matted to her naked body beneath with the blood and viscera of four strangers.

This wouldn't be the best moment for witnesses.

I rip my wet nightgown over my head and scrub my hands

and face as clean as I can with water from a stream. I'd packed a fresh white petticoat and a school uniform, but I hadn't anticipated a three a.m. summoning. Which means I've no appropriate sleep clothes to put on. I settle for the petticoat without the dress. If any of my housemates glimpse me sneaking back into bed, maybe in the darkness it'll look like an ordinary nightgown.

I bury my ruined clothes beneath some soft peat, the mossy substance abundant in Scottish bogs. Beneath the moonlight, a surge of strength flows through me. Even though I'm back in human form, I feel more powerful now than ever before. My mind is razor sharp. My exhaustion has vanished. I stretch like a cat, unleashing a fresh burst of energy. I've never been this wide awake in my life.

Maybe this little outing was just what I needed to prepare for my exams after all.

30

Despite the early morning interruption, I awaken before dawn. Careful to make no noise, I turn my head toward Ishbel to watch her sleep.

She's awake and watching me.

We both grin at being caught gazing at the other. I scoot my spine toward the wall and motion her over.

"Just so our voices don't wake the others," I whisper.

She nods and nestles her body into mine. "One must be considerate."

We lie spooned like that for a long minute, her derrière against my thighs, allowing each other's scent and warmth and softness to seep between us, blending into a single form.

"What do you plan to do after you graduate?" I murmur into the nape of her neck.

She's the same age as me, but ranked as a fourth-year in all subjects. Her first year at Floodbane will be her last. Whether I transfer away next year or not, Ishbel will be all done with school.

"Maybe I'll join Maisie's convent," she teases. "At least there should be plenty of girls there."

I tickle her ribs furiously until she shrieks with giggles and has to clap her hands over her mouth to stifle her mirth.

"My father could introduce you to the butcher," I tell her. "Or to Hamish."

"Good Lord. I'd rather sacrifice myself to the kelpies."

"A sign of intelligence," I confirm. "But seriously, what will you do? Where will you go?"

She twists to look at me. "Where will you be?"

All right, fair. I've no idea either. "What would you do if we could do anything we want?"

A wistful smile flutters at her lips. "Do you know, I'm a Lowland girl? I never visited the Highlands until coming here to Skye."

"Haven't you?" I'm in shock. I know it isn't fair—I was born in the Highlands, and never left. That land is such a part of me, that I cannot imagine any Scot never having set foot there. "I'd love to show you even more. It's magical."

"Then that's what we'll do," she says. "I'll find work and save money, and whenever you're on holiday from school, we'll rent a carriage and drive up farther into the Highlands to visit castles and to see . . . what else is there?"

"What else?" I sputter in indignation. "Only the highest mountain, Ben Nevis. And the beastie of Loch Ness. Not to mention Rannoch moor, the Culloden battlefield, the Glenfinnan monument, both the—"

"All right, all right." She grins at me. "I believe you. Leave some surprises for the trip."

"I hope you can drive the horses."

"Can you not?"

"I can ride sidesaddle and astride, but no, I've never driven a carriage. Only my father drives the cart." I am even more impressed with her than before. "You've had a charmed life."

She looks embarrassed. "Maybe a little. I've driven for as long as I can remember. As a little girl, my parents gave me a special driving outfit and driving gloves, and taught me how to control the horses with a flick of my wrist or the position of my hand."

It sounds incredible. "I'd love to learn all that. Teach me, too."

She makes a wicked expression. "I'll teach you anything you want to know."

"Anything?" I widen my eyes with faux innocence. "Even wicked deeds as—"

Thwump!

The entire house shudders to the sound of falling trees and gleeful hoots of male laughter.

Ishbel and I scramble out of bed and yank open the curtain in time to see four familiar forms dashing into the bowels of the woods. The metal blades of their handsaws glint in the darkness before disappearing with the boys into the deep forest.

"Those absolute *rotters*." Ishbel's body presses up against mine, her familiar softness and warmth incongruous with the harsh destruction below.

Overhead, the first streaks of dawn slither behind the mottled gray clouds hanging heavy in the sky.

Both our trees—our cherished rowan tree and hawthorn tree—lie on their sides in the dirt. Upon impact, their majestic branches cracked and separated. Their beautiful autumn leaves, flung free from their stems, shot into the air in a chaotic colorful cloud, like the aftermath of a bomb. Even now, they float in the air, mixed with decayed brittle leaves from the ground. Pockets of wind whip dust and shards of leaf against the windows and the side of the house.

The trunks are going nowhere. Our beloved rowan and hawthorn are dead. The boys destroyed them.

"We didn't protect our trees," I murmur to Ishbel. "And now they can no longer protect us."

She trembles against me.

The door to our bedchamber slams open. The other girls skid into the room in nightgowns and stocking feet.

Euphemia's face contorts with outrage. "Did you see what those cretins did?"

"It was the same boys who attacked you!" Sorcha jabs an emphatic finger toward the window. "Roderick and Angus and Mungo, and that prig, Fraser."

"We saw them." Four silhouettes rising up into the twilight like the enormous blocks of a stone circle. Each with a saw in hand and a contemptuous sneer.

"Those trees were for our protection," whispers Maisie, her eyes wild and frightened. "To ward away misfortune."

My molars sharpen into fangs and scrape blood from my tongue. I turn back to the window and narrow my eyes at the dark woods harboring my assailants.

"You're going to wish you cut *me* down," I whisper to the fleeing cowards beneath my breath. "If you fools dare come for my friends, I'll *show* you misfortune."

Euphemia's breath is uneven. "I could kill them!"

I smile. So could I.

"Our window is facing the opposite way, so we couldn't see what happened." Fiona's voice shakes.

I turn around. Her face is even paler than usual.

"We didn't have to see to know who it was," she adds bitterly. "The royal four are the only ones who still torment us."

Sorcha nods. "They probably hate us more than ever because our presence takes attention away from them."

"Catriona's presence," Ishbel corrects her, reaching over to squeeze my hand. "She's the queen of the school now, and Roderick cannot bear it."

"But *how* did she become queen?" Fiona demands with indignation. "None of the boys cared about her at first. She's not the richest or the brightest or the prettiest—"

"Of course she's the prettiest." Ishbel smiles at me. "Look at her."

Fiona glares at me, perplexed. "Was Catriona always the prettiest?"

Euphemia frowns in confusion. "I don't remember. Perhaps she blossomed into it."

"In less than a *month*?" Fiona is incandescent.

"Does it matter?" asks Ishbel, ever the peacemaker. "Thanks to Catriona, all six of us girls are the ruling class now, whether those four bullies like it or not."

"I'm glad they don't like it." Euphemia lifts her chin. "Off with their heads!"

Sorcha pats the smooth sides of her nightgown as if looking for her knife.

"What about our heads?" Maisie asks. "You can claim we're the ruling class of Floodbane if you like, but first ask the French how well that worked out for *their* royalty."

Fiona mimes having her throat cut by a guillotine.

The smiles are replaced by shifting glances and flickers of fear.

"No one's going to hurt you." I meet each individual gaze one by one. "Not any of you. Hear me?"

Ishbel's fingers have not unclenched from mine. "You have a good heart, but you can't be everywhere at once."

Mm, I'd say pretty bloody close.

"And even if you could," adds Fiona, "you could never defend against four lads at once."

There is a quartet of corpses the next village over that might beg to differ.

If they were still alive to voice complaints.

I gaze at my friends. Six barefoot nymphs in billowing white nightgowns. If we were a painting, we'd look like vengeful fairies.

My blood rushes. I get as much strength from our sisterhood as I do from being a monster. Our combined power flows through me, heightening my abilities and my senses. I feel like I could pull a tree up by its roots with my bare hands.

"Meet back here after school," I tell the others. "Behind the house. We'll practice defending ourselves."

"You mean fisticuffs?" Fiona looks horrified. "A proper lady would never—"

"Survive a single night at Floodbane," Sorcha finishes. "It's brilliant. I can teach you knife safety."

"And I've a brother with a short temper," I tell them. "I can teach you defensive positions, and where to strike with your knuckles or a well-placed knee."

I'd never imagined the scrappiest of my skills from home would matter at Floodbane. But here I am, teaching others how to fight dirty.

Fiona bites her lip. "Won't a strong, capable woman be less desirable to a man?"

"Always take care of yourself first," Sorcha tells her. "Find a man who rises to your level, not one who makes you sink down to his."

Good advice. I wonder if being a baobhan sith is an honorable ascension of status . . . or if the summonings pull me down to the same level as the men who prey upon us.

Saving women from ruin and pain *must* be a higher calling.

Which, aye, probably means I shall never rest.

"Do you think Roderick and his crew will brag to the other boys about toppling our trees?" Ishbel asks.

I roll my eyes. "He'll probably claim he caught a kelpie out front, and destruction was an unintended consequence of his relentless heroics."

Once we've all donned our uniforms with our crest-embroidered collars, we file into line, moving swiftly to arrive at school in time for our first exams. The gong sounds as we exit the forest. We dash across the grass, but we're the last bodies into the school.

I run to my classroom. As usual, my seat of honor is waiting for me. But the morning holds more surprises.

Half a dozen boys in the lecture hall are wearing bonny blue armbands, a swath of ribbon the same rich gorm hue as our Phoenix Sisterhood collars.

My confusion must be evident on my face, because the lad next to me leans close to whisper, "I hope it's the right shade. We're rubbish with embroidery, but we want to show we're on your side."

I stare at the five other students with armbands, then swivel my startled gaze back to the boy next to me. "You're on my side against Roderick and his lads?"

The boy presses a hand to his heart. "On the side of all six of you lassies, against whomever dares to threaten you."

I want to chortle with delighted laughter. If Roderick had expected praise and glory for tormenting us in the hours before dawn, I hope he's now cowering between two burly boys with blue armbands. For once, boasting will get him nowhere.

"Thank you," I whisper to my classmate. "Please keep an eye on my friends."

"It will be my pleasure." The lad flashes me a shy smile. "It was Dougal's idea, but there are more of us than you think."

Sweet Dougal. Naturally, this was his idea. He has such a pure soul.

But what could have been, cannot be. Dougal deserves a human girl, who won't disappear from the breakfast table, only to pop back moments later, dripping in blood—and too full to eat another bite.

"Now that you're one of us . . ." I fix each of them with my most persuasive sith smile. "How about dropping by the female lodging after church on Sunday? You're all such big, strong lads. We would so appreciate your help planting trees, and teaching us how to defend ourselves when you're not around to protect us."

Their words tumble over each other in their eagerness to agree with this plan. Helping us would be their honor, their duty, their delight.

I don't know if they really mean it, but at least one boy will be genuinely happy to visit. Once I tell Dougal he's in charge of the gardening efforts, he may never return to ordinary lessons again.

During the rush between classes, Mungo catches sight of me in the corridor. His face fills with fury. I'm guessing he's seen the armbands and heard whose protection they represent. His thick fists are already flexing.

Neck straining against his collar, he barrels forward in a blatant rush to trip me. I fix him with my most seductive smile. He trips over his own legs instead, tumbling to the floor at my feet.

Throughout the crowded corridor, a dozen boys with blue ribbons on their arms turn in our direction.

I don't need their help, though it feels good to know I have allies protecting my housemates. I offer a hand to Mungo to help him up.

He doesn't take it, though his fingers do twitch in my

direction. It must be awful to want to kill me, and have his own body disobey his murderous commands.

"You've not won anything," he growls, glaring at me with an intensity hot enough to smelt iron.

Fortunately for me, there's none nearby.

Mungo scrambles to his feet and stalks away, darting furious glances over his shoulder. Disarming his attack will make him and the other three bullies try harder. I will simply have to stay prepared.

There are even more armbands in my second and third classes.

When I meet the girls for lunch, the mood is euphoric. We have a veritable army.

Fiona bubbles over with excitement. "Tavish is wearing an armband!"

"Of course he is." Sorcha makes a face. "He's your suitor, not a simpleton."

"He's not the only one with a blue ribbon," Euphemia puts in. "At least ten percent of my classmates are wearing one."

"A boy in my class says Catriona personally requested for him to look after us," Maisie shares in wonder. "He said I should think of him as my private knight. I'm to call upon him at will."

I grin at the others. For the first time, Floodbane doesn't feel like a wish gone awry. Nor do my powers as a baobhan sith seem like a curse. The opposite. I feel blessed.

Maybe I *was* born to be queen.

31

At ten o'clock on Sunday morning, we welcome the boys into our hive. Euphemia has been up since dawn baking cinnamon buns and nut cakes. Our house may be an eyesore, but it smells divine.

As predicted, Dougal is delighted to be head gardener. No powers of persuasion needed. He struts around our pathetic grounds like a general overseeing a battlefield. He has come to conquer, and I'm thrilled to leave him to it.

"Remember our coat of arms?" I remind my friends. "Our rowan and hawthorn may be gone, but like the phoenix, they shall rise again. Today, we will plant a river of protective soldiers all around our house."

Dougal nods. "In time, it will grow into a thick wall of interconnected trees and vines. Your female housing will become a fortress, protecting you and future female students."

The girls' eyes light, and we scatter to direct our respective battalions in their chores.

To my shock, the blue-ribbon boys don't require my magical intervention either. A smile from any of the girls or a sweet cake from Euphemia is all it takes to keep them toiling beneath the ever-rising sun without a single word of complaint.

They're our real allies, I realize in surprise, then chide myself for taking this long to notice. Of course they are. I didn't force them to wear their armbands. Dougal came up with the idea on his own, and the others joined in because decent lads do exist.

My housemates assure me that Fiona's beau, Tavish, is the best of them. Though I've no time to meet him. Tavish and half the other lads are outdoors under Dougal's command, while the other half are inside the house with me.

Thanks to an intense midnight raid of the academy's supply warehouse, I've amassed a prodigious quantity of nails, tools, buckets, paint, brushes, and more. The girls and I do our best with a mop and broom, but with the boys' help, we can do more than surface-level tidying and make this a house worth living in. It takes hours to reinforce beams, buff all the wood, and add enough coats of varnish to cover up the scars of the past. By the time we're done, the interior of the house sparkles.

Exhausted, we wash our hands and stuff our gullets with cakes before heading out-of-doors to see how Dougal's crew is getting along.

Swimmingly is the answer! He's cleared away the fallen trees and the dead brush, pulled the weeds and cut the grass, and planted a garden that will provide beauty and nourishment for female students for generations to come.

I hug him. "Thank you ever so much. You really are a knight in shining armor!"

He goes bright red, but bows gallantly, pressing a kiss to the back of my hand in the process.

From the corner of my eye, I glimpse Ishbel watching us. She does not appear to be taking the moment in good fun. She looks ready to pick up a tree trunk with her bare hands and brain Dougal across the back of his head.

He lowers his voice. "I haven't found a spell to break your curse yet, though it would help if I knew what the curse *was*."

I shake my head. "Bad. I'll try anything."

He hands me a piece of folded parchment. "I found mentions in old manuscripts of potions to send negative energy back to their source. One involves thorns from a hawthorn tree, which you have in abundance. The other is a purifying bath. I can't guarantee either one will do anything—"

"I'll try them tonight," I promise. "Thank you."

He looks pleased.

Ishbel still very much does not.

"New teams!" Sorcha calls out. "Girls, plus any lads skilled in fighting, to the back to practice self-defense. The rest of you shall paint the exterior of the house."

"Yes." Ishbel stalks forward, glaring at Dougal. "Let's practice kicks and punches."

"Not me, I'm afraid," he says cheerfully, oblivious to her ire. "I'm deft with a paintbrush, though, and not afraid of ladders. I'll start from the roof and head down."

A few of the other lads wipe the sweat from their brows and exchange wary glances.

"And then we'll break for supper," Euphemia calls out before anyone can complain about the nonstop work. "For anyone who stays, I'm making haggis, neeps, and tatties, with raspberry cranachan for dessert!"

That settles that. No one wishes to miss Euphemia's cooking.

After waving goodbye to Dougal, I take Ishbel by the hand and drag her to where Sorcha and the others have formed a ring for practicing self-defense.

"Be kind to him," I chide Ishbel. "He's trying so hard."

She makes a face like rotten eggs, then sighs. "I know I'm being unreasonable. He's unobjectionable in every way. If he were a little less perfect, I'd likely hate him less."

"He hates books and can't fight," I offer. "That's why he's painting, instead of out here with us."

"I'm pretty certain that 'nonviolent' is a mark in his favor, not against him," she grumbles, though her face has cleared from its scowl. "Come hither, bonny maiden. *I* shall protect you from evil."

I don't have the heart to tell her that I'm the evil everyone on Skye needs protection from.

In fact, I hope she never finds out. I dread the day Ishbel looks at me with fear in her eyes instead of love.

She would never accept a monster.

32

Neither of Dougal's spells work. A fortnight trudges by. The best moments are those with Ishbel and our friends. After the school year ends, a few of my housemates will graduate. Others may choose not to come back to Floodbane. I'll miss them. There may be letters, at first.

And then it will be just me and the summonings.

They come more frequently now. I'm not certain whether men are getting worse, or my senses are just heightened. As my power expands, so does the geographic range in which I am summoned.

I've now seen every dark corner of Portree, the capital of Skye, though none of its attractions. I'm the most well-traveled person on this island, but haven't experienced its charms. All I see are slow-motion male faces, laughing, scowling, snarling. Cruel husbands, heartless landlords, utter strangers who feel entitled to anything they wish. What every victim has in common is complete disregard for women's dignity and autonomy.

Before they can register my presence, I leap through air to attack the tender spot in their necks between their vertebrae. I drain their blood, but dine less upon their flesh. No need to gorge myself when there will be another fresh corpse later.

Like tending fields and tying bales of hay, summonings are just another task I must attend to during the course of my day.

My feet give a warning twinge, and I make my excuses in the library. Headaches are a good fib. Megrims can come on without warning, like a summoning, and cannot be proven or disproven by squinting at my face.

I'm ensconced in the nearest empty broom pantry by the time my feet shatter and reform. For days now, I've been able to sense the hooves coming on, like the old country women who feel impending storms in their bones.

This evening, I'm deposited onto the twilit rugby pitch. Whatever game was played here earlier is long over. The remaining lads swagger about, passing a cigar and boasting of their bad behavior toward a few housemaids, slapping each other on the back with mirth.

One of them notices me and gives a shout to the others.

I do not hurry. This is a dance I know well. It will start when I'm good and ready.

Ignoring my targets for the moment, I shrug my satchel off my shoulder and fish inside for a fresh apron. My yellow Floodbane pelisse gets folded and tucked inside.

I take my time looping the frilly white garment around my neck and tying the strings tight behind my back. A leather butcher's apron would be better than a schoolgirl pinafore, but much harder to acquire and impossible to keep clean. Discarding and replacing this muslin sheath is easier than trying to explain how the devil I keep misplacing so many school uniforms.

By the time I'm ready, all the boys are looking at me.

I strike a suggestive pose, one hand on a jutting hip. They trip over each other with comical clumsiness in their frantic attempts to be the first to reach me. Dirt and grass fly from their heels as they sprint across the pitch.

"Thank you, gentlemen," I murmur. "For coming to me."

I wait until they're close enough to grab the bow at my waist.

Then I strike.

Claws. Fangs. Hooves. It doesn't take long to finish the handful of miscreants. In the past few weeks, I haven't had to start over once. I learned my lesson outside that pub: No dithering. If you're going to do something, then do it and be done.

I take pride in my work, now that I've the trick of it. I hope the fairies are pleased.

I keep the killings fresh with a dash of creativity. So as not to get bored, some mornings I decide it's Neck-Snapping Day, or Throat-Slashing Day, or Day of Disemboweling.

Thanks to the wild tales of the vicious monster Roderick and his band of evil brothers bravely battled off, my crimes don't even need to be covered up. A fictitious rabid kelpie is the built-in scapegoat.

Can kelpies even contract rabies? Who cares? Not my lie, not my problem. Even the authorities are convinced—correctly—

that the culprit is a monster, not a man. The more Roderick and his cronies embellish their tales, the easier they make it for me. A young girl all alone is less threatening than ever. I can show up, slaughter, and get on with my life.

After all, I've got exams to study for, and friends to go picnic with.

Today, I decide, is the Day of Crushed Ribs. According to legend, God gave Adam's rib to Eve. I wouldn't mind snacking on one myself.

With minimal effort, my fist goes through the first boy's chest, shattering his breastbone. I snatch out his red, juicy heart—not still beating, sadly; once disconnected, that process ends quickly—and take a big wet bite as if my teeth were ripping the flesh from a peach.

The other boys attempt to skid to a stop, but they're already so close that the first two crash into me. Out go my fists, snapping and crunching. I imagine that I earn an extra credit point for each fissure I cause. At this rate, I'll graduate with the top marks in anatomy class.

To my surprise, one of the boys whips out a knife. Before I can leap out of the way, he slashes it across my abdomen, slicing me open.

The pain is instant. The blood . . . is not? We all look down toward my bare belly, visible through the new gap in my clothing. The wound has already healed, as quick as it formed. Only a few trembling drops of blood give any indication of the blow I should've died from.

I snatch the knife from his shaking hand and throw it over

my shoulder. No one dives for the weapon. It wouldn't help in the least.

"I'm sorry," he gasps. "Please don't hurt me."

With his wrists in my iron grip, I dance the boy in a circle. In the space of a single rotation, his fear has been replaced with a fuzzy, spellbound expression.

He doesn't even flinch when I dart my teeth forward and drain his blood.

The other boys, however, flee like rats. I toss the bloodless corpse aside to give chase. This time, there is no dancing and seduction.

A few more bites of fresh hearts—*why are some juicier than others? I ought to do a more detailed tasting session*—and I must sprint forward a few steps to catch the last two boys before they scurry away.

The penultimate lad sobs as my fist shatters his ribs, spraying blood and chips of bone over his snot-covered face and neck.

Maybe I won't eat that one.

I spin toward the final boy, who is neither sobbing nor running away. His expression is more confused than anything else. He looks familiar, as if we shared a class together. We won't anymore.

Just as my fist connects with his breastbone, he croaks, "Catriona?"

I jerk my hand back as swiftly as possible, but it's too late. Shards of his own broken bones puncture his lungs.

His eyes fill with tears. "But . . . I came here to . . ."

It is then that I notice the strip of blue ribbon tied snug about his arm.

I catch him to my chest, cradling him to me like a mother consoling her baby. All that's left in my arms is the empty shell of a lifeless corpse.

He wasn't with the others, I realize far too late. This kind-hearted lad saw a pack of adolescent degenerates running toward a lone, unprotected woman, and chased after them to try to save her life.

By the time I shattered this boy's ribs, the summoning was over. He saw his murderer for who she really is: me, Catriona Cameron. The girl who was too busy making up games in her head so she wouldn't get bored whilst she massacred her targets. Rushing too much to look in front of her face and determine who the actual targets were. Causing me to attack . . .

An innocent bystander.

Dead. Because I killed him.

I really am a monster.

33

The next day is the Sabbath. I spent a long sleepless night hating myself for leaping before I looked. When morning comes, I can't bear to get out of bed and face the day. Much less my own reflection.

Ishbel drags me out of bed anyway. She doesn't understand my melancholy, but she tries to cheer me up. When Sorcha and Maisie head to the library, Ishbel, Fiona, Euphemia, and I stay home to have a Hair Day. Four luxuriant hours of taking turns sitting in a chair to be shampooed, brushed, braided.

"Pampered, like the queens we were always destined to be," announces Fiona.

Ishbel laughs. "We're on rickety wooden chairs in a tiny kitchen whose flimsy walls could fall down around us at any moment."

"I'll ask the boys to make new furniture and reinforce the walls," I promise.

"We're still being pampered," Fiona grumbles. "Maybe Ishbel could catch a suitor if she weren't so negative."

"Maybe I don't want one," retorts Ishbel.

Euphemia drops her voice. "Ignore Fiona. That's nerves talking. She thinks tonight, her beau might make their romance official."

Fiona closes her jaw with an audible click and folds her arms over her bosom.

Ishbel and I exchange surprised smiles.

"What about you, Catriona?" asks Euphemia. "Is Dougal going to declare himself?"

My grin slides from my slackened face. I should never have smiled. I don't deserve it. Like I don't deserve Dougal. The last thing I want is for my friends to know he *tried* to forge an understanding with me, and I turned him down.

Hell of a thing to attempt to explain.

"We're just friends."

Ishbel and I sit at the kitchen table to embroider Phoenix Sisterhood crests while Euphemia braids Fiona's hair.

Rather, Ishbel is embroidering. I'm having a devil of a time controlling my strength. I keep snapping threads when I try to sew, and now I've bent my needle.

Ishbel darts me concerned looks.

"What?" I toss my curved needle into the hearth. I was never going to be able to sew with it anyway.

"I don't know . . ." she says in that slow way that people do, when they definitely do know what they want to say, but don't want to still be sitting here when you react the way they know you're going to.

"Say it," I prod.

She puts down her own perfect embroidery and gives me the most vexingly kind expression. "You don't seem yourself lately."

Yes. Excellent observation. One hundred percent accurate.

I've never been less myself in my entire life. Since stumbling home last night, I've been so upset that I can't even control myself. The teeth inside my mouth keep shifting from molars to a mouthful of fangs, and I have to talk with my lips glued together lest I accidentally flash saber-toothed canines at my friends.

I'm saved from having to respond as our other two housemates come barreling through the front door. They look as though they've seen a ghost.

"What's wrong with you all?" asks Euphemia, glancing up from Fiona's braids.

Sorcha gulps. "Not us. We're not what's wrong. It's . . ."

The four of us wait expectantly. The two of them exchange distraught glances.

My claws come out on their own, and I shove my hands into my lap to hide them. Something is far from all right. The others might be missish, but *Sorcha* doesn't gulp or run out of words. For her to be this upset . . . Oh, God, *they* didn't stumble over the bodies, did they?

"There's been another attack," Maisie blurts out.

I want to slam my face into the wooden table repeatedly. The events of last night were bad enough without me traumatizing my friends with a field of five corpses.

"We didn't see it," Sorcha says quickly. "Dougal told us about it."

I relax somewhat. Dougal can be trusted not to share any more details than necessary. I hope *he* isn't the one who found the latest bodies. I didn't mean to traumatize him, either.

Maisie drops to her knees in front of Fiona, and tucks Fiona's hands into her own. "Tavish won't be taking you out to watch the sunset tonight. I'm sorry."

Fiona and I put it together at the same time. She lets out a long animal wail, this continuous keening cry of anguish, rocking in the wobbly chair and shaking her half-braided head.

I run to the closest chamber pot and retch.

The boy with the armband—the boy who tried to save me—was Fiona's intended. And I put my fist through his chest with enough force to shatter his ribs.

"What is wrong with you?" Euphemia hisses. "*Your* paramour is alive."

What's wrong with me? Hysterical laughter bubbles up with a fresh round of bile. Better question: What *isn't* wrong with me?

I wipe my mouth with the back of my hand and force myself to face the others. They're right. This is Fiona's pain, not mine. From their perspective, I'm reacting as though I'm the one for whom a whirlwind courtship with Tavish was going to be my ticket to a better life.

"I'm sorry," I gasp. "I'm sorry, Fiona."

She doesn't hear me. She's still rocking and shaking and making that godawful noise. Euphemia has her arms wrapped around her tight, while Sorcha and Maisie try to calm her.

I can't stand here and watch Fiona fall apart. Not without falling apart too.

Euphemia's eyes widen. "There's a boy I like who likes me, too. What if this kelpie . . ."

"It won't," Maisie assures her with false bravado.

"It might," Euphemia says, her eyes glassy. "It might kill everyone we love."

I'd like to claim that *no, it won't, I swear your beaux are safe,* but I cannot. Any minute now, I could be sent to destroy the object of my friends' affection . . . then an hour later find myself transported into her childhood home to kill her father or her brother. I could be dropped in the middle of the chapel on her wedding day to smite a couple of uncles whose intentions toward another guest were less than pure.

I'm not only dangerous to be around—it's dangerous for me to *exist.*

"I need to grab something upstairs," I croak. "I'll be right back."

Neither of these statements is true, but it doesn't matter because no one is paying attention to me. I edge to the stairs, then poof into my bedchamber the second I'm out of sight.

My solitude lasts for less than three minutes before the door flings open. Ishbel rushes inside.

"Go be with Fiona," I tell her. "She needs you."

"You need me, too." Ishbel opens her arms wide. "I don't know what's wrong, but I'm not going anywhere until you feel better."

I don't deserve her. But she's right: I do need her. I throw myself into her arms gratefully—

And then immediately leap backward, spine arched, like a cat fleeing a scalding hot roof.

Ishbel gawks at me. "Catriona, what in the—"

I gasp in pain, sucking in shallow, wheezing breaths as my molten torso knits back together. "What in God's name are you wearing? Some kind of iron chain?"

"Oh . . . a new necklace. Did it scratch you somehow through my clothes? I found it in the forest while we were searching for hawthorn and rowan seeds, and I thought it was beautiful." She lifts a length of familiar twine from beneath her bodice to reveal the tiny iron cross that's been handed down in my family for generations.

I stare at the talisman dangling from her fingers in disbelief. I'd left that cross at the site of my attack as a gravestone to mark the place the old me had ceased to exist.

And now it's come back to haunt me.

"You have a similar one, don't you?" she asks, moving toward the armoire. "I thought we could be twins and wear them together. I remember putting yours somewhere over here . . ."

My skin has ceased bubbling like a cauldron, but I can't make myself speak.

She spins around to face me. "This isn't . . . It's not *your* necklace, is it? Did you lose it in the woods? I didn't mean to steal it from you. Here, you can have it back."

I scoot backward again, palms up in the universal gesture for *don't you dare come any closer*.

Confusion lines her brow. "Do you not like it? I can put it back in the armoire."

"You should wear it," I manage. "It's yours now."

"Then it *is* your necklace!"

"Not anymore. The cross symbolizes God's protection, and the iron wards off magical creatures. To me, it means safety and love."

Her eyes narrow. "Then why wouldn't you want to keep it?"

"I want to keep *you* safe. Please wear it and never take it off. I swear it does its job."

"But why won't you—"

"Ishbel, I *can't*." My voice scratches. Wretched, tormented.

She stares at me, frozen solid.

I stare back in supplication.

"To keep me safe from . . . you?" she whispers.

"I would *never* hurt you," I say vehemently. "Never. I'd die first."

"But . . . you can't wear this."

I shake my head. "I can't wear it."

"That day when you cut your hand . . . You sliced it on this cross?"

"Something like that. It got better."

She rubs her fingers against the talisman. "The cross can't cut you. It's perfectly smooth."

I gulp. "Aye."

"But it hurt you . . ." She looks down at it, then back up at me. "When you hugged me, you said, 'What are you wearing, *iron?*'"

Now we're in the thick of it. The point of no return.

"That's what I said," I confirm bleakly. "Iron is precisely what I'm afraid of."

"Iron repels enchanted creatures. Meaning . . . You . . ."

I hang my head.

"Oh, Catriona, my love. What did they *do* to you that day?"

My face jerks up at how swiftly she put it together. Unshed tears sting the corners of my eyes.

She tugs the necklace up over her head.

"No! Don't remove it!"

She drops it onto her bed and reopens her arms in my direction. "I can put it back on in a minute. But first, you need a long hug."

I hurl myself into her arms, wrapping my own around her tight, until I no longer know where her embrace ends and mine begins. Our entire bodies are plastered together, thigh to thigh, bosom to bosom, wet cheek to wet cheek.

It is only then that I realize I'm sobbing all over her face.

Once I calm down, she tugs me over to my bed—well out of reach from the little iron cross—and sits me next to her, hip-to-hip on the mattress.

"Tell me," she says softly.

I tell her.

The attack. The wishes. The inexplicable pain in my feet, and the sudden burst of strength that allowed me to free myself and flee. How confused I was when the pain came back, and I discovered I had hooves. The nausea of disappearing from one place to appear in the next. The realization that I was cursed to become a baobhan sith, and that there is nothing I can do to prevent death by my own hands.

Her eyes are filled with horror, but she doesn't leap from me in disgust.

She doesn't believe me.

"Watch." I stick out my legs, hike up my skirts, and brace myself for the onslaught of pain as I force my feet to transform into hooves.

She stares at my deer legs, then glances up at me. "Is something supposed to happen?"

I wiggle my two-toed hooves. "You don't see this?"

"I see you've cleaned your boots. They don't have blood stains on them anymore." She gasps. "Did you discover one of the bodies? Is that what this is about?"

"Ishbel, listen to me. What I'm telling you is real. I'm the one who killed those boys and turned them into corpses."

She regards me for a long moment, then nods. "All right, you murdered them. But you didn't mean to."

I turn my hooves back to feet in relief. "Not at first. I tried everything I could to break the curse, to escape each scene without killing. But it's impossible."

"Because you keep popping back, again and again, until you do it."

"*Yes.* So, I gave up, in a way. It felt more humane to take care of business quickly, rather than toy with my prey like a cat with a mouse. Except I got too fast at my job. Because last night . . ."

"Wait. Mr. MacLeod *saw* the beastie. He said she was a white woman ten years older than you, with blond hair and blue eyes—"

"He saw what he wanted to see. That's the curse's camouflage. Men can look right at me, and their dazzled eyes will see whatever they think of as the most beautiful woman in the world, rather than a plain old country lass like me."

"Catriona." Ishbel cups my face with her soft hands, her deep brown eyes intense on mine. Her lips are close enough that I feel her feather-light breath against my own. "Dear heart, you have *always* been beautiful, since long before the attack. Do not let those boys take your light from you."

I swallow. "You have to say that. You're my best friend."

"Is that what we are?" She drops her hands from my face and straightens. "Your beauty isn't my opinion. It's a fact. Why do you think Dougal's in love with you?"

I shake my head. "It's far too soon for anyone to be in love with me."

"Who wouldn't fall for you?" Ishbel grabs my hand and tugs me off the bed and over to our tall mirror. "Anyone can see that you're—Jesus Christ! You have *hooves*?"

"Wait . . . what?" I stammer. "You can see them?"

I pull up my skirts. My human legs are still there.

Ishbel skitters away from me, one hand clapped to her mouth. "Your legs . . ." She frowns at my booted feet, then glances back at the mirror. "I see it in your reflection. Your legs look like . . . the hind legs of a deer. Spindly, with brown fur. Even your knees are bending the wrong way. And instead of toes, you have . . ."

"Hooves. That's what I said from the start. You didn't believe me?"

"I believed *you* believed it." Her gaze keeps darting from my human legs to the monster ones she sees reflected in the looking glass. "You're a . . . You truly did . . ."

"See?" I drop my skirts back to the floor to hide my legs from view. "I *am* an ugly person. Regardless of what your eyes see. The mirror *is* reflecting the real me."

"No!" She cups my cheek. The soft pad of her thumb wipes away my tears. "You are not your curse, Catriona. And yours will always be the most precious face that I've ever seen."

Ishbel lowers her hand and kisses my cheek.

She'll regret saying that once the full horror of what I've done—what I've become—fills her brain with images she cannot erase. I hate myself for driving her away.

Ishbel takes my hands. "It's not your fault."

I choke. "How can you say that? I've killed so many people. The blood . . . The sounds of their bones breaking . . ."

"It's not your fault," she repeats without letting go of my hands.

"I got used to it," I babble. Simultaneously needing her to comprehend how depraved I've become yet fearing the inevitable rejection once she understands. "Another day at work. Like farmers who don't mind slaughtering chickens, one after the other."

She nods. "It's not your fault."

"I'm a sith, Ishbel! A monster!" Now I'm shouting at the person I most dread to lose. I'm my own worst enemy.

"At times. But it's not your fault."

I throw my head backward and make a horrific grimace up at the unforgiving sky. My throat tightens. "If those boys hadn't made those horrible wishes . . ."

Ishbel's soft words of assurance never waver. "Catriona, it is not your fault."

My stomach roils. She doesn't realize how stupid I've been. How helpless to stop the nightmare to come. My eyes sting with unshed tears. "If I hadn't gone into the woods that day all alone . . ."

"It's. Not. Your. Fault." She squeezes my hands hard, her urgent gaze locking on mine. "You've no control over anyone else's words or actions. Not Roderick, not Angus, not Mungo, not Fraser . . . and certainly not the capricious whims of forest fairies. You're living with the consequences of their actions as best you can, but you didn't do it to yourself. *It's not your fault.*"

I need her to be right. For some small part of me to be worth saving. Worth loving.

She opens her arms again. I pitch forward, my breath hitching. I refuse to cry any more tears over what's been done to me. But what about what *I've* done to others? How can I live with that? How can anyone wish to live with *me*?

Ishbel strokes my back. "I won't abandon you, Catriona. I'm here and I intend to stay here. We'll find a way to undo this curse together."

I cannot risk her being caught in the crossfire—or being shackled with the same curse. "You'll wear the necklace for protection?"

She hesitates. "If I do, I won't be able to embrace you."

I swallow hard. What I want and need don't outweigh her safety. "Promise me."

"Very well." She sighs and lets go of me. "No touching.

I guess we have all the more reason to find a solution as fast as we can."

It's sweet of her to still have hope for a happy future.

And cruel of the Fates to make me yearn for what I'm certain we can never have.

34

For the next week, I throw myself into my education. Drowning out all unwanted thoughts with facts and figures from history, geography, mathematics. I finish the literature assignments for the rest of the school year.

And yet none of it erases who I am and what I do when the summons takes me.

At home, Ishbel tries her best to keep me safe. Before we sleep, she burns sage and rosemary for protection. Afterward, she takes off her cross and crawls into bed with me, throwing her limbs over mine, as though to physically stop me from being summoned.

It doesn't work. Nothing ever does. But if my middle-of-the-night disappearance and reappearance doesn't wake her, I fib and claim things are getting better, so that Ishbel believes she's helping and sleeps more soundly.

We now have tutoring sessions every evening and morning before school. Surrounded by burning pots of protective herbs, of course. I don't know how granddaughter-of-a-witch Ishbel found mugwort, but it's like a smelly version of sage, and oddly bitter.

Ishbel plays a dual role of protectress and tutor to distract us both. As though, if we focus on our studies hard enough, the darkness will no longer exist.

Instead, it's getting stronger.

Philosophy and geometry only have a temporary ability to mute the disturbing images haunting my head. The pull to be a sith is spiraling out of control. I'm summoned farther and farther, at least daily, sometimes twice.

I wonder whether my new reality is any better than what life would have been like if Hamish had never made the wish that sent me to Floodbane to begin with. I'd never have known a village bigger than the one I grew up in. I'd never have met Ishbel or the others. And I'd be betrothed to a butcher who slaughters animals for a living.

It sounds quaint compared to how I spend most nights now.

As for the days, my newfound popularity is a godsend. Lads jostle for the privilege to sit with me, to carry things for me, to carry *me* on their broad shoulders. All the boys are my tutors and eager handmaidens. They never even blink when my gaze is upon them.

There's no better distraction from death than a dozen voices clamoring to talk to me at once. Some lads come with compliments, some with offerings, some with school or social problems for me to resolve. I've made a name for myself. With four notable exceptions, classmates and professors alike bend over backward to make life easier for the girls of the Phoenix Sisterhood.

This blatant worship and sycophantic reverence isn't going to my head. Roderick and his trio of rats still spread bitter rumors. They cannot stand that despite the big lie of those four being the heroes who saved a helpless waif from peril, *my* popularity has outshined theirs.

I'm the Lass Who Lived. The one the kelpie wanted and could not have. The young woman *all* the lads want and cannot have.

Dougal doesn't seem surprised about this turn of events. Perhaps he knows it's linked to the curse. Besides, I haven't changed *my* tune. I told him before that I am not interested in courtship, and he sees me gently rebuff my classmates' romantic overtures.

Ishbel has become more protective. She'll give out withering glances to an annoyingly persistent boy and a sharp *Are you daft? She said no.*

I tell Ishbel that these advances are an unwelcome distraction.

Mostly unwelcome. The truth is, it's complicated. I would rather be sprawled on Ishbel's bed studying algebra than courted by boys from Philosophy class, but I cannot deny how flattering it is to be gazed at with admiration instead of revulsion. Still, I know they don't see the real me.

The next day at school, Roderick and his cronies manage to catch me in a deserted corridor as I attempt to take a shortcut between Religion and Geography.

"You think you're clever, don't you?" growls Roderick.

Out of range, they hate me and conspire over my doom. But within my direct sight, I can buff the sharp edges off their rage, coaxing it to simmer inside them rather than spill out into violence.

Due to the intensity of their hate, control requires constant concentration. And with these four, it often only works on one boy at a time.

Roderick darts forward to grab my arm.

I deflect the attempt with a flutter of my seductive lashes. "Have you nothing better to do with your time than to waste mine?"

"Slattern," he growls.

I snort at the trite insult. When in doubt, impugn a woman's purity. How tedious. "Too bad for you, if that's true. I'll spread my favors to every other lad in the world before I willingly suffer a single touch from you."

Roderick was expecting tears or anger. Perhaps an attempt to slap his cheek, which would bring me close enough for him to grab my wrist. The last thing he anticipated was a shrug and boredom.

I make a show of pulling out my invisible pocket watch. "If we're done here? Some of us have classes we're not failing."

"One day soon, you won't be *at* school when I find you," he warns. "Then you'll see what I'd do about your pert mouth."

I send him another unimpressed look. "I'm no longer afraid of you."

He sneers. "You should be."

I hold out my arms as if expecting to be nailed to a cross. "Go ahead. Do your worst."

"We will," promises Fraser. But he makes no step toward me. He cannot. I'm watching him.

"We don't want *you* anyway," pipes up Mungo. "We're going to pounce on your little friends."

Angus smacks him in the chest.

All my cockiness vanishes. My arms fall back to my sides, where my fingers curl into fists. "You leave them alone."

Fraser chuckles. "Do you think we take orders from the likes of you?"

I will myself not to claw their eyes out right here in this corridor. "If I so much as hear a single rumor that your worthless shadows fell within fifty yards of any of my friends . . ."

They are not cowed. They cackle and strut, preening at having crawled under my skin after all.

Abhorrent fiends. I wish them the worst deaths I can think of. Slow. Torturous. Starved for weeks whilst tied to a tree, watching helplessly as squirrels and field mice take bites of their flesh. Sharp little teeth flaying their skin in a thousand tiny places. Bleeding them dry, drop by drop, day after day.

Before the evil quartet can attempt to hurt me, boys in blue armbands flood between us, forming a protective wall between me and my tormenters.

"Dougal asked us to make sure each of you girls has special protection on campus," one of the lads tells me with a smile.

Their timely arrival certainly prevented me from being tempted into smiting Roderick and his crew once and for all.

"You won't always be flanked by your little blue army!" Angus calls out angrily, as the boys in armbands herd the four bullies out of sight.

He's right. I take the warning to heart. So should he.

"Proper demons, aren't they?" comes a voice right behind me.

I jump out of my skin.

It's Ishbel. Glaring over my shoulder as my repeated torturers once again saunter away without consequences.

"Do you ever wish you could take revenge for what they did to you?" she asks.

Only every bloody second of every bloody day. I force my rage to simmer down. Refusing to kill unless I'm forced to by a summons is the only way to keep a shred of my humanity. "Wishes are dangerous."

"The *wrong* wishes."

"That's the only kind there are." My stomach hollows as I contemplate all I've lost thanks to three different boys' remorseless words. I turn to give her a warning look. "Don't attempt to outsmart fairies. They've been playing this game longer than humans have existed on earth."

Her chin lifts. "Most wishers aren't thinking about fairies at all. If a desire was phrased right . . ."

"It would still lead to disaster. It's too great a risk. Fairies delight in making the world an even worse nightmare in new and inventive ways."

"You don't think it's possible to phrase a sentence in a way that it cannot be misconstrued?"

"Sure. I'm certain that with enough time and care, you could devise *something*. But it wouldn't help."

"Why not? They'd be forced to—"

"No, they wouldn't. They don't have to do anything you want. Most wishes go nowhere. Fairies grant the ones they please, in chaotic fashion. If you really were clever enough to make a foolproof wish, they'd ignore it."

Ishbel is undeterred. "What if we could wish for all men to be better humans, and for women to never again live in fear? We could wish away world hunger or wish for equality and better living conditions everywhere. Don't you think it's worth a try?"

"If it were really that simple, wouldn't someone have done so by now?"

Her jaw sets stubbornly. "Maybe they all phrased it wrong. There has to be a way."

"Don't you dare try to outsmart the fairies, Ishbel. It's not worth your life—or your humanity. There will be enough challenges in your future without taking the weight of the world onto your shoulders. Trust me."

Dismay replaces her zeal. "Oh! I didn't mean you weren't ridding Scotland of . . . I wasn't trying to imply that you weren't doing anything useful for other women. I meant . . . I thought . . . I *hoped* . . ."

"I once had hopes, too. Try to keep yours alive. Now come, or we'll be late." I loop my arm through hers and steer us toward our final classes, which share the same corridor.

After school is over, Dougal steps into my path in the crowded hall before I can reunite with Ishbel and the others.

Dougal looks as though he swallowed a toad. "Catriona, could I please speak with you for a moment? Alone?"

This sounds serious enough that I allow him to lead me into the empty auditorium where school plays are staged. Nothing as dramatic as my real life.

"What is it, Dougal? Is something wrong?"

"Aye." His eyes search mine. "Though I'm not sure what."

I try to keep my patience. "Please don't tell me you dragged me in here to tell riddles."

He looks at our hands, which are not touching. He has never dragged me anywhere. Dougal would never presume. He is a gentleman.

"I asked for a moment of your time because . . . I followed you yesterday."

Gooseflesh prickles the back of my neck. "Followed me? Where?"

"You left literature class early. Headache, you said. My mother also suffers from megrims, and I'd asked her for some suggestions that might help you. Her letter arrived yesterday morning. I saw you slip into the empty music room, so I followed you."

I don't say a word. I already know where this is going.

Dougal's forehead lines. "But you weren't there. I saw you go in. You didn't come out. Maybe you crawled through a window, though how you shimmied down from the second floor . . ."

"Yes!" I latch onto the unlikely explanation. "I love to climb. It's a favorite pastime."

"An hour later, two boys turned up dead."

My stomach hollows. Murder is a less favorite pastime. So is lying to people who care about me.

“I was shocked to hear about their unfortunate demise. You remember how surprised I was. You were the one who told me. We were in the library with a hundred other students. My headache felt better by then.”

“Aye. I remember your face when I told you. And I remember the dress you were wearing.”

“Well, it didn’t have any bloodstains on it!” I say.

I know this to be true, because blood had soaked through my apron, and I had to poof back into my bedchamber for a fresh uniform and pelisse.

I also realize, as soon as the unfortunate *but no bloodstains!* defense flies out of my mouth, that these are not the words of an innocent party, but rather of someone who expects to be accused of the crime.

“No,” Dougal says quietly. “No bloodstains. A dark spot from a cup of hot chocolate that had dribbled onto your bodice at lunchtime also vanished. You were wearing a new dress.”

“You shouldn’t look at people’s bodices,” I mumble.

We both know this isn’t the point of his story. His observations are sound.

I didn’t go home to change my clothes the day I was pelted head to toe with rotten fruit. So, the notion that, mid-headache, I’d crawled out of a window and scaled the tower of a castle to sprint by myself through a dark forest due to a minuscule speck of chocolate that I don’t even remember dribbling . . . Such an alibi would be ludicrous, at best.

"What are you accusing me of?" I manage.

"Nothing I wish to say aloud, now or ever. The sweet, pacifist lass I met on your first day . . . That's the real you. The lassie I write home to my mother about. Or used to."

I swallow. "Not anymore?"

"Catriona, you must know I cannot recommend she sponsor someone who . . ." He rubs his face, then looks at me pleadingly. "Surely there's some other way to solve your problems. Without violence."

My heart goes cold. He *knows*. Or at least has a horrible suspicion.

His eyes are stricken. "I can't help you break your curse if you don't want it broken. You must fight, too. Please think with care."

He turns and exits the auditorium, leaving me alone with a thousand empty seats and my own black soul.

I stare at the door swinging closed behind him. Find an alternate way to solve my problems?

Dougal's right. I haven't tried other options in a month. I'd forgotten they were available to me.

The noise from the corridors has vanished. Final lessons are over for the day, and students have dispersed to wherever they go after class. But administrators should still be in their offices.

I roll back my shoulders and prepare to poof to Headmaster MacKenzie's office, then stop myself before doing so. I'll walk there on two human legs, like a normal person. There's no sense getting caught in the midst of magic for no good reason. I've come to rely so much on my powers that I forget regular girls can be powerful, too.

It takes much longer, but I wind my way down the corridors to the headmaster's bureau.

The first time I was here, no one listened to me. I was no one yet. The second time I was here, the secretary was ready to usher me into an audience with the most important man at the school—only for a summoning to take me away.

I never came back. Whose fault is that? Mine.

Fraser is not at his desk. He's likely off with Roderick and the other two, stalking one of my best friends.

The secretary isn't here either. Perhaps that's for the best.

I hurry over to Fraser's desk and root through stacks of papers until I find the template for the incident report. I sit in his seat as I fill out the form, using his own pen and ink to damn him and his coconspirators.

Then I knock on the door to Headmaster MacKenzie's office.

"Come in," calls his gravelly voice.

My fingers are shaking as I close the door behind me and seat myself on the plush armchair facing the headmaster's large desk.

"What can I do for you, Miss Cameron?"

"I'd like to report an incident." I slide the paper across his desk. My writing fills both sides.

As he picks it up and scans it, his eyebrows shoot skyward. "This summary reports several distinct incidents. The first of which contains damning accusations, indeed."

He doesn't believe me.

"There is no kelpie!" I burst out in frustration. "That is,

kelpies may exist, but there were none that day in the woods. The boys made it up when the groundskeeper stumbled upon—"

"I am literate, Miss Cameron. If you'll allow me to finish reading?"

Right. "Sorry."

I slouch down in my seat, then catch myself and straighten until my spine is as straight and strong as a spear.

At last, Headmaster MacKenzie puts down my report.

"I see." He temples his fingers. "It's your word against their word."

A defeated sigh escapes my lungs. "I can't prove what happened—"

"And neither can they," he finishes, shocking me.

"You . . . believe me?" I ask in disbelief.

"Should I not?"

"It's true," I stammer. "Every word of it. If anything, there wasn't enough room to include every occasion they've frightened or harmed me."

He nods slowly. "I understand your ire, and you came to the right place. However, your incident is not the only trouble of late."

Ugh, blast! It *will* be difficult to drum up concern about misbehaving human schoolboys whilst a magical monster is out massacring his students.

"My attack was different," I mumble.

"That's true. Yours was the only attack on a female student. Whatever beast haunts this isle has had no difficulty mowing down multiple full-grown men." He looks down at my report.

"You're right. It's unlikely that the four lads mentioned here vanquished such a creature without suffering so much as a scratch."

I hold my breath.

He continues, "I'm headmaster of this school, not a High Council chair for Skye. I cannot protect everyone on the isle."

No, I'm the one trying to do that. Protecting women and girls from the men and boys who would harm them. Should not the school have a similar policy? If perhaps slightly less murderous punishment.

"As administrator, my role is to protect my students—and our funding."

Ah, yes. The endowment from Dougal's mother will reduce if all six girls are no longer present by the end of the school year. Ignoring me would be bad for the school's budget. If Floodbane Academy wants to be paid, Mr. MacKenzie must help.

He steeples his fingers. "Tomorrow I'm holding a special assembly to announce new precautions intended to keep students and faculty safe from the monster preying upon them. At the same time, I shall introduce an addendum to the current code of conduct, specifically prohibiting threats or aggressive behavior such as you've reported."

"What will the consequence be to boys who break the rules?"

"Expulsion from Floodbane. We shan't tolerate ungentlemanly conduct."

Ungentlemanly. That's one way to put it.

He pushes my incident report aside. "It appears Mr. Fraser's time as my assistant has come to an end. I shall announce that position's reopening tomorrow as well. Now, if there's nothing else, Miss Cameron?"

"Thank you, Mr. MacKenzie."

I stride from his office. The secretary is back and startles at the sight of me. I give a little wave and walk out into the empty corridor. The school is silent as a graveyard.

Dougal was right . . . there *is* another path besides violence.

35

The headmaster's promised assembly the next afternoon accomplishes what nothing else has managed to do in weeks: reunite the Phoenix Sisterhood.

We're all at the assembly. Ishbel and I sit surrounded by boys in blue armbands. Our other housemates are scattered throughout the auditorium.

The crowd suffers through a forty-five-minute lecture about anti-kelpie precautions, ranging from staying far away from bogs, swamps, rivers, the sea, and other bodies of water, to a brand-new school-wide curfew from sundown to sunrise, starting tonight.

I hope for everybody's sake that some of this works. I mean, I'm the monster, and I'll go where I'm summoned—not much choice in the matter—but if the males in this auditorium could cease being horrid, then they wouldn't become the curse's new target.

Which brings Mr. MacKenzie to his next point. Like a

minister on Sunday morning, the headmaster launches into a long sermon about the qualities that make a boy into a man. He emphasizes courteousness, and chivalry, and basic human decency. Trots out some biblical *Do unto others as you would have them do unto you* and tops it off with Scottish aphorisms like *We're a' Jock Tamson's bairns* to encourage equality and camaraderie, and a dash of *What's fur ye'll not go past ye* to remind the audience to expect to get what's coming to them, for better or for worse.

After informing the entire student body that any act of aggression toward any classmate, particularly female, shall result in immediate expulsion from Floodbane, he turns to the front row containing Roderick, Angus, Fraser, and Mungo, and asks pointedly, "Any questions, lads?"

Ishbel claps her hands over her mouth to stifle a squeal of delight.

The rebuke is subtler than I'd like, but in this crowd, Mr. MacKenzie might as well have marched all four lads to the stage to trap their head and hands in wooden pillories for a public stoning.

Every person in the auditorium now knows which specific quartet has been causing us the most trouble. If there was any doubt. As the "unfortunate incidents" with the beast have been piling up, the heroic tales Roderick and his crew spun have seemed less and less likely. Even the lads without blue armbands have started to wonder what really happened the day I was attacked in the woods.

Headmaster MacKenzie just gave them the answer.

Ishbel whispers into my ear with excitement, "With curfew an hour from now, Roderick and his gang of liars will be trapped in a dormitory with four hundred Knights of the Phoenix."

A delicious thought.

The rest of the sisterhood feels the same way. The mood is exuberant on our walk back to the female housing.

Sorcha chortles. "Our lads will beat them to a pulp tonight, and we'll be rid of those four forever by tomorrow!"

The rest of our evening is spent baking and eating hot fresh sugary cakes instead of a proper dinner. Our flimsy walls can barely withstand vibrating from this much delight and laughter.

The next morning, all four assailants corner me between Mathematics and Composition.

There's nary a bruise or black eye among them.

"Disappointed?" Roderick asks with a sneer.

"Frankly, yes." I try to push past them. "Move, or I'll be late to my class."

Whichever bully I stare at with all my might shuffles out of the way, but the others immediately close back in.

"'No aggression' means no aggression," Angus singsongs.

"Meaning your little beribboned bumpkins can't thrash us unless they fancy being expelled themselves," Mungo explains.

"Yes. I see the paradox. A quite unfortunate side effect. Now, if you'll let me pass?"

They do not.

"You can't do this," I remind them. "You were at assembly yesterday. Any act of aggression is cause for immediate expulsion."

"Am I aggressing?" Roderick asks his lackeys innocently.

"We're having a nice chat," answers Angus.

They step closer to crowd me into the corner, shoulder to shoulder, so that with my smaller height, I'm not visible to any passersby. Most of whom—if not all of whom—have already disappeared into their classes.

Roderick smiles. "Aggression before witnesses, aye, that'd be a serious charge. But if there's no one to see a thing, did it even happen?"

Fraser snarls, "This scheming shrew made the headmaster retract my permanent assistant position."

"*You* lost your own post by being a prick," I point out. "You don't appear to be learning from your mistakes."

"You shan't be learning at all," Roderick snaps. "I told you from your first day that you don't belong here."

Angus's sudden smile is chilling. "Relax. Removing you won't be *our* doing. It cannot be considered *our* fault when you're taken away to an asylum, never to see the light of day again."

He has about as much chance of keeping me locked inside a room as I do of flying a glowworm to the moon.

Nonetheless, something about this threat doesn't feel idle.

I narrow my eyes. "What are you talking about?"

Angus cackles. "Goodness, we've been talking *so much* today, with so many people. Lads, do you remember what everyone's been talking about?"

"Ah, yes," Fraser says, as if he's just now recalled a scrap of conversation. "One of our classmates is always dashing out of her lessons without explanation. What was her name again?"

"Catriona Cameron," Mungo supplies solemnly. "Who knows what ails her?"

"Headaches," I say quickly.

Fraser nods. "Aye, megrims. That's what she claims, although all four of us have seen her vomiting into chamber pots."

"What? You've never once seen—"

"Och," Roderick exclaims with exaggerated innocence. "Dear me, what could it mean when a girl of known loose morals suddenly starts bocking up her breakfast?"

"You're telling people I'm *pregnant*?" I exclaim in horror.

"Did I say that word?" Roderick asks his cronies with wide eyes.

They shake their heads gravely. "A gentleman would never say that word. Nor would a lady."

They smirk at me, the implication obvious: I'm no lady.

"Your rumor makes no sense. I'm too busy to waste time with boys. Who is the alleged father of my supposed child?"

Roderick's laugh is chilling. "No suitor? Even better. Who knows how many villagers you've lain with? Better yet, once word gets out about your loose morals, half the boys in this school will claim they know someone who had their way with you. I won't have to point my finger at *someone* if everyone believes the father could be *anyone*."

Fraser smirks while Mungo and Angus nudge each other smugly.

I glare back at them in fury. A pregnancy rumor is the last

thing I need. Damn them and their appallingly credible-sounding gossip! Their salacious explanation for my absences sounds more plausible than mine. Vomit down the bodice is a much better excuse for changing dresses than a sudden headache.

How could I disprove such vile rumors? Wait three weeks for my next menses, then wave around my bloodstained undergarments? That would get me expelled as quickly as—

Damn it, they're smarter than I gave them credit for. The merest whiff of unchaste conduct is grounds to be sent home from school. "Fallen" women are ostracized. They bring shame upon their entire families, often living the rest of their lives in seclusion.

Such as being locked up in a Magdalene Asylum.

Mere walls could not hold me, but nor could I return to Floodbane. It would be a life on the run. I'd never see Ishbel and the others or my own mother again.

A future of nothing but blood and loneliness.

36

After the encounter with my tormenters, I'm too enraged to sleep. I lie atop my narrow mattress staring up through the pitch blackness at the ceiling.

I can perceive each element perfectly. The seam between every board, the grain of every slice of wood. My night vision is unparalleled. Yet I see no answer to this problem.

At supper, I warned my friends about the boys' threats and made them promise to take extra care. But they are only human. Even if I tie a rope around their waists and make them trail after me everywhere like little train cars chugging down a track, they can still get hurt.

Unlike me. Idly, I extend a single claw, sharp as a razor and hard as steel. I drag it across the inside of my arm as hard as I can.

Yesterday, this action still drew blood—although the wound healed as quickly as I could inflict it. Today, I might as well be tickling myself with a feather.

Ishbel is not so impervious. She lies asleep next to me. Her soft skin is sweet-smelling and far too easy to damage. If one of those boys were to catch her unawares . . .

My heart gallops, a rampant stallion—no, a rabid kelpie. I force myself to match my angry breaths to her calm ones.

In . . . out . . . In . . . out.

I pretend Ishbel and I not only share the same bed, but also the same lungs, the same air, the same body. I want to infuse her with my strength, so that she need never feel pain or fear again.

Unfortunately, life doesn't work that way. Magic doesn't transfer mouth to mouth and skin to skin like measles and tuberculosis.

I'm stuck in my impenetrable baobhan sith shell the same way my sweet, beautiful Ishbel is trapped inside her hopelessly fragile human body. There's nothing I can do about it.

Or is there?

All ten claws spring forth and tap against my belly, poking fresh holes into my nightgown. Roderick and his pack of wolves are evil. It's only a matter of time until I am summoned to rid the world of them forever. But Ishbel and the others may not have the luxury of time before they're cornered and attacked in a shadowy nook, like I was.

The question is clear: Why wait to be summoned?

Before, the answer was: so that I don't lose my humanity. I am an unwilling monster, not a cold-blooded murderer. But as the summonings increase, the line has blurred. A baobhan sith protects women from evil men. That's not the act of a monster—it's evidence of a good person.

It would be unethical to wait for them to harm another innocent girl, when I have the power to stop them at my fingertips. Claw tips. Fang tips. I can decimate my enemies before they can do the same to me or anyone of my sex.

My head swivels toward Ishbel in the pitch blackness. I see every curl of hair and every curve of her silhouette, as though her body were lit by the brightest moon. I let myself watch the rise and fall of her breaths for the briefest of moments. Then I vanish from the bedroom.

Chaos rings through the castle corridors.

The male dormitories are the opposite of silent. I'm nearly caught my first second there because so many boys are scurrying about. Curfew might keep them indoors at two o'clock in the morning, but the rule does little to prevent them from being up to no good.

I pop from shadow to shadow to search for Roderick, Angus, Mungo, and Fraser. When I find them, they're off in the darkened refectory, gambling at cards by candlelight with a dozen other boys.

I watch from the darkness and wait for my time to strike. Half an hour goes by. My limbs no longer feel fatigue, but I tire of lying in wait. I want to act.

My time comes soon. A harried housemaster with an unshaven jaw and a crooked nightcap rushes into the refectory. Shaking his fist in anger, he shouts at the boys to get to bed. My assailants are the last four to leave.

When the housemaster stays behind to straighten the displaced chairs and tables, I slip into the corridor after my tormenters.

They are dillydallying, bumping and pushing each other amid boasts and guffaws. The other boys are long gone, having run back to their bedrooms in fear of the housemaster's ire.

My targets, however, have never been riper for the picking.

I step out of the shadows, forcing my silent feet to slap audibly against the marble flooring.

All four of them swivel toward me and stumble into each other in shock.

"*Kitty cat*?" manages Angus.

I flinch. I'm so used to appearing in disguise, I'd forgotten for a moment that the boys would see me for who I really am.

Cringing like a field mouse, I feign surprise and fear at their presence, then turn and run. Away from the safety of their crowded dormitories. Away from the watchful eye of the aggrieved housemaster. Into the emptiest part of the school, where the vacant classrooms won't see life again until tomorrow morning.

The boys are so delighted to find me alone and unprotected—and in my flimsy nightgown—that they never pause to wonder what the devil I'm doing beneath their roof in the darkest hours before dawn.

They chase me exactly where I intend to go—the cavernous auditorium. The perfect stage for the play that's about to unfold. The door shuts behind us.

Now that there's no chance of being overheard, I let out several dramatic whimpers as I scramble up on the raised dais toward the podium where the headmaster had warned the entire school against acts of aggression.

At the center, I "trip" and roll onto my back like an overturned scarab, kicking its useless legs in the sky because it is unable to save itself.

Bait that my tormenters cannot resist.

In a flash, all four of them loom over me, one on each side, like gravediggers piling dirt upon a fresh coffin.

Roderick chortles. "You can't get away now, can you, kitty cat?"

Angus and Fraser bump shoulders in celebration.

It's Mungo who asks the obvious question. "But how did she get inside?"

I grin and flash my claws. "I let myself in."

They shriek and leap backward. All four faces pale with shock and confusion.

"*You* did this to me." I smile wide, letting them watch my small white teeth lengthen into deadly fangs. "And now you will die."

I launch myself at them, a tigress toying with her food. A swipe of my claws here, a nip of the fangs there. Soon, the stage is slippery with their blood. They scramble and fall, again and again, tripping over their own feet or from the snap of a tendon.

No killing blows. Not yet. I want them to see what their idle words have wrought.

One by one, I seduce each bully to his feet, waltzing him in wild circles through the sticky pools of his comrades' blood. I sip at each neck before tossing him onto the pile with the others.

They long to resist me, but cannot. Not while I'm staring

directly into their eyes. They see what I'm doing, they feel the agony, they fear the next slice of claws or bite of fangs. But they are helpless to turn away. It scares them witless.

I love it. They deserve nothing less.

"What did you wish for?" I ask Mungo, licking his blood from my claws.

"W-w-wish?" His face is ashen, his lips trembling.

"That day in the woods," Fraser hisses. "You three were teasing her about wishes."

Roderick's jaw drops. "Oh, *we* were misbehaving, were we? What were *you* doing to her with your knife, headmaster's pet?"

I run my tongue over my fangs impatiently.

"What did you say to her?" Angus whispers urgently to Mungo.

"Not to me," I correct them. "I was powerless. It was the fairies who overheard your wishes. Mungo said something like, 'I wish Catriona were a magic fairy. Maybe then there would be a kitty cat for each of us.'"

He pales further. Mungo might not recall his exact words, but he clearly remembers making the wish.

Now he'll live to regret it.

I wiggle my claws at him. "Look. Magic! Just like you wanted. Plenty of me for each of you."

"What did *you* wish?" Fraser hisses to Angus.

He stares at me. "That she were bonny?"

"That's right," I confirm. "Thank you for your kindness. Some men have opined that I'm the most beautiful woman in the world."

"Mr. MacLeod said he saw—" Roderick gulps, his eyes

bulging. "*You've* been the one killing our classmates and the men in the villages?"

"Big brain! You've put it together so fast. Yes, I've been disposing of rubbish. Males that the world would be better off without." I flash my fangs at him.

The boys realize they shouldn't be bleeding out having a chat with me but rather running for their lives instead.

Unfortunately for them, no lad's legs run faster than a sith who can materialize wherever she pleases.

I pop in front of them, one after the other. Swipe my claws across their bellies, their heaving chests, their scared faces. It is the most fun I've ever had in my life.

How many times have I wished something bad would happen to my tormenters? I bite off an ear and swallow it whole with a smile. Wish granted. I *am* the Something Bad. I cackle.

School officials won't be shocked to find four dead bodies here in the morning. When I'm done with these pricks, there will be nothing left to find.

"Oh, Roderick," I coo, popping up before him as he tries to run again. I slam my hands to his head and rip off his scalp. "Drat, you've lost your crown."

Mungo makes a heaving noise somewhere behind me.

I help myself to a handful of Roderick's brains, letting gelatinous globs dribble from my blood-smeared mouth as I taunt, "Who's your king now?"

Angus and Mungo attempt to flee in opposite directions, though there's nowhere for them to go. The auditorium only has one unlocked door, and I can reach it long before any of them.

"I should have done this that day in the woods like I wanted to!" growls a voice right behind me.

I turn in time to see Fraser stab an eight-inch knife into my breast.

Or try, anyway. All that happens is the tip breaks off as though he'd attacked a slab of marble. The sharp recoil of the handle causes the knife to shoot from his startled hands.

I grab the knife out of thin air and slam the nicked blade into his own heart.

"That should've killed you!" he manages to gasp.

I smile sadly. "I'm already dead."

With a well-practiced twist and thrust, I gut him like a fish, spilling his wet, steaming organs all over the freshly buffed auditorium stage floor. I'll be back for those treats later.

Mungo and Angus are close to the exit.

"No leaving the party early," I sing. "Such unpardonably rude behavior."

I pop up in front of them, inches from the door, just as they were reaching for the handle.

In quick succession, I snap their necks like harmless chickens, drink them fully, then tear into their flesh with the hunger of a wolf. My spine slides down the door until I'm sprawled like a rag doll, two delicious corpses filling my blood-soaked lap.

I dine until my belly is so distended, I really do look pregnant.

When I cannot consume any more, I wipe my mouth with the back of my hand and transport myself into a frigid spring that bisects part of the forest. I forgot to bring my satchel of supplies along, but even if I'd remembered to don an apron, I'd still be scrubbing blood and viscera from my limbs in the closest river before returning home.

I do the best I can to clean myself. My skin is soon clear of all evidence of an altercation, but my nightgown looks like it was used to tourniquet a missing limb during battle. I can either go home naked or walk with soaking wet pink muslin plastered to my skin.

I opt for the nightgown. The wind is violent enough tonight that the wet fabric might dry by the time I cross the lawn. The material's new rose-colored swirls should at least be marginally easier to explain than strolling the woods as naked as the day I was born.

Maybe I'll claim it's menstrual blood. See? Not pregnant.

Rather than poof directly into my bed and risk staining that as well—or waking Ishbel, who believes she's halted the summonings—I materialize at the clothesline behind our house, where several petticoats were hung to dry. None of them are mine, but they at least look close enough like a nightgown to buy me the time I need to—

"Catriona?"

I spin to face the house in horror.

Ishbel is standing at what would've once been the rear servants' entrance, not that our female housing has employed any staff to help us. Her hair is mussed, and her feet are bare. The door is barely ajar, yet the wind whips her nightgown to and fro about her legs.

Her eyes widen. "Were you summoned?"

"No," I say quickly. "Go back to bed. I was just taking care of something."

The door opens wider, casting more moonlight on Ishbel's skeptical frown. "You had an errand to run at three o'clock in the morning?"

I realize my error and wish to the devil that this was a moment I could start over by running away. If ever there was a time to lie and say *Yes, exactly, an unexpected summoning, I have absolutely no control over anything that may have just happened* . . . this is that moment.

She's too clever and knows me too well for me to attempt to backtrack with white lies now. To buy time, I shuck my soiled nightgown over my head and reach for a fresh clean petticoat. I pray my unexpected nudity might distract her from this line of questioning.

It does not. By the time the new petticoat is over my head, she's out of the house and stalking toward me, her eyes flashing with anger and hurt.

"Were you out *hunting*?" she demands in indignation and horror. "On purpose? You said the curse forces you to act *against* your nature and your will!"

I reach for her. "Ishbel, I—"

She jerks her soft, gooseflesh-covered arm from my grasp and flees.

Ishbel. Running away. From *me*.

My batlike ears follow the sound of her racing footsteps up the stairs. Not into our bedroom, but to the one shared by Sorcha and Euphemia. The thin scrape of a wooden chair against the scarred floorboards indicates she's doing her best to lock me out of the room.

Sorcha and Euphemia mumble sleepy questions.

Ishbel sobs and says she can't tell them what has happened. That I've gone mad. That there's been a murder. That we won't know who died until tomorrow.

I can tell from their tones and their relaxed heartbeats that both Sorcha and Euphemia think Ishbel has had a nightmare. They push a pillow and a blanket onto the floor between them so that Ishbel can spend the night guarded on both sides.

Ishbel's nightmare is only beginning. In the morning, when the housemaster takes headcount in the dormitories and the first staff member walks into the auditorium to see the mess of corpses I left behind, Ishbel will know exactly what I've done.

I did it for love. I did it to protect her. To save her life.

And now she'll never again be a part of mine.

37

Morning arrives, and no one comes for me. Kirk bells ring in the distance. It's the Sabbath again. I brace myself for what is to come.

The house is eerily quiet. The others must have gone to church. Or to fetch an army with iron pitchforks.

I needn't wait for cavalry to arrive. I can materialize anywhere I wish to go.

But the only place I want to be is right here.

Ishbel never came back to our room, of course. I savored the still-warm sheets she'd vacated as long as I could, to feel her familiar scent embrace me one last time.

The news of the latest deaths must have broken by now. The identities of the lads who used to inhabit those fang-ravaged, dismembered corpses will have spread across campus like wildfire. If my housemates haven't been told the rumors yet, they will at any moment.

As soon as Ishbel hears the names *Roderick, Angus, Mungo,*

and *Fraser*, I am lost. Even if I'd had the wherewithal last night to lie about being forced to perform that smiting, she'll know *those* deaths weren't the least bit against my will.

Aye, I enjoyed it. I laughed. I smiled. I made jests. I delighted in the moment. It was the best night of my life.

I roll out of bed and shove my arms into a Floodbane dress uniform. Not because I'll be allowed on campus ever again, but because I have nothing else to wear.

My mother will be so disappointed to see me back home so soon. *If* they let me go home, that is. Her disappointment to learn I've given away her talisman will be nothing compared to her horror at why officials want to put me in iron chains.

Authorities can try to lock me into an asylum, and I can always escape. But I could never return to visit my mother. Home would be the first place they'd look for me.

The bedroom door swings open, and I jump out of my skin. It's Ishbel. She's alone.

"Come with me," she says instead of bidding me a good morning.

She doesn't look as though she's had much of a good morning herself, either. Her brown eyes are bloodshot and bleary. She's stuffed into one of Euphemia's too-short dresses. Dirt cakes her bare feet.

I go with her. What else can I do? I can never say no to Ishbel.

She leads me out of the house. Four of my five housemates mill amongst the smattering of newly planted saplings. Everyone but Fiona is here. And they're all wearing identical stunned expressions.

I was right. News travels fast at Floodbane.

"Is this about the boys?" I ask.

"No," Ishbel answers. "They're dead. This is about you."

I dart another look at my friends, none of whom are meeting my eyes.

None of whom are my friends anymore.

What sane person would befriend a baobhan sith?

"You told them?" I whisper.

Ishbel's jaw flexes. "Oh, did I break a confidence? That's ironic, since you more than broke my trust by going on a bloody rampage!"

I'm not sure if she means *bloody* in its literal or figurative sense. Probably both.

"I had to." I turn toward her. "I did it for—"

"Revenge," she finishes, condemning me to Hell in a single word.

"You wanted revenge, too!" I burst out. "How many times did I hear you say, 'I could kill them!'?"

"But I didn't kill them, did I? I wanted them to be pariahs, not corpses."

"It was never going to end. The only thing that could stop them—"

"Yes, a *thing*. A thing that killed without being summoned. That's not a smiting. That's murder. You're a murderer and a monster."

Well. All right. I have no convincing rebuttal to that argument. Ishbel's pronouncement is one hundred percent correct.

"Killing them was unnecessary," Maisie says quietly. "You'd already won."

I spin to face her. She's seated on the fallen hawthorn trunk. "Are you mad? In what world did I win?"

"The assembly," Sorcha answers. "We were all there, remember? Headmaster MacKenzie stared right at them and said—"

"He can say any words he wants," I interrupt. "Words don't change anything. Actions do. Those boys cornered me the next day and threatened all your lives."

"They would've been expelled from school if they'd tried," Euphemia says.

"No, *I* would have. They threatened to lie and tell the school administration that I'm pregnant."

My friends gasp.

"That wouldn't just get you expelled," Maisie says in a shaky voice. "After the label of 'fallen woman' follows you home, your entire life would be ruined."

"With no consequences for *them* at all," Sorcha adds angrily.

I nod. "Precisely. Just like nothing happened to them after they attacked me. If I've learned anything here at Floodbane, it's that a woman's words are useless."

"No." Ishbel shakes her head. "Your words *did* matter. Headmaster MacKenzie *did* act on them. His speech didn't bring about the desired result, but that doesn't mean you should give up on decency and start killing people."

"Obstacles mean try again," Euphemia says. "There are alternative consequences besides cold-blooded murder. Did you try reporting their newest threat? Did you see if any of our male classmates would confirm witnessing them back you into a corner?"

No. I did not. I slipped straight to preventative measures.

Maisie glances over my shoulder. "She's not coming?"

The others look up toward the top floor.

I spread my senses until I hear the racing heart and uneven breath up above. Fiona. I would have expected her to be first in line with a pitchfork.

Euphemia rolls back her shoulders. "We'll do it without her."

I gulp. "Do what?"

Ishbel turns toward the path into the woods. "Come with us."

I follow. There's no question what this is. My best friends are leading me to my death.

There's only one thing on this earth that can hurt me, and Ishbel knows exactly what it is. She's wearing the evidence around her neck.

It won't be a mercy killing. The effect of even a tiny flake of iron against my body is too extreme to be considered merciful. But nor is this act murder. These girls won't be killing a classmate.

They'll be putting down an animal.

"I didn't ask to be a sith!" I burst out beseechingly. "It's a calling. Literally. I cannot resist the summons. Unless I fulfill my duty to protect, I'll suffer on two painful hooves until it's done."

No one acknowledges this argument. It probably isn't much of one. Whether or not you agree that baobhan siths are avenging angels, doling out much-deserved justice, what I did last night . . .

I did as Catriona Cameron.

"Here we are." Ishbel motions me into a clearing.

I'm the first to step inside. I don't see any pitchforks or iron chains or weapons of any kind. Perhaps Ishbel told them there's no point attempting to subdue me. That I can vanish at will and escape any consequence I do not wish to suffer.

Or maybe whatever they have planned is worse than anything I could imagine.

"I know this place. This is where Mungo dragged me, when he trapped me in the woods. Where they tied me to a saw bench and thrust their knives into my flesh and clothing." I let out a shuddering breath. "This is where I died."

"Part of you died that day, yes." Ishbel and the others encircle me. They hold hands with each other. "But this is also where you are born again."

"As a sith, you mean?"

"No." Euphemia shakes her head. "That was then."

The girls raise their clasped hands.

"We are phoenixes," Ishbel proclaims. "This is a sisterhood. We can overcome any evil together."

Sorcha opens her mouth. Whatever she's about to say is drowned out by the soul-splitting wail of a banshee.

Fiona barrels into the circle, breaking the closest clasped hands, sprinting straight at me.

"You backstabbing bitch!" she sobs, windmilling her fists into me.

I stand there and take it. I won't bruise. It's Fiona's fingers that are in jeopardy. I trap them in my own hands before she breaks her bones trying to hurt me.

"You killed my suitor?" she screams. *"You killed my suitor!"*

"There was a summoning. I couldn't prevent it. One second, I was here, and the next I was there. I didn't mean to go anywhere near him. I didn't even know it *was* him. I'd never met Tavish—"

"At some point, you did realize." Fiona jerks her fists from my hands, her puffy face streaked with new and old tears. "Either while you were doing it, or after it was done. You hugged me in my grief and said nothing. You knew."

This is true. And only part of the awful truth. "You're right. I could have confessed, but did not. I didn't want to hurt you even more than I already had."

Fiona rubs her splotchy face, then takes a step backward to look at me. Her expression is that of a woman who has been utterly destroyed and will never be put back together. "Ishbel says you only kill bad people."

"I . . ." My throat closes up. "A sith is compelled by the summons to smite those who deserve judgment, aye."

A true statement, spoken as a lie. I wasn't summoned to smite Tavish. He was trying to save me. His final words were, *I came here for . . .*

I'd thought he was going to say *you*, meaning he'd come to my aid to rescue me, but now I think he was going to say *Fiona*. Tavish tried his best to defend me out of love for Fiona.

And I killed him for it. An honorable, kindhearted lad, who could've grown up to be a good man. A better future for Fiona. Her way out. Until I destroyed her dreams and his heart with one blow.

All of which makes me very much not a good person. I deserve Fiona's hate and so much more.

Her lower lip wobbles. Then she throws her arms about my neck and sobs. "Catriona, I can't lose you and Tavish both."

Tears flow down my own cheeks as I hug her to me as gently as I can.

After all we've gone through together, no revenge on this earth is worth losing the friendships I've gained.

She leads me to the center of the circle and pushes me down to the grass.

I sit and wait.

The five girls turn and rummage for items hidden in the shrubbery. As a unit, they spin around and sprint toward me at a dead run.

I flinch, but stay right where I am. I deserve whatever they have planned.

They attack. Not with knives and pistols, but with . . . flower petals?

One by one, each of my friends places a handmade crown of flowers upon my head. It is the ceremony I'd failed to achieve before. They are besieging me. Not with weapons, but rather with grace.

"It's all right to need help," says Euphemia, as she places her crown atop my head. "Next time, talk to us first."

My throat goes dry.

"The six of us are wiser together than any one of us alone," says Fiona, knocking the first ring of flowers into my lap to crown me with hers.

My eyes shimmer.

Sorcha is next, with a cheeky smile. "If we decide as a group that violence is the answer, then we take those steps together."

Maisie shoots her a quelling look. "But violence is rarely the answer. Be true to yourself and to your soul."

Perhaps my heart is not yet dead.

Ishbel is last. "Don't go so far down a path on your own that you can never find your way back."

They join hands again and form a circle around me. The folds of their skirts mingle with mine. Flower petals are everywhere. I'm not certain anything coherent sits atop my head.

They lean forward in unison, wrapping their arms around me and each other until we become an interlocking Gordian knot the likes of which even the gods themselves could never tear apart.

Sometimes family is all you've got, my mother used to say. *And sometimes family is the best thing you've got.*

A wise woman, my mother. When I met these lasses, I didn't yet realize I had found a family that would accept me more than I'd ever dreamed possible.

But unless I can undo the curse, I won't get to keep them.

38

"I'll find a way to break the curse," I promise the friends seated around me.

Ishbel studies me with cautious hope in her eyes. "*Is* there a way to break the curse?"

"There must be." I refuse to believe otherwise. I can't lose Ishbel and the others. "I've hunted through old tomes in the academy library—"

Sorcha snorts. "You think our boarding school lends out instructional manuals on magic?"

"They have books about legends, and tomes on Scottish history."

"Maybe the answer cannot be found in books."

"Then where?" Fiona asks. "Ancient Egyptian scrolls?"

"No," says Euphemia. "Fairies did this, not gods."

"That's right," Ishbel agrees. "Fairies did this, which means they can undo it."

"But they won't," I remind my friends. "Their entire personality is based around not giving you what you want. At best, fairies are like mischievous children. And at worst . . ."

Maisie sighs. "I wish—"

"Don't you *dare* use that word," I snap in terror. "This is exactly where I was tied up when I got this damned curse to begin with."

She claps a hand over her mouth and pales.

Sorcha crosses her arms. "I'm tired of men getting their way. Isn't it time *our* wishes came true?"

Fiona sits up straight, her eyes shining with fervor. "I'd wish for Tavish back."

"I'd wish for money," says Euphemia. "More money than I can spend in a lifetime."

"I'd wish for Arthur's sword," says Sorcha. "And the power that comes with it."

"Don't be so selfish," Ishbel chides them. "The thing I wish is that Catriona would stop murdering people."

She realizes her mistake the second the words come out of her mouth.

A blanket of terrified silence smothers the air from our lungs. Everyone's faces fill with panic. Ishbel didn't say what she *would* wish, hypothetically. She accidentally made a real one.

"And not be magical in any way," she adds loudly. Then lets out a choking sob and covers her face with both hands.

"Retract your wish," Euphemia hisses, her eyes wide. "Invoke God's protection!"

"It's too late," murmurs Sorcha. "She added to the wish instead."

All six of us are still and silent as tombstones for a long, protracted moment, staring at each other's terrified faces beneath the dappled shadows of the forest.

"They didn't hear us, did they?" Maisie whispers. "The fairies?"

No one speaks.

"I don't think so," Sorcha whispers back. "Nothing is hap—"

I can barely hear them. I squint in concentration. All I hear is the rustling of leaves from the wind, and the occasional cry of a bird overhead. My senses are muted.

"I can't hear your heartbeats," I blurt out. "Or the blood rushing in your veins."

Fiona recoils in disgust. "You could hear my *blood*?"

"And the air expanding your lungs. But not now." I hold up my hands and deploy my claws. Nothing happens. I try harder and harder.

"What's wrong?" Ishbel asks nervously.

I hold up the backs of my shaking hands. "My claws are gone."

Maisie lets out a squeak. "You had *claws*?"

Ishbel grabs both my hands and brings her face to mine.

"It worked?" she whispers, her eyes shining. "You're human again?"

I wrap my arms about her waist and press my cheek against her chest. The tiny iron cross suspended there presses into my flesh, cool and light. There's no pain.

"I'm human again," I reply in wonder.

Ishbel hugs me so hard, we can *all* hear the air whooshing

from my lungs. Then she leaps to her feet, dragging me up with her. She dances me around the clearing in a drunken, rhythmless waltz, laughing and crying and peppering my cheeks with kisses.

With delight, the others join us in celebration. Whoops fill the air as they take turns hugging me tight, then spinning me amongst them in dizzying circles.

My conflicting emotions are too big to fit inside my body. Now that I got what I wanted, my unmagical limbs feel heavy and sluggish. My fingernails are just fingernails, and my feet are just feet. And my corset is too damn tight. I can feel pain again, and I don't like it.

Ishbel cups my face with her hands. "It's all right to need time to get used to being yourself again."

She understands me so well, it's frightening.

I press a kiss to her cheek in return. "Thank you."

"Oh, Catriona, I didn't mean to wish out loud at all. When I—" She stumbles.

I catch her by the shoulders.

Confusion flickers over her face, followed by a wince of pain.

My human heart races in concern. "Are you all right? Did you sprain an ankle? We can stop dancing."

Euphemia lets out a shriek behind me, followed by Fiona and Maisie.

Ishbel slips from my useless human fingers. All five girls thud to the ground like dead apples falling from a tree.

I'm the only one left standing.

Breathing shallowly, I turn in a slow circle. My friends

writhe on their buttocks or their backs, kicking off their shoes to rub desperately at their feet.

"No," I whisper, darting my gaze toward the shadowy bushes in sudden understanding. The careless cruelty of the fairies. The irony. "You wouldn't have!"

But they did. It's done.

I know intimately the pain that's assailing my best friends' delicate bones. The crushed-glass sensation of standing on shattered feet. It's what I felt for the first time right here in this clearing.

The price for turning me human again . . . is for them to lose their humanity.

Ishbel is the first to put it together. "I'm a *baobhan sith*?"

"We all are," sobs Euphemia.

Fiona sends me a dark look. "Not Catriona."

Sorcha wiggles her fingers. "When do I get claws?"

"Undo it!" Euphemia shouts. "I didn't ask for this!"

Maisie simply hunches over her shattered feet, weeping. Her curved spine heaves again and again.

Ishbel gasps and stares at me, wide-eyed. With alacrity, her fingers scrabble behind her neck to undo the knotted twine.

She hurls the talisman in my direction. It falls at my feet, harmless. Ishbel rubs her chest, which had no doubt begun to burn.

I could leave the cross where it lies. A shared grave marker. My death was much earlier, but thanks to the fairies' sadistic intervention, all six of us have lost an irretrievable part of ourselves on this trampled grass.

"Do something," hisses Euphemia.

Ishbel shakes her head in horror. "Don't you dare say a single word, Catriona. It won't turn out right. Save yourself, now that you can."

I bend over, wincing at the pinch of my corset, and pick up my mother's cross. It doesn't burn. It feels cool and familiar. I press it to my bosom and imagine I still feel remnants of my mother's warmth and love.

A cool breeze caresses the back of my bare neck. I can wear my family talisman again, but I'm not certain I deserve to be protected. Not after all I did when it no longer graced my throat.

I glance over my shoulder at the place where I'd been tied up and tortured. The place I returned to, less than a fortnight later, to scream my head off.

That day, I'd shouted my wish to be human over and over, begging the fairies to let me be my old self. I'd prayed to them and the church alike for me and my friends never to need be frightened of anything again for the rest of our lives.

This was not what I'd had in mind.

I turn back to Ishbel, who rocks in place, her feet in her hands.

"Would it help if I rubbed them?" I ask quietly.

"We don't want our bloody feet rubbed," Euphemia snarls. "We want to be human again!"

"I don't think she was talking to you," Fiona whispers.

Ishbel shakes her head. "Don't touch me."

Her words hit like a punch to the solar plexus. Every time a wish comes true, I lose more of my family.

The cross in my hand now feels small and insignificant. No part of it scratches me. The warm metal is smooth and even. I'm not a monster anymore.

I tie the twine about my neck loosely. The talisman nestles above my bosom, as it always used to do. It feels foreign now. No longer a symbol of my mother's love, but of the five other hearts lost to me today in these fairy-poisoned woods.

Fiona says bitterly, "I hate this, and I hate you. It's not fair. We must suffer, while *you* get to live happily ever after with your one true love."

Baffled, I dart my gaze toward Ishbel.

"Dougal will be thrilled," Ishbel murmurs, without meeting my eyes.

Oh. Right.

Dougal is a good person. He was there for me before, and he'd be here for me now. He and his mother can make all my dreams come true. Now that I'm human again, the future I yearned for will happen. My mother, safe at last.

All I need to do . . . is go and live.

No doubt, Fiona and the others would understand that the only sane choice for me is to run as fast as I can toward a happy ending.

But what about them?

39

"Catriona?" Maisie says in a tiny voice. "What are you going to do?"

It's hard to think inside this human body. My brain isn't as fast as it was. I roll back my shoulders and shift my weight from side to side to get the blood to flow.

Euphemia sighs. "If I were Catriona, I'd go home for Christmas holiday and never come back."

"And leave us?" Maisie says in disbelief. "She's human, and we're not!"

"We are for the moment," Sorcha says, staring at her legs with disgruntlement. "My hooves haven't solidified."

"It takes about a week for claws," Ishbel informs them. "Catriona's powers came on gradually over the first month or so."

"Thank you, professor," mocks Fiona, though she's glaring at me rather than Ishbel. "It must be nice to have been kept informed of what the *devil* was going on."

Probably still not the best moment to confess I'd killed her paramour by mistake.

She'll find out about the hunger soon enough.

Or must she? Ishbel warned me against it, but I *could* make a wish of my own. Though if the fairies answer at all, it's unlikely to be in a way that any of us would want.

What do *I* want? The answer floods my mind with colorful images and familiar scents.

Simple. I want things to go back to the way they were, but better. Six human girls, studying and dining together, sharing chores and hair bows and secrets. Ishbel and me, tucked in our cozy bedroom. Talking all night long, cheek to cheek, hand in hand. Falling asleep on the same pillow once more.

But that cannot last forever. Do I really think Ishbel and I will be sharing a pillow next year, much less when we're eighty years old? More importantly, do I really think the fairies would grant such a simple, perfect wish without twisting it into a nightmare for us all?

The other option is to say nothing. Not to Ishbel, and not to the fairies.

Return to school.

Now that I'm human, I can live up to my full potential. Spend the rest of my life teaching and giving girls like us better opportunities. With a boy who gardens at my side.

"Cat?" Fiona says tentatively.

There's no breeze, but the leaves rustle all around us. Something is in the bushes.

The fairies haven't gone far. They're hiding just out of sight. Listening. Waiting. Rubbing their gleeful little hands with anticipation.

"They're watching us," Ishbel whispers.

I nod. "I know."

I shudder at how she'll feel at her first summoning. She'll probably run away as I tried to do, again and again. But it won't work. It never does. Justice isn't served until the hunger is satisfied.

The smitings will never end until all the worst offenders are dead. Or until men learn to be less terrible. Perhaps that's the real purpose. Boys shall be forewarned, and make different choices in the future.

"Go," Ishbel says brokenly. "Your curse is broken. You're free."

Maisie says in a small voice, "I thought us lasses were meant to stick together?"

"The rest of us will," Euphemia assures her.

Fiona sniffles. "Catriona has a human she wants to spend the rest of her life with."

In the same tone you might use to utter, *Wench, I hope you walk straight off the nearest cliff and die,* Sorcha sneers, "True love."

The words echo around us.

I turn to Ishbel.

She gazes back at me.

I want to save her more than I want to save myself. I want Ishbel's company, now and forever. Her hugs. Her smiles. But if I'm going to make a wish, it cannot be a selfish one. I must strive to aid the most people possible. Just as I've always wanted to do.

"Ignore the fairies," Ishbel urges. "Walk away. Now that you're human again, this may well be the last chance you get to put your own desires first."

"Really?" Maisie hisses. "Shouldn't we *try* to become human again, now that we know it's possible?"

"I doubt that *is* possible," Euphemia says bleakly. "Women rarely get what they want out of life. Not with men, and not with fairies. Our words will always be twisted. Be the exception, Catriona. One of us should live a life of her own choosing."

Fiona wipes her nose. "Aye, go ahead and choose love, while you can. Nothing else matters."

Choose love. In that case . . . I turn to Ishbel and smile. My decision is made.

Her sad, sweet eyes don't leave mine.

I tilt my face up toward the treetops and let my voice ring out loud and proud.

"I wish I were a fearless baobhan sith—and that the unstoppable Phoenix Sisterhood shall never die!"

Without regret, I hurl my mother's talisman to the fairies. This is the last time anyone will take something from us that we don't wish to give. I grin at my sisters as my feet crumble beneath me.

May we all thrive with power.

EPILOGUE

Winter Solstice

Just after midnight I allow myself a moment to materialize in my mother's bedchamber while she sleeps.

She is alone now, and much happier for it. The furniture is simple, the walls free of adornment, but the narrow bed is so comfortable that she has never once woken to find me hovering by her side like a guardian angel.

Ironic to think that five months ago, it was she who waved goodbye as I was ferried off to a boarding school far away. Now she is the one living in the new on-site dormitories for grown women at the Morrison Institute for Promising Ladies of All Ages. Like my mother, every woman in this wing has a private room to call her own, and has access to all the food, education, and resources they could dream of.

According to a brief visit I had with Dougal's mother, mine has taken to books like a selkie to water. She'll be catching up to her peers faster than any of us dared to hope. In the meantime, Mother earns a small but respectable allowance as part of her scholarship terms. When she graduates from the institute, for the first time in her life, she will have options to choose from.

When I last dropped by, she told me Hamish had returned home to the Highlands to work with Father rather than continue living in Edinburgh. I wasn't there to see my father's reaction to the news, so I'll never know whether he welcomed his baby bird back into the nest with open arms or yelled at Hamish for wasting the family savings on an education he doesn't intend to use. Dougal is taking a sabbatical from school and following his dream to become a gardener. Not at his childhood home, but here at the beautiful Morrison Institute. He and his beloved bilberry bushes are thriving.

Without waking my sleeping mother, I cross the room to press a kiss to her forehead, vanishing as soon as my lips make contact.

My bare hooves touch grass.

"Took you long enough," grouses Sorcha. "We were about to start the hunt without you."

"No, we weren't." Ishbel holds her hand out to me. "Ready?"

I entwine my fingers with hers. "Ready."

Euphemia grins. "Dinnertime!"

Some siths hunt alone, and others hunt in packs. Our group prefers to stick together, at school and after. Not for safety—we're untouchable—but because together our instincts unfold like a dark ballet, an intricate performance of the finest dance of bone and blood.

The six of us flit through the darkness, no longer waiting to be summoned before going wherever we're needed.

The men are always, always happy to see us. Some of the comments that escape their lewd mouths . . . are downright improper.

But don't worry, ladies. We'll make sure every one of them learns from their mistakes.

ACKNOWLEDGMENTS

This book would not exist without the support of many wonderful people: My fabulous editor, Bria Ragin, whose brilliant ideas put everything into motion. My rock star agent, Lauren Abramo, for the wisdom and support. The team at Random House Children's Books, including Elizabeth Cervantes, Shameiza Ally, Jamie Johnson, Cathy Bobak, Angela G. Carlino, and Tamar Schwartz, as well as the cover illustrator, Elena Masci. Any mistakes are my own.

Unending gratitude to the irreplaceable Lacey Reid, for literally everything. For decades, you were the best friend a girl could have. Thank you for cheering me—and this book—on, until the very end. I love you so much, and will miss you forever.

The biggest of bear hugs to Shauna. You saved me time and again with all your support and friendship, as I struggled as a writer and a human over the past couple of years. You are amazing, and I am so grateful to have you in my life.

I am indebted as always to intrepid assistant (and awesome

mom) Laura Stout, my stalwart right hand in the United States, handling everything I cannot from Costa Rica.

Muchísimas gracias to sweet, silly, snuggly Roy Prendas, for the countless ways life is better with you in it. Te adoro, mi popolote.

And heartfelt thanks to all of you amazing, marvelous book lovers: readers, reviewers, educators, librarians, booksellers, and anyone who gushes about their latest read or gifts a book to someone else. You are the very, very best.

Thank you all!

This horror novel will have you hanging by a thread!

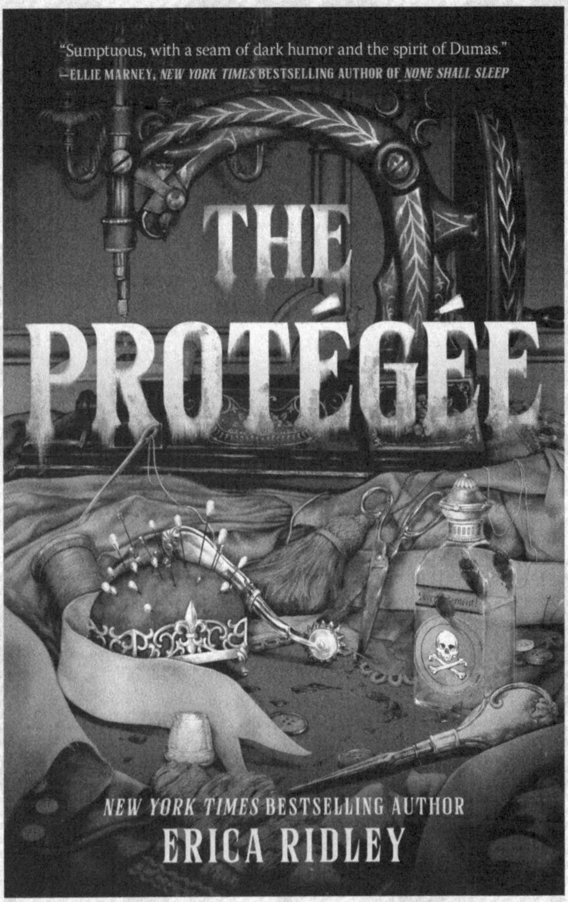

"Revenge has never looked so chic."

—Lydia Gregovic, *New York Times* bestselling author of *The Monstrous Kind*

CHAPTER 1

Paris, France
18 September, 1850

Jagged shards of sunlight stab through my lowered eyelashes, and a needle plunges into the tip of my finger.

For a moment, I'm tempted to leave it in there. Why not? I've suffered worse.

There's no blood. Not yet. Not while the slender silver needle protrudes from my flesh, vibrating with joy at having bested me in a rare moment of inattention. Old memories are to blame again. My brain flashed to an unbidden image of the gruesome day I lost my father, and the needle saw its chance to remind me of pain.

"Keep sewing, Angélique," snaps Mademoiselle Jacqueline.

The other five girls dart their eyes at me, quick as cockroaches. They don't bother to hide their titters. They want me to hear their ridicule. To know I will never belong.

They have worked here for years. I'm almost finished with

my six-month trial in this windowless room with its hive of sewing tables in the center. Ankle-high scraps like piles of dead leaves line all four walls. We are newborn chicks in a giant bird's nest.

Baby egrets, to be exact, known for killing their siblings before they can learn to fly.

I stare at the needle again.

"Angélique," Mademoiselle Jacqueline says in warning, flipping her long pale hair over her shoulder.

She's not the owner of this luxury dress shop. That distinction goes to famed modiste Madame Violette, who is fitting clients in one of the plush dressing chambers at the front of the store, helping to turn yet another wife of an industrialist into a queen dripping with bespoke wealth. Every sign of excess is calculated to generate the maximum amount of envy from each client's peers, who will then descend upon the shop en masse, eager to glitter like diamonds too.

"Yes, Mademoiselle Jacqueline," I say dutifully. After all, she is Madame Violette's protégée—and our taskmistress. This provisional junior seamstress post is the best thing that's ever happened to me. I cannot afford to lose it.

Literally. It's this or beg for crumbs on the street.

"Well?" Mademoiselle Jacqueline prompts.

I stare at her thin blond hair, the color of an apple slice left in the sun. The strands are dry and brittle. I have a recipe for hair cream that would help, though I know from experience none of the girls in this room cares about my opinions.

The other seamstresses are watching me. Not a stitch is being sewn, but there are no harsh words for anyone else.

They have been waiting for me to err, to prove myself unworthy, since the moment I sat amongst them.

I pull the needle from my flesh. The hot silver quill sticks a little before popping free. A bubble of bright red blood blossoms to the surface, trembling as it grows. I touch the tip of my swollen finger to my tongue. The taste is salty and metallic.

For the entire six-month probationary period, I have foiled my coworkers' fervent wish to see me fail by excelling at every task, no matter how menial or time-consuming.

Madame Violette was so impressed, she instructed Mademoiselle Jacqueline to cease wasting my sewing talents on cleaning duties and allow me to work on the fine garments with the others.

The girls could not despise me more. Every day, they giggle amongst themselves and snap at me to go back to the factory, where "my kind" belongs. No one in *their* families has ever had to dirty their hands to pay the rent, much less wonder if there would be food to eat tomorrow. According to society, well-dressed young ladies like these are born better than humble girls like me—and they never let me forget it.

"Look, the poor baby injured herself," one of the girls coos, her saccharine words unable to disguise her delight.

The rest join in gleefully, mocking me. Even Mademoiselle Jacqueline smirks in appreciation at their jests.

Instead of listening, I shut off my ears—a trick I learned when I started work in the textile factory at age twelve. A shudder racks my flesh as unwanted memories bombard me. The enormous, clanging spinning machines . . . The startled yelps from other workers when the looms' automated teeth very nearly catch a finger . . . The sound of my father's screams when—

Madame Violette materializes in the open doorway. Panting, as though she sprinted five kilometers across a barren desert to arrive. But this is how she always looks. Rushed, winded. Rich mahogany skin, one shade lighter than my mother's. Startled brown eyes, like those of a doe hearing the crack of a hunter's rifle. Carefully ironed black hair escaping at odd angles from her coiffure. A sumptuous velvet gown bedecked with flounces in every color of the rainbow. A mad genius.

Our spines straighten. The giggles vanished when she entered. Our fingers become industrious.

Although we all work in the same room, we are far from equal. I am the youngest, at eighteen; the others are one to four years older. Half are Black, half are white. I am the only one who's a combination of both. All seven of us are French to our bones. But there, the similarities end.

Mademoiselle Jacqueline wants to show that she has us under her control. That she should rise from the role of assistant and be made a full partner.

The other five girls openly covet Mademoiselle Jacqueline's position as protégée. Its many privileges. The eye-watering salary.

Moi? I only need to survive until the end of the month. The promotion to full employee comes with a commensurate increase in wages. The glorious moment at which Madame Violette presses my new, no-longer-provisional salary into my hand.

The money I will soon earn is four times the pittance I received at the loud, stinking Fournier Fabrics factory. Which means my mother and younger sister will soon be able to quit their dangerous positions there and seek work that does not demand they risk their lives daily, even if the pay is lower. *I* will provide for my family.

Like Papa used to.

Madame Violette sweeps past each of our tables, inspecting our handiwork with a keen eye. My task is a full-torso whalebone corset, as fearsome and constricting as a serpent.

"Well done," she pronounces at last.

The relief in the room is palpable.

"Especially you, Angélique." Madame Violette holds up the hem I've just finished. "Such precise stitches, and completed so quickly."

Waves of hate roll off the other girls, battering me like a tempest tossing a sailboat.

"Merci," I murmur, ducking my head to shield my vulnerable eyes from their piercing gazes.

Madame Violette plucks a long strip of bone-white silk from my table. "What's this?"

"Left over." I gesture to one of the colorful discard piles lining the sewing room. "Shall I deposit it with the rest?"

She tilts her head. "Why don't you take it home, if you'd like."

A gasp of disbelief claws free from my throat.

If I'd like! Six *years* sweating in that god-awful textile factory, creating reams of material none of the workers will ever be able to afford in their lifetimes. A ruined finger, a dead father, yet never so much as a single precious thread was allowed out of the owner's greedy hands.

I lift the ribbon as though presenting my firstborn child to the heavens. A moonbeam, caught in my hands. The silk is soft, shiny, weightless. If I cut it carefully, there might be enough for four matching hair ribbons: one each for my mother, both of my sisters, and me.

We are exiting our final month of mourning, though the wound is as fresh as ever. It's about time a scrap of something bright and happy returned to our lives.

"Mes filles, that's enough for today. I'll see you all first thing in the morning." Madame Violette whirls to her protégée. "Jacqueline, would you help me with the comtesse?"

"Of course." As the women leave the sewing room, Mademoiselle Jacqueline tosses a triumphant look over her shoulder, smug in the knowledge that she alone is trusted in the same room as fine aristocratic ladies like the rich and fashionable Comtesse de Centre-Fleur. With her ebony tresses, smooth maple-brown skin, and enviable curves, the comtesse is a flawless model who elevates any piece she wears. I would love to fit her one day.

But no one else seems concerned with our client. As we rise to our feet, I discover all five of my bitter colleagues staring at me with glittering ratlike eyes and oversized wolfish grins.

"What—" is all I manage.

They pounce.

Ten fists fly at me at once. Not to strike me with tepid, girly blows but to snip my nicest dress with their shears. Quick as arrows, they corner me, trapping me in place as their sharp silver instruments carve holes in the best gown I've ever created.

"You're not better than us," one of the girls hisses beneath her breath.

"You're nothing more than a raggedy mop," snarls another.

"Quit now," a third whispers into my ear as she rips my thin yellow sleeve. "You'll never be worth anything."

They snap their scissors closed and place them back where they belong as if nothing of import has happened. Then they flounce from the room, cackling.

I neither cower nor sob. Simple shears will not defeat me. Those girls aren't half so dangerous as the weaving machines I conquered.

As I roll back my shoulders, a slow smile spreads over my face. Their petty insults and threats have only made me more determined than ever to prove them wrong. To make *them* quiver in fear.

To show the entire world what I'm really made of.

ABOUT THE AUTHOR

ERICA RIDLEY is a *New York Times* and *USA Today* bestselling author of historical romance and horror novels, including *The Protégée.* When not reading or writing, Erica can be found riding camels in Africa, getting hopelessly lost in the middle of Budapest, or zip-lining through rain forests in Costa Rica, where she lives with her husband.

ericaridley.com
@ericaridley